Dead Lands

Azarel Chronicles #2

Dead Lands

M.C. Ashley

Edited by John Transylvania

First Printing: 2021

ISBN : 978-1-7923-3086-5

www.starvingwritersguild.com/

Cover Design by EbookLaunch.com

Edited by John Alexander Erdely (dba John Transylvania)

Special discounts are available on quantity purchases by corporations, associations, educators, and others. For details, contact the publisher at the below listed email address.

U.S. trade bookstores and wholesalers: Please contact M.C. Ashley at mca@starvingwritersguild.com

DEDICATION

I dedicate this book to my grandmother Linda Lutz Rhinehart. Over the years, you have always blessed me with love and support I never deserved. God will be taking you soon from me in accordance to His love, plans, and designs, but just like Grandfather, I know I won't truly be losing you. One day, we will meet again and rejoice in the God who will remove all pain and suffering from the world and we will praise His Name forevermore.

"Jesus said to her, 'I am the resurrection and the life. The one who believes in me will live, even though they die; and whoever lives by believing in me will never die. Do you believe this?'"
—   John 11:25-

ACKNOWLEDGMENTS

This book never could have been made without the generous donations of my friends, family, and the kind people who've taken a chance on me by buying this book. Thanks to all of you so I can continue pursuing this crazy dream.

PREVIOUSLY…

Blake Azarel found himself flung into the future with the inability to remember the past seven years of his life. Formerly a member of the clandestine supernatural group once known as the Gray Forum, Blake discovered that his fellows had been wiped out thanks to an attack ordered by the empathic vampire organization known as the Sanguine Collective.

Under the direction of a mysterious figure known as Nathaniel David Parker, Blake entered Vice City, a renamed Corpus Christi that was one of several strongholds of the Collective and led by Zoë Slinden, who ruled the humans with an iron fist. Living now with a death wish, Blake was saved by Zea Accorsi, who, like him, was called Christened—those gifted with supernatural powers meant to defend others. She took him to the hidden headquarters of the Gray Forum, allowing him to meet with Mara Van Denend, who now lived as the Archivist who held all remaining records of the Forum.

With their help, he discovered some of what had happened in his absence and learned that the Collective would soon murder hundreds of humans in an event known as the Feast, where they would be sacrificed to the Interlopers: the strange, eldritch beings that empowered the Collective to victory over the Forum. Seeking allies under Nathan's orders, Blake found Nathaniel Freeman—an alternate version of Nathan—and Clooney Dressler—a mysterious wind Christener with an unknown agenda.

Now gifted with more help, Blake organized his fellows to find Cinderella Young, a young, mentally-broken woman who wielded fire invocations and would be the cause of the deaths of those sacrificed in the Feast. Blake managed to contact Cinderella and was able to give her hope she had long lost, which proved to be their advantage once the Feast was stopped thanks to her intervention.

However, Zoë revealed she was working with Beleth, a demon working with a rogue group known as The Thirteen. With the help of his allies, Blake was able to kill Zoë and Beleth, claiming Vice City as his own in resistance to the Collective. He then dubbed his new group Excelsior, ready to move ever upward to save a world lost to destruction.

CHAPTER 1

1

I really hate paperwork.

Although I should say that I hate bureaucratic work in general. I'm not cut out to be a politician.

Yet that's what I am these days.

I just wanted to kill bad things for a living. Now I was supposed to be a leader. I knew that I wouldn't like it and yet I still announced it on what counts for national television these days. I really need to learn how to shut my big, fat mouth.

"Are you listening, Blake?" a voice asked, snapping me back to reality.

I was sitting at my desk in my office located on the third floor of the Silver Fortress, former headquarters of the Gray Forum and current home of my new team: Excelsior. It had to be about noon, but I had no idea without a watch, which I still hadn't bothered to obtain since I'd found myself here. I looked up to see my secretary, Dorothy Alexis Alduino, staring back at me. She was holding a stack of papers in one hand and a pencil offered to me in another.

"I'm sorry," I said, cracking my neck. "I am so out of it today."

She rolled her eyes. "Blake Azarel, you may be the leader of this organization, but you really suck at your job," Dorothy said.

A part of me wanted to laugh. Just a year ago Dorothy had almost killed herself because of what the Sanguine Collective had done to her and her fellow slaves. Now here she was, glaring at me with murky brown eyes that had finally regained their strength, a far cry from the ones I had looked into while convincing her to not fall to her death. I smiled.

"Is this funny to you?" she asked.

"No, it's not this," I said. "I'm just reminiscing."

"Well maybe if you kept your mind focused on the present and not the past you could get more work done. The Free-Zone ambassador will be here within the hour."

"Wait—that's today?"

Dorothy placed the pencil on the table and rubbed the bridge of her nose. "Blake, what is today's date?"

I paused. "Uh…the month is May."

"No, that was last month. It is June 4th."

"Oh, huh."

I sat back in the chair and propped my feet on the table.

"If that's the case then don't you think we should've already left for summer vacation?" I asked.

"What's a vacation?"

I nearly fell out of the chair. I was still getting used to being a living anachronism to these people. Then I chided myself for not thinking that joke through. No one here in Corpus Christi (formerly Vice City) had ever had the slightest inkling of what a vacation was. The fact that they could walk around in the open without fear of reprisal was still a novel concept to them even though it'd been a year since I'd helped liberate them from the Sanguine Collective.

"Nothing," I said, regaining my composure. "Just a joke. What is it you need me to sign?"

"I just need you to initial here and there," Dorothy said, handing the paper and pencil to me. "These documents are the basis of what we expect when it comes to potentially allying with the Free-Zone. You should know what's in there, seeing as you wouldn't let anyone else touch them for weeks. Your handwriting was atrocious, and you misspelled the ambassador's name seven separate times, but I was able to fix that when you weren't paying attention to them."

"Everyone's a critic. You try spelling Niseweynu without a Google search." I paused. "You don't know what that is." I huffed. "No one understands me anymore."

I accepted the pencil and paper and did as instructed. For someone who was supposed to be in charge I'd gotten used to being ordered around by everyone else. Then again, I had a soft spot for Dorothy, as the girl had a pretty obvious crush on me. It was only natural given how we'd first met, but I had done

4

everything I could to gently shoot down the idea. I wasn't in a good place to start dating, especially since I was technically married to someone I couldn't remember.

I paused, trying to conjure the long-lost memories to my mind, but—like all the other previous attempts—I failed. There was just the same gloomy blackness as before. If I didn't know more about the man who had sealed away my memories, I would've been madder, but Nathan-Prime always had his reasons for doing what he did. Self-righteous egotist that he was.

"Is something wrong?" Dorothy asked, as I shook my head.

"Thought about what I couldn't remember," I said, signing the papers. "Made me sad for a second."

Dorothy bit her lip. I had made it common knowledge that I knew very little of what had happened to me before I had found myself in the future. The last consistent memory I had came from when I was twenty. I was twenty-eight now, having spent the last year in Corpus Christi with very few flashes of what had happened to me in the seven-year gap Nathan-Prime had blocked. It was annoying to be sure, but there was very little I could do about it. Nathan-Prime was one of those sink or swim mentors when it came to figuring out what he wanted me to do sometimes. I just needed to figure out what it was I needed to do to get them back.

"Well, this seems to be in order," Dorothy said, examining the papers.

I opened my mouth to speak, but felt the presence of a friend about to enter the room. I watched as Nathan Freeman—this reality's alternate version of Nathan-Prime I mentioned before—barged in, breathing heavily. I raced up from my chair and ran to his side. Nathan's hazel eyes greeted me when he lifted up his head. The kid was only eleven years old, but he had seen more and had fought harder than most of the kids my age had done back when we could afford to be lazy.

"Survivor..." Nathan said, panting as Dorothy offered him some water. "Thanks." He drank some and calmed down. "The Dead Lands."

"The what?" I asked.

Dorothy recoiled in horror. "No one ever leaves the Dead Lands," she said. "No one living anyways."

"One did," Nathan said, looking at me. "Her name's Sedecla.

5

She collapsed outside of town. I was there patrolling like you wanted me to."

"You were what? You let him do this? He's eleven!"

"And more than capable of handling himself alone," I said, coldly. "We don't have the resources required to patrol this city effectively with mundane help, so I authorized Nathan to do it in my stead since I'm stuck up here in this godforsaken room instead of doing what I should be all day."

"You cannot seriously be defending the idea of letting a child do this! What if the Collective got word of where he was? They could snatch him up before you could do anything about it!"

"This is not open for discussion. Until we find more Sentinels and Psionics we need to use what we have to protect this city. Unless you have a better idea, Dorothy, then I suggest you shut up."

Dorothy flinched. She was used to my temper, but rarely was it ever directed at her.

Nathan and I were what the Gray Forum classified as Sentinels. Basically, it meant that we were able to channel the energy of creation by invoking the help of God. For people like me, our specialty was invoking light or darkness, while for Nathan it was mostly illusions, dream creation and manipulation, and telepathy. Others with us were called Psionics, which were noted for their more destructive power. To an outside observer the two classifications looked like two different names for the same thing, but once you saw a Psionic and Sentinel in action, you'd note the differences immediately. Sentinels channeled their power quickly, using fast strikes to slay their enemies, while Psionics spent time charging up, doing in one blow what a Sentinel could do in fifty. I had done what I could to train my fellows, but I was finding it harder to do, especially since I was constantly forced into my office to fiddle over some new administrative problem that the city had. This was a welcome intrusion.

"Continue with your report, Nathan," I said.

"Yes, sir," he said. "Sedecla was wounded, so I tried to heal her. I could only do so much. I used this thing" he pointed at the walkie-talkie on his belt "that you gave us and used its magic to contact the Fortress."

I suppressed a chuckle. Despite my lectures to the contrary the people of Corpus Christi had no idea how to use what had been considered modern technology one hundred years ago in my time. The Sanguine Collective had only allowed a select few mundanes—people without supernatural power—access to it and most of them had been killed thanks to the efforts of my team a year ago when we stopped the Feast. A lot of people were convinced that electricity was something inherently magical in nature and could only be understood by people like me.

"I was able to reach Zea," Nathan continued, "and she's healing Sedecla right now. I rushed up here to let you know what was happening."

I smiled. Zea was perfect for the job. Being one of the first people who I'd met in the future who wasn't actively trying to kill me, we had formed a quick bond despite her initial distrust of me. If she was healing Sedecla, then she was in good hands.

"I'm on my way," I said, grabbing my trench coat and hat. "Cancel my appointments for the rest of the day, won't you, Dorothy?"

Dorothy sighed. "No, sir," she said. "You will meet with the Free-Zone ambassador in an hour."

I huffed. "Fine. Never gonna get my way ever again, am I?"

Shaking my head, I left my office behind, ready to figure out more about our new visitor.

2

Zea Sophia Accorsi barely acknowledged my presence when I entered the room, far too focused on her patient to worry about me. I stood silently, watching her work on the woman on the hospital bed, who I assumed to be Sedecla.

Zea was twenty-one years old, had red hair that was held up in a ponytail, cobalt blue eyes, and was a couple inches shorter than my six-foot-two frame. She had light olive skin, a gift from her possible half-Iranian origins, although this was mere speculation on my part, as neither of us knew what her parents looked like. Sedecla, on the other hand, was a woman in her late sixties by the look of it. Her eyes were closed and she was making small breaths that made it seem like she would give up the ghost at any moment. Zea had taken off the woman's robes, but had left her undershirt on, as Zea's medicinal invocations required her to see what she was working with.

Finally sensing where the wounds were, Zea moved to Sedecla's right and touched her lower abdomen with both hands.

"Balm of Gilead," Zea said, as white lights flashed from her hands and into Sedecla's body, sealing up the wound instantly.

Sedecla coughed and tried to sit up, but Zea forced her back down. I approached the bed and nodded at Zea.

"Where am I?" Sedecla asked. "What happened?"

"You were dying," Zea said. "I healed you. You're welcome."

"Excellent bedside manner there, Zee," I said, using my lazy nickname for her.

Zea studied me for a moment, mulled over what I said, and then turned her back to me so that she could reach through her knapsack that was on the table beside the bed. She hurriedly pilfered through it to locate a book—entitled Common Idioms and Their Meanings—and flipped through the pages. I resisted the urge to laugh.

Zea had never been what you'd call a quick study when it came to understanding past idioms. Granted the girl didn't exactly have a normal upbringing, given that she had been forced to live in hiding with only one other person to talk to for the first eleven years of her life. When we had first met, I had infuriated Zea with my countless usage of phrases that were common in my time, but for which she had no context for. So, to help the poor girl out—and to stop face-palming every time she failed to understand what I said—I had managed to procure one of the few surviving books from my time and gave it to her for her birthday. I'd never seen her happier, as she had only learned what a birthday was when I had to explain the concept to her.

"I see," Zea said. "I am not being friendly with my patient. I should be nicer." She turned to Sedecla. "Your hair is a nice shade of white."

I lost it. Zea stared at me as if I was mad, but I couldn't help it. It was always one step forward, two steps back with her, but that was one of the reasons I liked her.

"I'm sorry," I said, straightening up. "You did well." I turned to Sedecla. "Nathan tells me you came from some place called the Dead Lands."

Sedecla stared at me, shivering at the last few words I'd said. "Yes," she said, finally.

"No one ever leaves the Dead Lands," Zea said.

"I almost didn't," Sedecla said. "I was with a group of people who were attempting to escape. Before we got out we were attacked by an army of living skeletons."

"Living skeletons?" I repeated. "Oxymoronic, no?"

"The Dead Lands are said to be possessed by a group of necromancers who are adept with necrotic and entropic evocation," Zea explained. "The Sanguine Collective kept up many supernatural barriers to prevent them from attacking, but that's all I know."

"I don't know how I managed to survive," Sedecla said, staring at nothing. "I watched as we were all slaughtered. Men, women, and children. None of them made it out alive. Except for me. I was struck by one of their blades and I assumed that they must have thought me dead, because they did not search my body. I woke up hours later and managed to get away. I barely made it here alive."

I paused for a moment, recalling a map I had seen on the television screens Zoë Slinden—the deceased former ruler of Vice City—had used in the broadcast for the Feast. It had shown the regions of North America that the Collective owned, with the southern part of what had been the United States marked in another color, denoting the Free-Zone. But there had been a section of the map left uncolored, one that had covered parts of Oregon and all of California and Baja California.

"Do you remember the map Zoë had on the big screen last year?" I asked.

Zea turned to me and nodded. "That was the Dead Lands," she said.

"You traveled here all the way from there?" I asked, looking at Sedecla.

"Barely," she said, weakly. "Were it not for your young ward's help I would be dead now."

I smiled and turned to my "young ward," who was shaking her head when she saw my smile turn into a smirk.

"No," Zea said.

"No to what?" an older woman's voice said from behind us. "What is he trying to do now?"

I turned to see Mara van Denend—Zea's surrogate mother and keeper of the Gray Forum's Archives—standing in the doorway to the patient's room. Mara carried herself with an air of mystique, barely offering hints as to how long she had been here in the Silver Fortress since the Collective had destroyed the Gray Forum a hundred and one years ago. She had short gray hair and blue eyes and was a little shorter than Zea.

"Nathan found a wounded woman and brought her here to the Fortress," Zea explained. "She claims that she escaped from the Dead Lands, which, of course, means Blake is now interested in exploring them."

"Why wouldn't I be?" I asked. "It's been a while since I took care of necromancers." I turned to Mara. "I am so cooped up in here. I haven't seen action in weeks. Just give me a month to go explore. I'll only need half that to dismantle whatever's going on there. I'm efficient."

"Out of the question," Mara said, as she stared at Sedecla. "But this is a conversation to be had elsewhere."

Taking the hint, I walked with Zea out of the room and closed the door behind us. Mara stared at me without saying anything, but I could practically hear her call me stupid.

"Obviously something's going on there," I said. "We can't let necromancers just have their way with the world."

"And why not?" Mara asked. "It has been this way for a hundred years. The West Coast is a wasteland. I doubt there would be many people worth saving."

I opened my mouth to speak, but Zea spoke for me, "'If there's only one person there worth saving then I want to go.' Does that sound about right?"

"Am I that predictable?" I asked, frowning.

"As always," Mara said. "You have far more pressing concerns here. We need to ally with the Free-Zone. You are the legitimate leader of Excelsior and a symbol of the resistance against the Sanguine Collective. If you do not show up to these meetings than I feel that they will fail. You may not like it, but you are in charge. The High Court never left the Fortress behind unless it was well defended. We are all that remains of their legacy. To lose a single one of us would endanger the future, especially when there are far better battles to fight."

10

"This is just as bad as the time you stopped me from investigating that massive wall of flames that cuts off the southern part of this state from the north. Clearly there's something in there that wants to control what's on the other side and given what we deal with that can't be good for us now that the Collective's gone."

"And yet nothing has come from inside the flame barrier. Whatever is responsible seems to be content to hold onto what it has."

"Well...maybe, but we don't know that."

"And for now it must remain that way. We are safe for now."

"And if they intend to attack later?"

"Then we must defend Corpus Christi and what remains of the Sentinels and Psionics. A suicide mission into discovering a way past a gigantic fiery barrier is a waste of our time and resources."

"Yeah, yeah, I know. That's how you won the last argument we had."

"And yet it would appear you haven't learned your lesson. Are you so desperate to put yourself in harm's way that you would willingly want to go into a region of the world populated by the undead?"

"Well you heard her—there are still people alive there. People we're responsible for. That's what Excelsior stands for."

"It will stand for nothing if we all die," Zea said.

"But...there's a mystery," I said. "I solve those."

"You used to solve them," Mara said. "You are simply too valuable a resource to lose. The Dead Lands do not threaten us now. They are contained as they always have been. The Sanguine Collective made sure of that. You cannot rush out to every brush fire there is in the world if you expect to ever restore it back to what it once was. This crusade of yours could take years. You might not even live to see it come to fruition. You need to learn patience. There are many sacrifices you need to make in the coming days, and you need to accept that quickly. You are our leader. Act like it."

I rose my finger to try and rebut her, but I had nothing to offer. She was right.

I sighed. "I understand," I said, walking away. "Way to take the wind out of my sails."

I stalked forward, using all of my willpower not to throw a

temper tantrum in the middle of my own building. I heard footsteps behind me and turned around to see Zea trying to catch up with me. Curious, I stopped and allowed her to reach me.

"I almost forgot," she said, taking a breath. "There's something I need to talk to you about after you have your meeting. I…I hope it makes up for killing your sails earlier."

Part of me didn't want to laugh, but she made it very difficult to remain angry at her if she was still going to screw up simple idioms, especially since I had just said it not ten seconds ago.

"I look forward to it, sweetheart," I said, as I put on my best diplomatic face, ready to enter the Embassy Chambers of the Silver Fortress and talk to the Free-Zone ambassador.

CHAPTER 2

1

On my way to the council chambers to meet the ambassador, I stopped to check in on Sedecla in the infirmary, only to find that she was asleep. I sighed in defeat, knowing that my questions would only serve to further fuel my desire to escape the responsibilities I'd given myself.

Leaving the infirmary behind, I ended up in the gardens. The Silver Fortress was a massive building, stretching over five hundred thousand square feet, or so it had been when I was twenty. For all I knew there had been expansions made in the gaps of my memory. I hadn't had the time to explore the whole place in the year since I'd come to the future.

I'd always enjoyed spending time in the gardens, as it served as an unofficial meeting place for all the Psionics and Sentinels of the Gray Forum. In-between missions and various assignments, we would catch up with one another there and gossip about the latest items of interest. The gardens were a hub of sorts, where our teleportation circles were directed should we need to enter the Fortress from far away. It also served as a practical jumping off point, as you could access any part of the Fortress from the seven hallways that connected to the gardens. Now the gardens had fallen into disrepair, although that was unfair to our latest tenants, who were busy restoring the whole Fortress back to its former glory.

I waved at the workers as I passed by. Most of them smiled back at me, but then returned back to their work.

Most of the workers there had been survivors of a human trafficking caravan led by The Horde, a group of ghoulish vampires allied with the Sanguine Collective. In one of my more inspired ideas, I had saved them, almost dying in the process, which, to be honest, wasn't unusual for me.

Laughter nearby alerted me to the presence of Clooney Dressler and Cinderella Young, a storm Psionic and fire Sentinel, respectively. I walked over to them, having not seen them since training with them the night before.

Clooney was busy telling a joke to Cinderella, but, given the face she gave when she noticed me, I had a sinking feeling I was the punchline. This was further reinforced when Clooney smirked at me the moment I crossed my arms in front of him.

He was a little younger than me, but by how much I didn't know. He had soulful dark gray eyes, stood a little taller than me, and was garbed in the attire of an Initiate. Cinderella, meanwhile, was twenty-four years old, had strawberry blonde hair, and green eyes. She too wore Initiate robes, but those for Sentinels. Mara had designed both robes in her spare time, as the ones from my time had all withered from age.

Both of them had helped me take down Zoë Slinden a year ago. Cinderella had once been under Zoë's thrall, forced to become a tracker—a Christener trained to locate other Christeners to be fed on by the Sanguine Collective. Thanks to Nathan, we had managed to help Cinderella overcome her brainwashing and she had proved herself to be a valuable asset against Zoë. Clooney, on the other hand, had saved my life in the earlier battle against The Horde. Of the two I knew less about him, mostly because he rarely offered information unless he deemed it proper to speak about.

I had been training the both of them for the past year, helping to hone their natural abilities. Clooney was skilled enough to not need the simpler lessons I gave Cinderella, but he endured it for her sake, knowing she was handicapped, comparatively, in her growth. Were it not for Zoë's constant psychic torture of her, Cinderella would've been able to quickly catch up to Clooney. However, it had taken her a while to grasp things a five-year-old learned intuitively when the Gray Forum had been around. Still, she hadn't let this affect her training. If anything, it made her push herself harder, which was something I admired about her.

"Have you heard the news?" I asked.

"About what?" Clooney asked.

"We have a visitor. From the Dead Lands."

"Impossible," Cinderella said, shivering. "No one ever leaves the Dead Lands."

"Yeah, about that. It seems they've gotten rid of their old motto. People really took it to heart, so no one ever visited. Really decreased tourism; left a lot of good people out of work."

"What?"

I laughed.

"He doesn't mean it, Cinderella, dear," Clooney said. "He just wanted to get a reaction out of you."

"Yeah, I think I'm starting to pick up on that more," Cinderella said. "It's really annoying."

"Seems a tad bit pathetic, don't you think? Obviously, he craves attention."

"All right, enough," I said. "We can psychoanalyze me later. Don't either of you realize how important this is?"

"It's...troubling if true. No one ventures in or out of the Dead Lands. The Collective has barriers up to prevent those very things from happening."

"What if they're not up anymore?" Cinderella asked. "What if this is their way of getting back at us?"

I paused, having not considered the idea before. It made sense if it were true. What better way to get back at us for wiping out a Slinden than to get an undead army to kill us without a single Collective casualty?

"That would make sense," I said. "Good catch, Red."

Cinderella blushed as Clooney rolled his eyes. I laughed inwardly. Cinderella had quickly latched onto the nickname I'd offered her, given that she had never been given a positive one before.

"But there's very little we can do about it in our current position," Clooney said, as he gazed into my eyes. "Ah, I see now. You want more support."

"Support for what?" Cinderella asked.

"He went to Zea and Mara first and they shot him down. Now he wants us to mention the Dead Lands to them and hope to persuade them to let him have his way."

"I am not!" I yelled. "I just wanted to keep the two of you informed!"

"Calm down, Blake. Your power is seeping again."

I noticed a faint glow around my hands and calmed myself

down gradually. It was a nuisance, but for people as strong as me, we continually leak out Christening energy if we don't actively keep it in check. Getting too excited or distracted easily breaks this concentration and the end result is a clear sign to anyone checking the supernatural aether that you were a target.

"You do understand why they told you no, right?" Clooney asked once I'd calmed down.

"Yes, but that doesn't mean I have to like it," I said. "Honestly sometimes I wish I was as laissez-faire about this as you."

"Ah, but I can afford to be that way because of what you do behind the scenes. I'm not a leader; I'm just a grunt. Always have been."

"Well this just makes me feel so much better." I shook my head. "I hate this job."

"Then you never should've labeled yourself a leader to the entire world last year. If you wished for true freedom you would've handed this job to someone else, but, since you knew how poor of an idea that was, you decided to take the burden on yourself. We are few in number. To lose a single one of us is to destroy the future of the Christened. The best thing we can do is keep Corpus Christi safe from harm with what resources we have. Like allying with the Free-Zone."

I sighed. How many times was someone going to lecture me today?

Cinderella stepped forward and placed a hand on my shoulder. "Are you okay?" she asked.

I shook my head. "No, but I'm gonna have to be," I said. "Listen, if you guys aren't busy, would you mind surveying the city for me? I want to make sure nothing followed our visitor here."

"Anything for you, Blake!"

"I shall accompany her," Clooney said. "It would be a shame to lose a woman of such exquisite beauty."

Cinderella blushed and I rolled my eyes.

"You really need some new material," I said, shaking my head. "Thanks, you two. Be safe out there."

They nodded at me and went to prepare for their trip, leaving me alone. Sighing, I went towards the direction of the council chambers, wishing I'd done more preparation for this meeting.

The council chambers of the High Court of the Gray Forum had seen better days. Even after the help of the mundane residents of the Silver Fortress, it still bared some of the scars of the attack that had destroyed the Forum. Now that Excelsior was in charge, I had tried to spruce up the place to make it look more appealing, but some things still remained to attuned eyes.

To my right was a death mark—the last remnant of the life of a Christener. When we died, we left behind parts of our power. In this case it was the remnants of Hubert Woodcock, one of the members of the High Court. His actual body had been flung elsewhere by whatever had killed him, but the death mark placed itself where he had actually died.

I paused to look at it, frowning. For Christeners like myself, who were tremendously strong in comparison to our fellows, it was very tempting to access the death mark and absorb some of its power. Zea and I had managed to exorcise most of the death marks in the Fortress without problem, but at a slow rate, given the mental torture of experiencing the last moments of people like us. I'd been wary of the process, knowing I selfishly wanted to learn as much as possible about the incident that had killed everyone I'd known before coming to the future.

Hubert had been one of my earliest teachers, sensing my potential and—fearing that I might be tempted to misuse it—he'd instructed me about the dangers of abusing the Christening. We believed that our powers were directly given by God and we invoked them in His Name in an effort to offer glory to the source of our strength, rather than to fall into pride.

I sighed. One day I'd have to get rid of his death mark too. Another part of my past erased for good.

The door to the chamber opened and Dorothy held it for a Native American man dressed in a black suit. He towered above both of us, easily beating me by about seven inches. He had dark black hair and a rather simple mustache that ended right where his top lips stopped. I steeled myself as he approached, wishing I had more experience with politics as I shook his hand, hoping I wasn't doing so too roughly and wondering if maybe it wasn't rough enough.

"Ambassador Niseweynu," I said, nodding politely. "Welcome to the Silver Fortress."

"It is a pleasure, Guardian Azarel," he said, displaying a wolfish grin.

I motioned over to the meeting table and took a seat in front of him. Dorothy stood beside me, diligently waiting to reprimand me for any potential diplomatic incident I inevitably caused. Niseweynu took out his briefcase and placed it on the table, taking out several documents and a pen. I whistled in approval, having not seen a pen in over a while.

"Now that's a luxury I miss," I said.

"Yes, many things were lost in the aftermath of the Sanguine Collective's destruction of the Gray Forum," Niseweynu said, nodding. "Although I've rarely heard of anyone outside of the Free-Zone having access to things like pens, Guardian Azarel."

I started to say something, but I saw he was pondering about another thought and shut up.

"Guardian Azarel," he repeated.

"Is there a problem with my title?" I asked.

"Why not Sage Azarel? I was given to believe the leader of the Gray Forum was known as the Sage."

"I don't have the years required nor the experience to even begin to think of myself as Sage material. Besides that was what the Gray Forum used. We're Excelsior."

"'Ever upward.' An interesting ideal. Some would say that with your arrival humanity has nowhere to go but up. Others would say you have spelled their end."

"Then I intend to prove the latter wrong."

Niseweynu barked with laughter. "So it would seem," he said. "Forgive my laughter. I find it so odd to be dealing with someone so straightforward in my line of work. Normally I have to be on the lookout for tricksters and liars, but you—I like you. An honest man. I shall treasure this meeting."

I laughed. "I'm sorry," I said. "Honestly, I have no idea how to go about this meeting. I'm more used to blowing up my problems."

Dorothy froze in despair, but another laugh from Niseweynu calmed her down.

"Oh, this is such a rare treat," Niseweynu said, wiping a tear from his eyes.

"All right, since I really have no talent for this, as we've noticed, I'll just get to the point: we need your help," I said. "Corpus Christi has done well for the year we've held it, but that hasn't been without its hiccups. We had a rogue Sentinel try to seduce the masses with a crusade led against the Collective that would've gotten them all killed, an infestation of some kind of sludge golem things I barely managed to stop from overrunning the sewers, and a whole city filled with people that literally have no concept of the idea of democracy." I sighed and pinched the bridge of my nose, but then turned to look at Niseweynu. "I mean, seriously: I had to go to each individual voting station and convince them that no one was going to kill them if they voted for the person that I didn't."

"Guardian Azarel, it would be wise to withhold such information," Dorothy said in a whisper, clearly annoyed. "It is unbecoming of the leader of Excelsior to be acting like this."

"Dorothy, I think we both know that even if I tried to start off this meeting like I knew what I was doing that Ambassador Niseweynu would've seen right through it."

"Then what was the purpose of you making me read all of that material from the old time that dealt with how to properly handle diplomatic situations?"

"So that one day you'd be able to help coach me to be a respectable diplomat instead of a boorish, slack jawed idiot who can't even be bothered to try to pretend like he knew what he was doing."

Dorothy sighed and shook her head.

"He has a point, Miss Alduino," Niseweynu said. "Diplomacy isn't something easily learned, especially in such delicate proceedings as these. It's important that you feel comfortable during them. As he has no experience with these sorts of meetings, Guardian Azarel is making himself comfortable by resorting to his regular self, which has helped him deal with whatever insecurities he might hold. But far more important is for you to make the one that you intend to negotiate with feel comfortable as well. Despite his...eccentrics, Guardian Azarel has done an admirable job at making me feel welcome."

"I have?" I asked.

"Trust me. It has been some time since I have had the pleasure of feeling so at ease at the negotiation table. Normally I deal with those who would rather threaten my life than offer me the pleasantries you have extended my way. It's quite…refreshing."

"I…thank you. I feel a lot better now."

"Good, because I have some disturbing information to relay."

I gulped. That wasn't good.

"President Barrett does not like you," Niseweynu said.

Boone Barrett was the democratically-elected leader of the Free-Zone. I had done some research on him before this meeting, knowing that he'd been a former slave of the Sanguine Collective who'd escaped into the Free-Zone, which was situated in the southeastern region of what had been the United States. I had hoped to meet with him face-to-face, but he'd insisted on sending Ambassador Niseweynu instead.

"And why is that?" I asked.

"He wonders where you've been all this time and why you chose now to come out of hiding," Niseweynu said with no judgment in his voice.

"I didn't choose to come out until now. I…well—it's complicated."

"I'm on a political vacation, Guardian Azarel. I have all the time in the world to listen."

I sighed. "I was born one-hundred and twenty-eight years ago. I have only been alive for twenty-eight of those years. I was a member of the Gray Forum before they were wiped out by the Sanguine Collective. I should've died there, but an extradimensional traveler calling himself Nathan-Prime plucked me out of there and erased seven years of my memories for reasons I still don't fully understand so that he could put me here. I found Corpus Christi under the control of vampires and the Silver Fortress in ruins, so I decided to do something about it. Hence what happened at last year's Feast. That sound good enough to you?"

Niseweynu made no judgmental movements and seemed to simply be absorbing the information. "I see," he said, finally. "I will of course have to check the records we have on the Gray Forum to verify your story, but a lot of it will be impossible for us to believe, I'm afraid."

"I could meld with your mind; let you see what I saw."

"If I did that, I guarantee you I would lose my job. For all my superiors know you could've just turned me into a sleeper agent."

I eyed him intently. "You're very well informed, ambassador."

He smiled playfully. "Yes I am. I believe you will find a lot of people are more informed than they ever were in your day."

"Yeah," I said, mulling the idea over. "I'm beginning to wonder if we shouldn't have involved mundanes sooner."

"Mundanes?"

"Non-Christeners. People with no power."

"Is this some kind of fantastic slur? Because believe you me I've heard more than my fair share in life."

"It's not like a race thing; it's just—a way to distinguish between people with powers and those without."

"I'm sure my superiors will see it differently."

"Your superiors sound like a bunch of asses."

I flinched, realizing what I said. I could practically hear Dorothy's heart enter cardiac arrest.

"Oh, well, too late now to take it back, so I stick by what I said," I said.

Niseweynu barked with laughter. "Oh, that will be sure to get them riled up," he said. "If I included it in my report."

"If?"

"I'll be honest with you, Guardian Azarel: we need each other to survive. Excelsior may be in a fallen state, but we are no different. The Free-Zone cannot survive for much longer in its current existence. I have had to deal with emissaries from the Sanguine Collective, The Horde, and too many other evil supernatural entities than I care to admit. We are very much alone in the world. Now you won't hear anyone say this in the Free-Zone, but everyone knows it to be the truth. Europe has gone dark, Israel hasn't left its borders in years, Africa and Asia are under the thrall of The Horde, Central and South America are complete unknowns, and Japan and the whole of Oceania are too spread out to form a complete nation.

"While it is true that America was able to stall the advance of the Sanguine Collective and maintain its sovereignty in the form of the Free-Zone without the help of your Gray Forum, it is also true that we were turned into a protectorate of the Collective. They simply fought in a war that they could not fully understand. Had they had even a small number of Sentinels or Psionics fighting for them I imagine the fight would have been changed in their favor, but, alas, this was not so. Now we realize your power, having read the files that you sent to us from your Archives. For two thousand years you kept groups like the Collective from turning the world into its current state and the moment you were removed things went to hell." He frowned. "I will not lie. There will be resistance to allying with you, because of your supernatural nature, but you must adjust to the force of the tide as it comes. I promise you it will fade over time. The more victories you gain with us the more we will learn to appreciate what you stand for.

"But I cannot promise that will happen over the course of a single conversation. We must still talk about—"

The door to the council chambers burst open, a distressed Zea standing in front of them. She looked up at me with fear and I immediately stood up, entering a defensive position.

"Clooney and Cinderella just contacted me on the walkie-talkie," Zea said, catching her breath. "We're being attacked."

"By what?" I asked.

"A horde of skeletons and living corpses."

"I knew it!"

I pumped my fist, but refrained from saying "I told you so." Now was not the time.

"Dorothy, get Ambassador Niseweynu to safety," I said. "Take him to my room. You know the password to get in. Barricade yourselves inside and give the general alert to everyone here. No one leaves or enters the Silver Fortress except for Zea, Nathan, and myself."

"Yes, sir!" Dorothy said, standing beside Niseweynu. "Ambassador, if you will follow me. I will escort you to safety."

I nodded at them and rushed forward to Zea, running outside with her.

"Nathan's in the gardens," Zea said. "What's the plan?"

"We get out there and get the civilians to safety," I said. "If anyone in the Guard wants to assist us, then tell them not to. They can't handle this yet."

The Guard was a collection of Corpus Christi citizens who'd been trained in self-defense by me and the human enforcers who

22

had defected from the Collective to join us. They were small in number and wouldn't be a competent policing force for another year, but they were the best we had.

Zea and I rushed into the gardens, finding Nathan standing next to a teleportation circle. He beckoned us forward as I heard Dorothy announce over the newly-installed PA system exactly what I'd instructed her to say.

I bent down over the teleportation circle and waited for directions. We had hidden several teleportation circles all over the city in order to access multiple points in moments should the need arise.

"They're in the west side of the city," Nathan said. "Near the old airport."

"All right, then when we get there, we—"

I felt a freezing sensation coursing through the ring finger of my left hand. I knew its source before I looked down, seeing the skeletal ring with a bony dragon on it was now pulsating with dark purple light. That wasn't good. So far as I knew I had only had the ring for over a year's time, but I knew it was bad news. True, it had helped me out of several sticky situations last year, but it had also done a number on my body in the process. Sometimes I heard the voice of its owner talking to me, but I always ignored it, knowing that using the ring was never worth the price. I hadn't found a way of removing it from my finger, save an amputation, but I liked my digits to be even when added up on both hands, so that was out of the question.

"Are you using it?" Zea asked, making me turn my attention to her.

"No," I said. "It just started glowing."

"That's not good. Please don't use it. I don't want you to end up like last time."

Zea had seen its power firsthand. She had never directly described what I had looked like while the ring was possessing me, but in her hesitation I could tell that it had terrified her to see me like that.

"Well it can glow all it wants," I said, activating the teleportation circle. "I'm not using it."

CHAPTER 3

We ended up at the airport, having teleported inside one of the old hangar bays. As one, we left the hangar bay behind to locate Cinderella and Clooney, whose spiritual presences we could sense as being several hundred yards away from us to the northeast. But they weren't alone in the supernatural aether. Hundreds of foreign presences were there, a dark and twisted energy running through their bodies, if they could be said to have that.

I shivered, feeling a strangely familiar realization of what the energy belonged to enter my mind. Ignoring it, I pressed on, running faster than the others.

The Christened have superhuman speed and endurance. A marathon to us is no more taxing than a jog in the park. Even Nathan—being younger and less trained than Zea and I—was keeping up with us without breaking a sweat.

"They're up ahead, near the apartments!" Zea announced.

"Right!" I shouted out. "Stick together! There's no telling what these things will be able to do!"

Looking forward, I saw the apartment buildings that Zea had indicated. They, like most buildings in Corpus Christi, were old and dilapidated, having not seen any kind of maintenance in a hundred years. Some of the rooms looked like they had been broken into, most likely as a result of the inevitable looting that had taken place after the Gray Forum had fallen. There were signs of life around, given the fires that were still lit on some of the balconies.

A strong gale erupting from nowhere on the opposite side of the buildings alerted us to Clooney's location. I could hear shouting and screaming, as well as the panicked sounds of people trying to get away from the spectacle. I rushed forward, ready to help the others out.

On the other side of the buildings, in what appeared to have once been a playground, were several civilians desperately climbing up on a geodesic dome, hoping to avoid their attackers. I resisted the urge to let fear enter my mind when I saw what we were up against.

A horde of moving skeletons had surrounded the dome, some of which were attempting to climb up it to kill the civilians. Several skeletons were armed with swords, which were about as old and shoddy as they were. Others had bows ready to fire at the civilians, while others still were aiming at them with what appeared to be submachine guns.

That was new.

Near the edge of the apartment complex were Cinderella and Clooney, who stood back to back as they attacked a man garbed entirely in black.

"Take out the archers and gunners first!" I shouted out.

"Right!" Nathan and Zea responded.

Holding out my right fist, I pumped it forward, filling it with light, as I yelled, "Fiat lux!"

Instantaneously, a beam of light erupted from my fingertips, heading straight into the nearest contingent of skeleton archers. The moment the light collided with them, the skeletons burst into flames. To my right, I saw Zea throw her spatha towards some of the skeletons, while simultaneously powering up a lightning invocation that passed from skeleton to skeleton, as she summoned her spatha back into her hands. Nathan remained behind us, attempting to use his illusion invocation to disorient the enemy.

However, at that same time, the skeletons I'd hit with my light attack stood back up and nocked their arrows at me, which were also now on fire. Realizing what this meant, I tried to craft a telekinetic barrier to deflect them, but settled for collapsing into the dirt, since I still wasn't skilled enough to do what I wanted. The arrows fell into the grass around me, setting it on fire as well.

I grunted, rolling to my left, only to realize I'd ended up next to several of the gun-toting skeletons, who trained their weapons on me.

"Seismic Finale!" Zea called out, sending a wave of earth into the air.

The skeletons, unprepared for her attack, had already started firing their weapons at me, but the bullets were instead swept up by Zea's earth invocation. I noticed that whenever the skeletons fired their guns, their bodies seemed to be too lightweight to sustain the kickback and their aim was off by a tremendous amount.

One of the civilians cried out in terror, alerting me to their plight, as they were struggling to stay out of the reach of their skeletal pursuers on the dome. Realizing I couldn't reach them in time, I held out my hands.

"Ageg!" I shouted, summoning an ethereal bow of light to appear in my hands.

Aiming at the closest skeleton, I pulled the bowstring back and let loose an arrow made of concentrated light that hit its target without fail. The skeleton's head fell off and the body soon crumbled afterward. However, one of the other skeletons managed to reach its target and bit into the throat of an older man, who'd pushed a child out of the way of the attack. The older man convulsed, dying of blood loss not too long after the blow had ended. I shot another arrow at the skeleton that had killed him, managing to get rid of it as well. The remaining civilians huddled together on top of the dome, watching in horror as the old man's corpse was suddenly covered by a veil of black energy that swarmed around it, twisting the corpse into a mockery of life that was now a mindless thrall greedily looking at the people who had once been its friends and family.

I nocked another arrow, but a sudden sense of danger made me duck, as I barely avoided a swinging fist that had belonged to a mundane who'd died and been turned into a walking corpse before we'd gotten there. Ageg disappeared once my focus was gone. I held up my fists, glad that my clothing would help stop any attempt on their part to bite into my flesh, save for my face and hands. For the briefest of moments, I looked back to the trapped civilians, only to see that the skeletons and corpses had abandoned them and were now running in the other direction. Puzzled, I looked over to Nathan, who was directing them elsewhere with his illusions. For now, the civilians were safe.

I, however, was not.

The corpse ran forward and I grappled with it as I tripped and fell onto the ground. Furiously, it attempted to sink its teeth into my neck, but I was stronger than it was and I could keep it off of me without it getting too close.

"Tenebris regni!" I invoked, sending forth darkness from my hands into the corpse's body, sending it flying off of me.

The corpse landed into one of the broken apartment buildings, causing a collection of dust and debris to end up in the air. Breathing heavily, I shook my head and stood up, seeing that Nathan was guiding the remaining civilians away to safety, while Zea was doing her best to wipe out the remaining undead around us.

"Fire's the only thing that seems to work on them!" Zea cried out, summoning several flames around her body to prevent them from getting close to her.

Hearing movement ahead of me, I watched as the corpse I'd sent flying had recovered and—while having clearly taken damage from my attack—it was still no worse for wear.

"Of course it is," I grumbled.

I sucked at fire invoking. I'd studied it for years, but had never mastered more than lighting the end of my thumb as an ersatz match. That definitely wouldn't be enough fire to set the corpse ablaze before it killed me.

It charged me once more, but I sidestepped it this time, and took the time to bring out my pistol, shooting the undead beast in the head. I held out my pistol—a Jericho 941—and pointed it at the corpse. The bullets it held had been coated with silver, which I knew wouldn't really hurt these walking corpses, but it still packed a big supernatural punch, as most creatures didn't like it. The corpse wasn't moving. I kicked it in the side and there was no response.

Glad that my gambit had paid off, I let out a sigh of relief and watched as Zea dispatched the remaining skeletons and corpses with fire. I ran to her side and helped her stand up. Unlike me, she wasn't used to sending out attacks in such quick succession. The process always tired her out.

"Great job, Zee," I said, letting go of her once I felt she could stand without help. "Turns out a bullet to the brain does the same job as fire."

Looking over to where I'd been, Zea pointed at the corpse and summoned a fiery blaze to consume the corpse.

"Just to be safe," she said, once her attention returned to me.

I nodded and was about to speak, but we both felt a prickle of danger incoming and turned around to barely catch Cinderella and Clooney as they flew out of the sky right into us. Knocked down on the ground, I shook my head and pushed Clooney's feet off of my face. I pushed myself upwards, realizing that Cinderella's face was on my chest. Her head slumped off of my chest and into my lap when I moved up and she stirred, groaning in pain. Gently, I picked up her head and placed it on the ground as I swiftly stood up, looking over to where they'd been fighting.

I watched as the black-garbed man from earlier slowly walked towards us. Every fiber of my being told me this guy was going to kill me. As he approached, I got a better look at him, seeing that he appeared to be of Palestinian or Egyptian descent, had black hair, and brown eyes. He stood about three inches above me and was grinning ear-to-ear at me.

Behind me, Zea stood up with Clooney, who'd recovered faster from the blow than Cinderella had.

"Some kind of concussive force blast," Clooney said, spitting out dirt. "Took us both by surprise."

"Understood," I said. "Take Cinderella away from here and heal her. Then take Nathan and the civilians with you. Zea and I will handle him."

"Got it."

Clooney stood up and picked Cinderella in his arms. She tried to protest and say she could still fight, but Clooney ignored her pleas and ran off to find Nathan.

"What's the plan?" Zea asked.

"He looks like he wants to talk," I said. "We'll use that time to charge up our energy. Then, when he's busy talking I'll rush forward and make him fight me. You'll use that to get him while he's distracted. If he's summoning corpses and skeletons than there's no way this guy's going to be reasonable, so don't even bother trying to take him alive."

"Yes, sir."

I held out my hands in front of me, but the man was still walking towards us, as if we weren't a threat. I felt a dark energy inside of his body, another sense of familiarity entering my mind. Then, when we were ten feet away from each other, the man held

28

out his hands, and bowed slightly. Unprepared for this, my politeness overrode my incredulity, and I bowed back to him.

"So the Christened truly are back," the man said, smiling.

He placed a hand on his chin and stood still, looking us over. He seemed to be pleased by whatever he saw and nodded his head.

"So they have you to thank for their being able to invade these lands," he said.

"Who does?" I asked. "Who do you work for."

"My current employers go by Morior Invictus."

"'Death before defeat'? Or is it 'I die undefeated'?"

"I believe both are quite apt. There are some who would even say it means 'to conquer death'."

"Then they'd better fire their Latin tutors because that's not how it goes."

The man laughed, throwing his head backward. "Not that I care, really. I just enjoy the pay."

Angered, I pointed around me. "This is enjoyment for you? People died here today!"

"And you only have yourself to blame."

I flinched. What did he mean by that? However, before I could answer that question, I heard shouting behind me and I dared to look back, seeing that Clooney, Cinderella, and Nathan were running back with the civilians, as they were pursued by an undead horde.

Feeling someone near me, I looked back to see that the man was right next to me, and holding onto my left hand. He was reaching for my ring and seemed to find a way to remove it from my body, but, at that same time, Zea swung at him with her spatha. The man leapt backwards, flipping elegantly in the air to land perfectly several yards away from us.

Zea stood in front of me, holding her spatha out to protect me.

"We never could have come here without your help," the man said, cackling.

"And what's that supposed to mean?" I asked.

"Normally the protective barriers set up by the Sanguine Collective would've prevented their forces from leaving the Dead Lands, but thanks to you the Collective removed them."

"Why? What does that have to do with me?"

"The Collective has withdrawn from all of their holds near the border of the Dead Lands. Anything in-between here and there is now Morior Invictus' territory. I think they want us to eliminate you for them, but my employers have other things in mind for the only free Christened left in existence."

Clooney and Cinderella shouted out invocations against the undead horde coming near them. I didn't dare turn my head for fear that I would get attacked again. I had to settle this, but I needed information.

"Who are you?" I asked. "Why are you doing this?"

"Me?" he asked, pondering for a moment. "When I was by myself people called me the Dark Thief, but now that I have an extra passenger, I go by Valefar."

"Valefar? As in the demon? Wait, are you a member of The Thirteen?"

The Thirteen were an alliance of demons who had been mired in the shadows of my world, creating havoc and destruction for their own nefarious goals. I had met one such member when I'd killed Zoë during the liberation of Corpus Christi. She had been possessed by a demon named Beleth, who had been incredibly difficult to kill and had claimed that he was the weakest member of The Thirteen.

He smiled. "Yes...and no. It is true that I am in league with my fellows, but I hold no true allegiance to them. If anything, I am glad to be rid of Beleth. He was far too much trouble for his worth."

"Just what I'd expect from a demon: a complete lack of empathy."

"Well, you can hardly—"

I rushed him, managing to close the distance quickly so that I had pinned him to the ground. I raised my right fist to crash down into his face, but the moment the blow landed it instead hit the dirt. My body fell towards the ground, as I realized that Valefar's body was no longer in-between mine and the earth. Rolling around to my left once I'd completely fallen, I barely missed getting hit by a strange claw that had exited Valefar's upper wrist. The claw retracted into his body and he shrugged, more bemused than upset that his plans had failed temporarily.

"Winter's Embrace!" Zea called out, summoning a cone of ice that flew towards Valefar.

30

Valefar noticed the attack and managed to bob and weave his way through it at blinding speeds that I could barely register. It was inhuman. Even if he'd managed to avoid the solid ice, he still would've been affected by the cold of the blast. Yet, he'd gone through it all with no sign of damage.

"Impossible!" Zea cried out.

Valefar held up his right index finger and wagged it around playfully. "Not if you know what you're doing, my dear," he said.

Grumbling in anger, Zea held out her hands and shouted out, "Lightning Reign!"

Three arcs of lightning jutted out from her fingertips, only to pass through Valefar harmlessly as the sound of thunder reverberated in every direction. Valefar grinned and Zea's face drained of color.

There was no way he was faster than lightning. This was a trick. A ruse. Speedsters existed here, but the immense energy necessary to perform such invocations took an enormous toll on the body. I could move about seventy miles per hour if I concentrated my energy into the sole purpose of moving fast, but it was such a chore that it was more responsible to just move at half that rate to get around.

But this wasn't that. He was reacting to things he shouldn't. Zea's conjured lightning moved slower than the real thing, but was still swifter than someone's normal reaction time. There was no way Valefar was moving that fast without ripping apart his body and killing all of us without a second thought in the same second, so what was the trick? What if he didn't move as fast as lightning, but was reacting to something else? I had to think smaller.

What was he responding to? He seemed to be focusing his sight on Zea alone, but I knew this was misdirection, because he'd be a fool to ignore me; he just wanted me to think he didn't care about me. Did it have to do with something he sensed at a rate faster than even we could process? But which of the five primary senses was it? What was I missing?

Zea sent a blast of earth at Valefar's face, making him turn his back to me, while also avoiding her attack with ease. She invoked again, this time bringing fire his way, which merely singed the grass around his feet.

A stray question entered my mind. Which sense would allow

him the greatest edge in this fight? Something that could allow Valefar the chance to move away from danger if he knew it was coming his way. I had an idea, but it was a long shot.

"Ageg!" I shouted, summoning the bow.

Firing off the first shot I could, I made sure to make as much noise as possible. The arrow flew forwards and merely missed its target when Valefar had taken a step back. He continued to ignore me, but it was obvious that he'd known what to do to avoid my attack.

Hearing. Hearing was the fastest of the five primary senses. Not by much, but those precious milliseconds were exactly what Valefar needed to beat us. But what if he couldn't hear something?

It was a risky gamble, but I had nothing else working for me right now. I took out my pistol and aimed it at Valefar's right arm. His back was still to me, so he couldn't see what I was doing.

To my knowledge, I'd never actually done what I was about to perform before, but I knew the basics behind masking sounds. I'd never been a stealthy person, but it had been required training at Sentinel camp to at least know how to hide yourself not only by sight, but by sound as well.

Holding my hand over the pistol, I whispered, "Silentium."

Amazingly, I'd managed to localize the lack of sound around my pistol, rather than the entire body as I'd been taught. Grinning greedily, I continued aiming at Valefar and then fired.

Two things happened then. The first was that the bullet traveled half the distance it needed before my concentration over the invocation failed and I was suddenly greeted by an uncontrolled outburst of the gunshot, which hurt my ears. The second was that the bullet managed to hit its target, albeit a little higher than I'd aimed.

I fell backward, nursing my ears because of the sound, which seemed to have somehow gained power after being hidden for so long. I didn't pretend to understand how that worked. I was in too much pain to think straight. Holding my hands to my face, I muttered a weak healing invocation that barely reduced the ringing in my ears, but allowed me enough presence of self to stand up off the ground.

I looked ahead, seeing that Valefar was looking back at me with something akin to pride on his face. He was nursing the wound on his arm, which was slowly being healed by a black energy that coursed through his body.

"Well, aren't we the clever one?" Valefar remarked. "Seems like you've got me figured out."

"I'm full of surprises," I said. "Beleth had that diamond armor skin, so if you're a member of The Thirteen, you also had to have some kind of unbelievable ability, which also meant you had to have a weakness too."

"Oh, I'll be the first to admit we all have our weaknesses. Like you, for instance." He pointed behind me. "You might want to do something about that."

Cursing myself for falling for the most basic trick in the book, I turned around, only to see that he'd actually been warning me of danger. Cinderella had gotten separated from the others and was fighting hand-to-hand with a skeleton wielding a sword with one hand, the other having been blown off of its body by her fire invocation. However, the now free-roaming hand was acting on its own and had leapt up to strike her while her guard was down.

"Behind you, Red!" I called out too late to save Cinderella from the skeletal arm that penetrated her body underneath her left armpit. "No!"

Without thinking, I ran forward to her location, not caring that in-between Cinderella and myself were twenty skeletons. They all aimed at me with their weapons of choice, but I ignored the danger. A surge of energy ran through my body and I yelled fiercely, the energy crafting a circle of pure power that sent every skeleton in the vicinity onto the ground. Ignoring Zea's cries to focus and remove the energy safely I raced over to Cinderella's position, holding her in my arms. I located the wound and ripped a piece of her shirt off so that I could use my medicinal invocation properly. The blow had made her lose a lot of blood and I doubted I would be able to make her body manufacture enough to put her back in the fight.

But I didn't care about that. My friend was dying and I was the only one who could save her. Clooney appeared to my right and deflected a bony arrow with his dagger as he crafted a wind invocation that destroyed the archer that had sent it our way.

I focused the entirety of my mind on fixing Cinderella's wound. I knew I wasn't as good as Zea, but I was the best she had at that moment, given that Zea was preoccupied with Valefar.

"Blake—switch with me!" Zea pleaded.

I barely heard her, too focused on saving Cinderella to bother caring about what was going on around me.

I watched the blood pour back into her body, having received my commands to help her heal her body. The wound slowly closed behind the blood, the damage being repaired swiftly. I felt more energy than I needed to use leaving my body, but I wasn't paying attention to it. Finally, once I felt the danger had passed, I let out a sigh of relief, as Cinderella had started breathing normally again.

It was done. I had saved her.

I looked up to watch the fight and saw to my horror that Zea had been stabbed by one of Valefar's claws. She fell to the ground looking in my direction, confusion all over her face. I stood up and prepared to race after her, but Valefar snatched Zea's body before I could lunge after it. He jumped into the air and cackled madly as he bounded over to the next building, eventually disappearing from sight.

"If you want your friend back," Valefar's voice rang out in the air with no clear origin, "then you'll give yourself up to Morior Invictus, boy. We'll be waiting."

"Zea!" I shouted, picking myself up from the ground.

I started to run off after her, but a firm hand prevented me. I glared back at the source, finding it to be Clooney.

"You can't leave us here alone," he said. "Nathan and I aren't enough to stop these undead and protect Cinderella."

"He took her, Clooney!" I roared back. "I have to save her!"

"She wouldn't want someone to die just because you tried to rescue her! Now get over here and help!"

Rage built up inside me. There was nothing I could do for her. I had been careless. Why hadn't I switched places with her? She was more suited to healing Cinderella than I was.

"Tenebris regni!" I yelled, sending a dark wave of energy at the closest skeletons, shattering them into dust instantly.

Taking my lead, Clooney danced in place, summoning the energy necessary for a vortex of wind to appear from nowhere, which collected the remaining undead in its high-speed grip. The cyclone swirled faster, grinding the skeletons against each other until there was nothing left but a white powder. Waving his hands around, Clooney sent the wind outwards, releasing the powder and dust, without a single undead surviving the strike. Tired from the attack, Clooney held his hands on his knees, but then recovered and went to Cinderella's side. He held her right hand in his arms and called out her name, but there was no response. She'd fallen unconscious sometime after I'd healed her.

Movement behind me alerted me to Nathan's presence, as he was checking over the survivors of the attack. No one of them seemed to have been bitten, but they were all still clearly traumatized over the incident.

A sudden rush of energy appeared beside me and I watched in confusion as Mara appeared from nowhere, having used a one-way teleportation circle to reach our location. She was holding an assault rifle I'd never seen before as well as what appeared to be grenades. She gazed throughout the scene, looking frantically for danger, only to realize that she'd showed up too late to help. She looked around further, trying to locate Zea, but when she didn't see her, she looked at me, helplessly.

I frowned. "They took her, Mara," I said, fighting back tears. "They took Zea. They took her to the Dead Lands."

Mara's pale face lost all of its color. She dropped her assault rifle and held onto me for support. I held her up as best I could, trying to sense Zea's spiritual presence, but the only inklings I got were short blips that told me nothing more than that she was alive, which I tried to take solace in for now.

"What happened?" Mara asked, looking up at me.

"We came here to help Cinderella and Clooney," I said. "We did, but the undead they were fighting were led here by a member of The Thirteen who calls himself Valefar. He said that he worked for Morior Invictus—the necromancers who lead the Dead Lands. He said that the Collective had broken down the barriers that stopped them from invading, because of what I'd done. We fought them together, but Cinderella got hurt, so I went to heal her. Zea screamed at me to let her do it, but I didn't listen. I was too angry. Then when my back was turned he took Zea."

I watched Clooney pick up Cinderella and walk towards us. He was angry, but not enough to let it stop him from making sure she was safe.

"This is all my fault," I said.

"No, this is the Sanguine Collective's fault," Mara said. "They were the ones who willingly removed the protective barriers so that we would be attacked. This is their revenge for what happened to them."

"That wouldn't have happened if I hadn't of interfered."

"Nor would you have saved the lives of over seven thousand people who were supposed to be sacrificed if not for your impetuous nature."

I clenched my fist. "Fortress. Now."

CHAPTER 4

I stormed into the Court Chambers of St. Jude the Apostle, scaring two workers who were attempting to paint the formerly mold-covered walls. When they saw the glare on my face, they left the room immediately, even though I hadn't once looked in their direction.

My hands shook fiercely, and I went to the biggest chair in the room, sitting down in it. I continued glaring, waiting for Mara, Dorothy, Clooney, Nathan, and the now stable Cinderella to enter the room and close the door behind them. Cinderella frowned when she saw my glare and avoided my gaze as she sat down.

The rest sat down and waited for me to say something. I tried to quell my anger, but it wasn't a hard-fought battle. Instead, I looked around the room, which had been the secret meeting place of the High Court before the fall of the Gray Forum. Before I had made Excelsior, I could count the amount of times I'd been in this room on one hand. Mostly when I'd been forced to give accounts of different missions I'd went on that had involved the deaths of a fellow Christener.

In the center of the round table where everyone was assembled was a marble statue of St. Jude. Like most rooms and hallways in the Forum, this room was named after a famous saint of Christendom, even though in my day very few members of the Forum were Catholic. I didn't know which smart aleck member of the Forum had decided to name this room after St. Jude, but I wanted to strangle them for making the patron saint of desperate situations and lost causes stare back at me after all I'd done.

I felt a stirring in my mind—a faint trace of the mental link Zea and I shared. Her thoughts were foggy and vague, as if she'd been given anesthesia.

I sighed. This was getting us nowhere. I needed to stand up and talk.

Looking up from my seat, I stared at the others, barely managing to suppress my rage.

"I'm going to get her," I said.

"And how do you propose doing that?" Clooney asked. "For all we know that demon's taken her straight into the Dead Lands."

"Even he's not that fast. I can still sense her."

"As can I," Mara said.

I furrowed an eyebrow. Sometimes I forgot that Mara had a smidgen of the Christening in her. There was a reason she oversaw the Archives after all.

"I still don't know what's going on," Dorothy said. "All I know is you left, came back, and Zea wasn't with you. Can't someone tell me what happened out there? Oh, and Ambassador Niseweynu is fine, thanks for asking."

"We went to help Clooney and Cinderella," Nathan said. "Some maniac calling himself Valefar was using zombies and skeletons to attack the city, but I don't think that's what he was really after."

"I agree," Clooney said. "He seemed more interested in you, Blake."

I frowned, recalling his attempt to steal the ring. I stared at it and grimaced.

"But then why did he kidnap Zea?" Dorothy asked.

"Because he couldn't get to me," I said. "I'd started figuring out a way past his defenses. It was only a matter of time before I told the others. But I was distracted, so—"

"It's because of me!" Cinderella cried out, silencing all of us. "It's because I got hit! I'm so useless!"

Cinderella burst into tears, hiding her face from the rest of us with her hands. Her body trembled violently and if I hadn't known better, I'd have thought she was suffering from an epileptic seizure. Dorothy swiftly rose from her chair and stood beside Cinderella, speaking softly to her and reassuring her that she wasn't to blame.

I stood up as well and smashed my fist into the table. Everyone turned to look at me, even Cinderella, who was still crying, but looking more confused now than ashamed. I gazed directly at her and tried to put my thoughts into words.

How could she say it was her fault? I was the idiot who'd

screwed everyone over. How could she have expected to be able to take on so many creatures she'd never seen before that moment? If anything, she should feel proud of the fact that she'd done so well.

But how did I say any of this out loud?

Then I realized I didn't have to.

Cinderella and I kept looking into the others' eyes, which was always a dangerous idea for the Christened. If your mind was unfocused you could tap into memories and thoughts that weren't your own; rather, they were the property of the one you were looking at. But a good effect eye contact had between people like us was that they acted like a lie detector. The moment our eyes connected, Cinderella knew that I bore her no ill will and it seemed to calm her enough to breathe somewhat normally, although the crying had not stopped.

"We can sit here and blame each other all day, but we really know they're the ones to blame here," Clooney said, as I sat down. "Obviously, none of us woke up today and decided today would be the day we wanted Zea to get kidnapped. They did."

"Who's they?" Dorothy asked.

"A group calling themselves Morior Invictus—the rulers of the Dead Lands," Mara said.

Dorothy gasped. "The undead masters? The ones said to have lived for thousands of years because of their necromantic magic?"

I looked at Mara. "Do the Archives have any mention of any human necromancers of such talent before the Fall of the Gray Forum?" I asked.

"Yes," she said. "Known human necromancers or Christeners with the ability to head down that path at the time before the Fall were limited to these individuals: Zvi Aharoni (slain in the Fall), Abdul Alhazred (presumed deceased after a fight with the last Joab), Blake Azarel (current leader of Excelsior), Lucien Azarel (slain in the Fall), Circe (current member of the Red Council), Aleister Crowley (slain by the Dream Team), Jannes and Jambes (current members of the Red Council), Koschei the Lich (slain in gladiatorial combat by Lucien Azarel), Medea (current member of the Red Council), Morgan Le Fay (current member of the Red Council), and Atanasio Mortis (slain in the Fall)."

I nodded. That list was a lot shorter than I imagined, but it wasn't without its surprises. Mara had gone above and beyond my limited selection. I presumed that I was on that list because of the ring. It didn't particularly offend me; I would've put me on that list on principle, but the fact that my father was on that list interested me.

Always a private man, my father had never gone too in depth into his past. My mother, Nane, had always told me that he was deeply ashamed of what he'd done before he'd met her.

"I believe we can remove anyone from the Red Council from our list of suspects," Mara said. "Given that they control Europe now and would have advertised their rule over anything the Sanguine Collective craves."

"Makes sense to me, but why exclude any potential deities from the list or even members of the Fair Folk?" Nathan asked.

"Because any deity who couldn't break the barrier the Sanguine Collective made wouldn't be worth suspicion," Clooney said. "Besides, deities that aren't the Almighty are humans brainwashed into thinking they're divine. They need people to worship them to keep having power. Enthralling your potential worshipers into mindless corpses isn't a good business strategy." He paused. "As far as the Fair Folk are concerned, I can't say that we can wipe them off the suspect list yet, but this does have a distinctly humanistic feel to it. The Fae are vain; they too would like people to serve them as willing participants, not mindless automatons."

"Initiate Dressler speaks fairly," Mara said. "The likelihood of our culprits being any of the other candidates is unlikely, given that you would have no desire to both lead a necromantic army as well as an organization devoted to destroying groups like that."

"Darth Sidious, I'm not," I said, surprised that I'd even had the will to crack a joke. "So that leaves who then?"

"People from the Forum who fled from the Collective?" Cinderella proposed.

"Or necromancers from before the Fall who weren't on the Forum's radar," Clooney suggested.

"The truth of the matter is we don't know who these people are, but we can determine their motivations," Mara said. "They came here to spread their diseased magic in an effort to find you, Guardian Azarel. I think you have already figured out why."

I grimaced and gently placed my hand on the table so that everyone could see my ring. "This thing here," I said. "Valefar tried to steal it from me, but Zea stopped him."

"And why would they want your ring?" Dorothy asked.

I paused, realizing I hadn't explained what it was to her and realized I'd reflexively done it to not ruin her perception of me.

"This abomination seems to hold the spirit of a magical practitioner," I said. "Given what it can do, I'd hazard a guess that they were a necromancer in life. I have used its power before to attack others and escape from bondage, but was never in control when it happened. It's...dark. Evil. A complete desecration of what we stand for."

"Which is precisely why people like Morior Invictus want it," Nathan said. "So—"

I wandered off into my own thoughts, pondering on what this all meant. Every now and then I could still feel a faint trace of Zea's thoughts enter my mind and cringed. A vague memory of a location I had never been before entered my vision only to be swiftly replaced by the scene of the meeting room. Realizing what this meant, I jumped up excitedly and spread my hands over the table.

"I have a plan!" I announced, grinning.

Everyone turned to me, wondering what had caused the sudden outburst.

"I can track down Zea," I said. "I can always sense where she is. It's fainter now, but soon she'll have to wake up and then I can use a teleportation circle to find her and bring her back before Valefar gets the chance to stop me."

"That's assuming you can even track her down in the first place," Clooney said.

"Correct," Mara said. "The odds are against us. The chances we find Valefar and Zea before they enter the Dead Lands are slim. For all we know it was their intention to kidnap someone and force you to come after them so that you could be led into a trap."

I frowned, but shook my head. "That's why we have to get to her before Valefar gets to the Dead Lands. If we leave now, we can catch up with them."

"I volunteer to go!" Cinderella declared. "We have to move fast to get to Zea!"

Cinderella tried to stand up and winced in pain.

"You will do no such thing," Clooney said. "You need more time to rest and heal."

Cinderella looked from him and then to me. She bit her lip and sat back in her seat in silence.

"And besides, even if you did leave, Blake, who will stay behind to defend the city?" Dorothy asked. "What if this is some ploy to get you to leave to allow the Sanguine Collective to sack Corpus Christi in your absence?"

"That won't happen," I said. "Some of us will stay behind to safeguard the city while I go to find them."

"Of course, leave a child, a librarian, a wounded ingenue, and me against the entire Collective," Clooney said. "As always you think everything through before you act, Blake."

"They're expecting me," I said. "If I send anyone who's not expected to go find her then Zea's as good as dead. At least this way I can guarantee her safety."

"By yourself? You're stronger right now than we are, for sure, but you have to know that you can't do this alone."

"I don't like this situation anymore than you do, Clooney, but we have to face facts. I'm the only one who can do this."

"I am coming with you," Mara said.

I turned to face her. Throughout the entire conversation, she had managed to maintain her composure, but all of that had been a well-crafted façade. In her normal, stoic face was now one filled with a concentrated determination born of anger and fear. However, I—true to form—didn't notice any of this until it was too late.

"Mara, I'm saying this as kindly as I can, but what the hell do you have to offer me besides a portable encyclopedia?" I asked.

"She is my daughter, boy," Mara stated, a hint of a growl in her voice. "No one takes her from me. No one else needs to come with us. They will need to stay and protect the city."

I stepped back involuntarily as Mara glared at me. Although they weren't blood-related, Mara and Zea might as well have been. Mara was not an overly affectionate person, but being around Zea was one of the few times she let her guard down. If I thought I was pissed off about this whole ordeal, I could only imagine what was going on in her head.

"I see," I said. "Welcome aboard."

I turned to look at the others, too fearful of her wrath to question anything else she did. They were all worried. I had to do something to calm them down.

"I'm not gonna sugarcoat this, guys," I said, wishing I believed in myself as much as they thought I did. "This whole thing sucks. I—"

Nathan suddenly convulsed and cried out violently. I rushed from my seat and joined his side. He held onto his temples and he opened his eyes, which were now pure white. I instantly knew he was having a vision of the future, although I'd never seen him react like this before.

"No!" he shouted out, shaking his head. "That can't happen!"

Then, just as suddenly as his ordeal had started, Nathan paused and looked me in the eye, saying, "He says you have to go or else the world is overrun with the dead."

I nodded and helped lift him off the floor and back into his seat. I looked over at the others, who were figuring out the identity of the one who'd sent the vision in the first place.

"If Nathan-Prime says I need to go, then there's no way in hell I'm not," I said. "He only gets involved when the situation's just that dire. Nathan, what did you see?"

Nathan shook his head. "I'm not saying it out loud," he said, panting. "He said it was only a vision of a possible future, but I won't say what it was. All those poor people. Those fools don't even know what they're doing. They don't understand the madness."

I placed a hand on his shoulder. "Then you don't have to say anything. I'm going with Mara. I'm gonna stop Morior Invictus or die trying."

"Then take me with you!" Cinderella protested, regaining her resolve. "I can help!"

"No," I said, staring once more into her eyes. "Mara is right. The more of us that go the weaker Corpus Christi becomes. I'm the strongest. I have the most experience. This is my fault. I have to go. I need you, Clooney, and Nathan to protect the people here. There's no telling what the Collective might do once they get wind that I'm not here to help protect you. Besides, you're wounded. You need to stay here and rest, especially since we don't have our strongest healing invoker with us." I bit my lip and tensed up.

"Will you listen to me or not?"

Cinderella sat back down with a hurt expression on her face.

"And pray tell how are we supposed to contact you if something goes wrong here?" Clooney asked. "Or what happens if you don't come back? Should we send a search party or start setting up for a funeral?"

"There will be no contact between us," I said. "I go with Mara and we get Zea back or we die. Dorothy is in charge of the administrative needs. Defer to her as you would to me. If you don't hear back from me within two months' time assume we are dead. Mourn us and move on. There are still Christeners out there who need to be taught. Excelsior must not fall."

"Regrettably, I must disagree."

"You what?"

"That is not part of my arrangement. My job is to keep you safe. Should you fall in battle my family would be very displeased with me. And should that happen I would have more pressing concerns than teaching prospective students, as I can assure that you that I would be quite dead, thus I would not be around here. Cinderella and Nathan would be all you would have left as a legacy."

I looked at them and then back at Clooney. "Then that will have to suffice," I said. "The rest is in God's hands."

"Blake, please be careful. There's a lot I need to—" Clooney suddenly stopped, holding a hand to his throat.

"What?" I asked. "There's a lot you need to what?"

"These lips are sealed."

I eyed him intently for a moment, but ignored him. I had better things to do than worry about him.

CHAPTER 5

1

Within the hour, Mara and I had gathered enough supplies between us to support us as we left Corpus Christi behind. She was done before me and had waited in faux patience for me to finish packing my belongings. She was not wearing her Archivist's robes, but was instead garbed in a burqa-esque outfit complete with shawl over her head, looking anxious and ready to just accept anything I brought to the table. However, when she saw my attire, she scoffed and shook her head.

"Guardian Azarel," she said, coldly, "you will not leave this place looking as you do."

I rolled my eyes. I was wearing my standard set of Sentinel clothing, which would be more than able to protect me from the heat on our way to track down Valefar.

"You may bring this uniform with you, but you must not wear it until we are nowhere near other people," Mara said.

"Why?" I asked.

"Because your face is the most recognizable on in the entire area and seeing you in your usual attire will only solidify the fact that Blake Azarel is heading west. We need to conceal ourselves. Come, I will arrange for other clothes for you to wear. We must not waste any more time."

2

Mara and I eventually left Corpus Christi behind, two hours before the sun would set. We were not alone, however. With us was a traveling caravan, which had been in need of muscle to protect them on their journey west. In total there were eight others

45

with us, all led by an older man named Benedict who had a gruff voice and a knack for lowballing on his negotiations for hiring bodyguards. Not that I needed the money, mind you, but it was more the principle of the matter.

The caravan was on its way to Phoenix, which seemed to have been right outside the sphere of influence from both the Sanguine Collective and the Dead Lands. Upon asking, the caravan leaders weren't concerned with Phoenix being dangerous, as it was supposedly well protected. Their main worry was what might attack them on their way there.

My horse whinnied and I brushed its hair with my right hand, trying to calm it down. It had been some time since I had ridden a horse, but this stallion of mustang stock had little of its ancestor's desire to never be broken. Instead, it had been far too easy to acclimate him to me and he had accepted me as if he'd known me his entire life. Most of us were on horseback, but others were inside their wagons, letting the horses tied to the reins do the work for them.

I, of course, was no longer wearing what I had before leaving on this trip. Mara had, with much patience, managed to convince me to wear far less conspicuous clothing, or at least her definition of the term. I now wore clothes more in line with the other caravan workers, who were dressed in jeans and t-shirts, which was what the cowboys of old used to wear as well, according to them. I wore my silver sunglasses to prevent eye contact with them and to block out the sun, while wearing a tan cowboy hat I'd been heavily encouraged to buy as part of the hiring process for this trip. I rolled my eyes, knowing full well that I was far too naïve to expect people to be looking out for others even in these trying times. If I'd been in a jovial mood, I would've cracked a joke about looking some like low rent cowboy cosplayer, but my heart just wasn't in it then

Mara had almost been forbidden to come, but she had revealed her massive arsenal, in order to prove her worth as a defender. I had meant to ask her where she'd gotten it all from, but I was too scared of her wrath to speak with her. She was never exactly warm to me even when she liked me, but I could tell that there was some barely hidden anger in her that was most likely directed at me. I couldn't say I blamed her. She wouldn't have had to do this if I'd just listened to Zea and let her do her job.

I cringed, feeling a pulsation of Zea's thoughts in my mind. She was closer to us, now that we had traveled westward, but I had no idea how to triangulate the psychic signal. This was new territory to me.

"Is she in pain?" Mara asked, surprising me, as she had been patrolling the opposing side of the caravan on her horse moments before.

Regaining my resolve, I said, "I don't know. It's faint."

Mara sighed. "I feared as much. She must still be unconscious. Whatever toxins placed into her body are too much for her to fight."

"She's strong. She'll break out of it before too long."

"I am grateful for your faith in her, Blake, but we must face reality. Were these normal poisons then she would awaken soon, but even her enhanced physiology will need to fight more than it ever has before to fight something that doesn't exist naturally."

I grunted.

Before Mara could speak, Benedict halted in front of us and ordered the wagons to be stopped so that we could rest for the night. We weren't far out of the city and I wanted to beg him to keep moving, but he would want to know why, and I had no answer that didn't reveal who I was. Besides, he was the expert here. The smart thing to do on a regular excursion was to camp before the sun went down.

Sighing, I joined Mara in guarding the fledgling camp, eventually joining them when my watch was over, falling asleep.

3

It's a curious thought to have, but I was beginning to hate the idea of being inside my own head once again.

The dreamscape around me was far too familiar to be comforting. When regular people slept without incident, I would routinely be forced into a representation of my own mind to talk with someone who had an incessant need to be as unhelpful as possible, while paradoxically being the most helpful person in the whole of reality.

I looked around, seeing that the dreamscape was not as well-defined as usual. Sometimes I would be greeted with a representation of the Silver Fortress, other times by a vibrant rainforest teeming with life, or some other locale that had something vaguely to do with whatever problem I happened to be dealing with at the time.

But that wasn't a thing right now. Instead, the misty swirls of my mind were almost entirely black. I was lost, having little light to see anything ahead of me.

"Nathan-Prime?" I asked. "Are you there?"

I knew it was a stupid question, but I was too tired and angry to bother with his usual jocularity.

A bright light appeared beside me and then a swirl of rose petals formed, transmuting themselves into the form of a human being, one who smirked at me. Nathan-Prime was the same as he'd been the last time we'd talked: tall, with dirty blond hair, and hazel eyes. He looked at me and sized me up, as if ready to diagnose everything wrong with me at a moment's notice, but then, just as suddenly as he appeared, he disappeared in a flash of light and rose petals, leaving me alone in the dreamscape. For the briefest of moments, he was replaced as he left by a young girl who I could only see from the side. I didn't have time to accurately remember everything about her, but I did recall seeing her long, blonde hair with white streaks in them. She turned to look at me, but she was gone right before I could see any more.

Before I knew it, I had woken up. I stared upwards, seeing the stars shining brilliantly in the sky above me. I watched them, noticing that I could see Scorpius, Lupus, and Centaurus, amongst other constellations easily apparent in the summer night sky. I had trained many years before to recognize the constellations, so that I could place myself anywhere in the world in case I got lost. My mother had been my private tutor in this regard and she herself said that she had a particular attraction to finding Centaurus in the sky, as it reminded her of friends that she had not seen in years from her native Armenia.

But then I paused, recalling the girl with the blonde hair with white streaks. I had seen her before, hadn't I? I shook my head, wondering why I couldn't recall her at all. Did she have something to do with my lost memories? Was Nathan-Prime using her image

48

in the dream to try and trigger memories for me?

Hey, kid, it's me; just chiming in to say cryptic things are coming, the voice of Nathan-Prime said inside my mind, his voice traveling from every single direction.

I instantly jumped up and looked around for him, even though I knew he wasn't allowed to physically manifest himself in my reality.

So he'd finally decided to make a vocal appearance. I grumbled and shook my head. I found myself wishing he'd have just said this in the dream, but I calmed myself down as best I could. If he was speaking to me now it meant that the "cryptic things" he was warning me about were coming soon and that I had to be on my guard and there had to be some reason he wanted to deliver the message this way.

"What is it?" Mara asked, having awoken thanks to my sudden movement. "What have you sensed?"

"Nathan-Prime just spoke to me," I said. "He said, and I quote, 'Cryptic things are coming.'"

"How very unhelpful."

"I'm glad I'm not the only one disappointed, but we need to be on our guard. He may be a jerk, but he wouldn't have said something unless he thought we were going to be in trouble."

"I know. I am just…I wish he had spoken more about Zea's welfare instead."

I nodded. "You and me both."

Brushing these thoughts aside, I cracked my neck and prepared myself to take over the next watch, ready to engage anything that tried to attack under the veil of darkness.

CHAPTER 6

The next few days were mostly uneventful. Outside of the occasional coyote or puma prowling about in the night, there was nothing to worry anyone as we traveled along the ruins of Interstate-10. But I knew differently. Ever since Nathan-Prime had decided to contact me, I was sure something was going wrong. Trickster that he was, even he wouldn't talk to me after so long just to screw with me. This was the closest we'd been to Sanguine Collective territory since we'd started this trip.

My unease was noticed by the other caravaners, but for the most part they just thought I was on edge because this was my first time. But others had given me uneasy glances, as if they thought I might suddenly go rabid and attack them.

We had stopped for water, ending up at where the Pecos River reaches the interstate. My eye was out on the river, waiting for any stray alligators that thought they might make an easy meal out of one of our horses, or worse, a person if they were starving enough.

I expanded my awareness, hearing and seeing things none of them could perceive. I heard the river flowing swiftly to the south. Inside the water, I felt the joy of life, as several minnows swam by, nibbling on the verdant plants that thrived underwater. A rogue thought entered my mind and I zoomed-in on them, finding to my delight that it was a group of silvery minnows, a species that had almost gone extinct during my original life, but was now taking back what had once been theirs. I grunted, glad that at least the end of the world had been good for one thing.

My vision grew glassy and I shook my head, chastising myself for my carelessness. Christeners and water had an uneasy relationship. For some reason it short-circuited our powers, making it difficult to invoke near moving water. By pressing my vision into the water I'd gotten what I wanted, but I had also sent too much power that way, which the water was now absorbing. We weren't suddenly powerless in its presence, but it was far more straining to perform the simplest of tasks near it, even sensing our surroundings.

I rubbed my eyes, now seeing clearly once I had stopped looking into the river. However, I felt a sting of pain, as if a needle had entered my radial artery. I let out a gasp of discomfort and grabbed my wrist, seeing that I hadn't been hurt, but I felt another consciousness fading away, realizing too late that Zea must've woken up and been put back under with whatever sedatives Valefar had forced into her body.

I frowned and looked to my right, finding, to my surprise, I was no longer alone, as Mara had ridden her horse and stopped it beside mine.

"You would do well to respect water's power," she said, morosely. "Many a Christener has fallen prey to its natural cancellations and found themselves unable to fight those who tricked them to battle in such unfavorable conditions."

I nodded, mad that she'd figured me out so easily and gotten the drop on me once more. I opened my mouth to speak, but sensed Benedict heading towards us, also on his horse, which had just finished drinking from the river. Once he reached us, he took off his hat and wiped his head of sweat.

"Would you scout ahead?" Benedict asked. "Got a feeling we're being watched."

"Odd that we have not," Mara noted.

"Look, once you've been out here as long as I have, you learn to trust your gut. Now are you going or not?"

"We'll go on ahead," I said.

Mara and I eyed him carefully, but, as he too was wearing sunglasses, neither one of us could look into them to see if he was telling the truth.

Our horses trotted forward at a moderate pace across the mostly flat terrain. Once we had gotten two-hundred yards ahead of the group, I noticed Mara was trying to speak up, so I stopped my horse and went off beside the riverbed, so that she would follow. All alongside us were tall goatbushes, obscuring our view slightly.

"Have something on your mind?" I asked.

51

Mara gazed at me solemnly. "If you can tell how I feel, I must truly be transparent," she mused and then sighed. "Yes, I do, but I do not know how to approach the subject."

"Then just spit it out."

Mara paused, looked out at the water, and then asked, "Why do you think that you have gained a mental link with Zea?"

I flinched, unprepared. "I don't understand the question," I said.

She nodded. "An unfair question; you are right to be confused. Perhaps it would be best if I asked what you knew of bonds between Christeners first."

I nodded back, placing my right hand on my chin to mull it over. "Hmm, well, from what I remember it's very rare. Happens only between people who're close to each other or have gone through similar traumatic experiences. It's the ability to hear the thoughts, feelings, and whims of another person, as if you were them and they were you. A permanent connection that binds people together. I always figured my parents had one, because I could swear they talked to each other silently all the time, but maybe that's just a long marriage at work. Can't say it's happened to me before now, but obviously I don't know."

"So, based on what knowledge you do possess, why would you say that you and Zea have acquired such a link?"

"Well, I suppose it's because we were firsts for each other. Like, she was the first person I connected with when I found myself here and I was the first Christener who wasn't you."

Mara sat silently on her horse for a moment, mulling over what I'd said with an odd sense of forlornness. Eventually, she nodded and turned to face me.

"I thank you for humoring my questions," Mara said. "You must understand that I only ask them because I am concerned for Zea."

"I understand," I said. "You've raised her since she lost her parents. It's only natural you'd be worried."

"No, Blake, it goes beyond that, because I also have concern for you."

"How so?"

"It is not that I believe that either of you is incompetent, but I have seen bonds harm others in the past. I have seen those who

52

establish them wound others by what they think, even when the other was nowhere near them. I simply wish for you to be mindful of these effects."

"I see, but why bring this up now?"

"Because it has already started with Zea, although she has not realized it yet."

I paused, thinking over what she'd said, waiting for her to continue.

"Do you know what she spends an hour doing every day without fail?" Mara asked. "No. Wait. You must promise me something first."

"Anything," I said.

"You must never repeat this to her. She told me this in confidence. I am merely using it to help you understand something."

"Agreed. So what is this thing she does? Praying?"

"No, but with you around we probably should be doing more of that." She sighed. "She reads that book you gave her and studies the words in there as intently as any assignment I ever gave her as a child. And do you know why?"

"No."

"Because she wants to impress you. She knows how much you value using your oh so hilarious turns of phrase to make fun of anything that walks in front of your path. It infuriates her that she cannot understand everything you say, so she reads that book to get the context for all of it, even though she knows it won't be enough to understand everything that comes out of that mouth of yours. She values your input and wants to make you laugh like you make her laugh. I know she doesn't always laugh aloud, but she always does inside."

"She laughs at my jokes? I knew it!"

"That is not the point to take from this," Mara said, eyeing me closely.

"And what is?" I asked.

"That she will do anything to please you. She has never had a friend, let alone been with a man for a long period of time. She trusts you implicitly and follows every order you give. If she has reservations about them, she quiets herself, because she does not wish to hurt you. In short, I ask that you be mindful of these things when you speak with her. I…have not been the best teacher when it comes to interacting with others. I am afraid that she will obsess over things that are not important to her growth. She has long needed someone like you in her life, Blake. Do not betray that trust."

I nodded. "You have my Word."

Mara blinked twice in surprise. To all Christened individuals, we took what we said seriously, but even we could lie and spread half-truths. One of the ways we held ourselves accountable was by giving our Word. To an ordinary human being, the only thing they would suffer from spreading lies after promising to tell the truth might be the loss of a friend or a temporary falling out. However, for us, it went far deeper. To give your Word was to sign away a part of your power if you failed to keep it. Perhaps I had been too hasty to promise something like that, but I'd meant it. Zea was my friend. Nothing was too much for her sake.

"I…I see," she said, nodding. "You are a good friend, Blake. But remember that your promises have consequences."

"Zea was the first friend I made here," I said. "I'm not letting her down, especially after all she did for me."

Mara smiled softly. "I am glad to hear it, Guardian Azarel."

We stood in silence, the only noises being the occasional grackle call and the rushing waters of the Pecos

"Mara, I have a question for you," I asked, breaking the silence.

"I will answer, if I am able," she said.

"Did you ever have a link with someone else?"

A sudden sadness overcame her face. Mara motioned her lips as if she were about to bite them, but stopped herself.

"Yes," she said. "One that haunts me to this day."

"So—" I started to say, until my danger sense alerted me to some unknown threat.

I gazed around, cursing myself for being so close to the dense foliage and water.

"I hear it too," Mara said. "It is distant to my ears, but I hear movement. Something is skulking out there and watching us with intent."

"Get behind me," I whispered. "Weapons drawn. Silver bullets if you have them."

I held out my hands, sensing something coming from in front of us. Whatever it was had sensed that we had suddenly been alerted to its presence, but not enough to dissuade it from continuing its plans. I stared into the goatbushes, ready for the moment something came out of them, only to feel a slight tremble in the earth. Barely reacting in time, I smacked the right side of my horse, scaring it enough to rush forward, right as a dust cloud swarmed upward from beneath us, revealing a trapdoor that had been disguised under the desert sand. Out of the trapdoor emerged three men, wrapped up in cloaks. Two of them headed toward me, while the other went for Mara, only to be greeted by a hail of gunfire that riddled his body full of 9mm silver bullets courtesy of Mara's Colt 9mm SMG.

The other two, unprepared for her swiftness or mine, reacted with concern, but were still heading towards me, intent on knocking me off my horse. Of course, none of them had expected me to jump off my horse and land behind them with the grace of an Olympic gymnast. To further their confusion, they howled in surprise when my hands glowed with the light of creation.

"Fiat lux!" I shouted out, sending twin beams of light into each of them.

I hit the one on my left dead-on in the right shoulder, searing the flesh off far more than if he'd been human. The second bolt landed its target, incinerating the second assailant's right kneecap, severing it from his body and causing him to land on the ground, face-planting when he couldn't stop himself from doing so.

None of them had expected such deadly precision, but neither of us had ever been under the impression that we were under attack from mundanes, thus we'd had no reason to hold back. Our thoughts were further confirmed when the one Mara had shot got on his feet despite his injuries and lunged at her, only to be greeted by the silver saber Mara had taken out of its sheath. It ran right through his wide-open mouth, killing him instantly.

I took out my pistol and fired into the one with the singed shoulder, while placing my left foot on the neck of the other one. The first one spasmed violently, the silver bullet's mystical qualities shutting down whatever healing factor he had as he suddenly stopped, moving no more. Then, to make sure it was over, I sent a smaller bolt of light into the back of his skull, finishing him off.

Pressing down harder with my foot, I looked down into the sand to see the face of the other one start regenerating, revealing its original, vampiric state.

"Sanguine Collective," I said, venom dripping from my voice. "How did you know we were here?"

"You're not supposed to be here!" he shouted. "We were promised mundanes, not your kind! This isn't fair!"

"Promised? By whom?"

He strained to look back at me, grinning madly with his teeth fully on display. "I think you know." He paused. "And that just pisses you off, doesn't it?"

Realizing what was about to happen, I took my foot off his neck, but was too slow. The empathic vampire grasped onto my leg with an iron grip. Then, to further his assault, he sent out a negative wave of energy, one that exacerbated my anger to uncontrollable levels.

My eyes grew red as everything that had ever gone wrong in my life replayed over and over in my mind. My failure to stop Zea's kidnapping, my inability to get back into the field before this moment, and my powerlessness to access my memories of the past.

The world bled over, the sun burned the land with red rays of destruction, and I gave into the rage. Yelling out madly, I sent a bolt of darkness into the sky above, not even bothering to form the words needed for the invocation or to escape the vampire's grasp as he fed off of my bloodlust.

I could hear voices that were not mine speaking, sounding vaguely like Mara and the vampire, but I didn't pay attention to them. Nothing mattered except the primal, irrefutable need to pay back those who had wronged me. I cursed Nathan-Prime for his vagueness. I roared with fury at Mara for daring to hold me back when I knew what was right. I conjured up images of those who had harmed me in the past and rushed after them, ready to murder them for their transgressions, not knowing if this was real or if these events were something only I could see. I didn't care. I wanted revenge. For everything. It wasn't fair. I deserved better. I was the greatest. I was the best. I was—

Gunfire roused me from my rage, as I felt a hand slipping away

56

from my ankle. Looking down with fury bursting from my eyes, I saw that Mara was standing over the vampire who'd been feeding off of me as she decapitated him with her saber.

The world was white again and I stumbled about, the disconcerting nature of what I'd undergone overwhelming me. I fell backward, hitting the sand harshly. Coughing up dust and sand, I looked up at the sky. The sun had returned to its normal coloration, blinding me with its brilliant light. Groaning, I tried to get back up, but was too dazed.

"Blake!" Mara cried, as I felt her getting on her hands and feet. "Get up! Now!"

I opened my eyes, seeing the concern on her face. She then held out her right hand and I grasped it, working with her to help pick myself off the ground. I exhaled violently, feeling as if I was about to enter that strange madness at any moment, but it didn't return. Its source was dead; I could only handle its aftereffects now.

At that moment, I became aware of movement to where we had originally come from, finding that the trade caravan had made their way to us. However, instead of relief, all I could see was disappointment and fear. Benedict was turning a new shade of red in his frustration.

He looked at me and shouted out, "You lied to us!"

"What?" I asked, flinching.

"You didn't tell us you were wizards!"

"We're not wizards. We're Christeners."

"Same difference. Why wouldn't you just do what you were supposed to?"

"The words you're looking for are 'Thank you,'" I said, anger rising. "You know, because I saved your sorry selves from death via emotional sapping."

"We were safe!" Benedict yelled.

"What? How?"

"Because we have a deal with them! We hire extra hands and let the vampires capture them so that we can continue on our trade routes unmolested! A few die so that we can get the job done! They have tunnels heading back to the Collective all over the desert here! Now they'll target us instead!"

I stopped, allowing his words to wash over my mind. I hadn't

57

heard that right, had I? No, it was impossible. No one who lived in Corpus Christi would dare consort with the very people who'd been draining them of their lives and freedom for a hundred years. It was unthinkable. But then I saw the expressions on the others in the caravan. It told me all I needed to know. How many people had they led to their deaths because of their selfishness? The earlier rage that had started to subside within me broke out again and I stood up without Mara's help, glaring at them.

"You traded human lives for money!" I roared. "How could you? After all I've done for you! After all I sacrificed to bring you freedom! This is how you repay my kindness? I'll slaughter every one of you!"

I gathered energy around my hands as they lit up brilliantly. Yelling out furiously, I watched as they all cowered before my might and I started laughing. At the same time, the ring on my left hand glowed with a black light, ready to join in with me. But before I could follow-through, I felt a kind hand clutching my right shoulder.

"Stand down, Guardian Azarel," Mara said, firmly, but without raising her voice.

"How can you say that?" I asked, feeling a trickle of blood pouring over my left eye, a consequence of my unbridled power. "They're killers by proxy! No better than the Collective or the necromancers! They should pay for what they've done!"

"It is not for us to concern ourselves with. They are liars and thieves and God will judge them on His time, not ours. Be thankful that we came out of this unscathed and can still continue our search. Don't let the rage that the vampire made you feel consume you. You would never act like this in your right mind."

"I refuse! They're mine to dispel justice to!"

"And this is what Zea would want for you?"

I froze in place. My ring stopped glowing and the light that had surrounded my hands shot out into the sand, crafting two small craters where they landed. Feeling the blood that had rushed over my left eye, I placed a hand over it, wiping what I could away. What had I almost done? I looked over to the caravan, wanting so desperately to ask them for their forgiveness, but couldn't bring myself to say it out loud.

"Leave here," I said. "Go back to the city. Tell the Guard what you did, and you can walk away with your lives. Now."

Knowing just how providential it was to still be alive, the caravan team said nothing more and turned back towards Corpus Christi. I watched them leave, still trying to overpower my anger at them. I should've known better. I was the perfect target for a vampire that fed off of wrath.

"Come, we must continue," Mara said, getting back on her horse. "Lest more time be lost before we reach Zea."

I nodded, knowing that despite it all, we had wasted more time here and that if we ever hoped to reach her soon, we would have to travel faster and on our own. Reaching my horse, I got up on it and ushered it forward, ignoring what had happened so I could focus on Zea.

CHAPTER 7

1

Mara and I traveled the next three days with little rest, even though she required far more than me. I had a large generator to feed off of when it came to my inherent power, but she had nothing of the sort, even with what little Christening she possessed.

The first day was the easiest. I could feel Zea's spiritual presence despite the gap between us and follow Valefar's path. When Mara had grown tired without sleep, I carried her on my back and continued running with her sleeping, invoking the energy necessary to keep going without wearing myself out. Her arsenal that she carried on her back did little to help us, but we both knew how important it was to have the extra firepower, so I avoided complaining about the extra weight. However, we all have our limits, and while mine would outlast most, it was still a hindrance to our quest, so we slept for four hours. When we awoke, I was desperately aware of the distance that Valefar had traveled while we stayed there. It was clear he didn't require as much rest as we did, which meant he had to be gifted with immense spiritual reservoirs of power, most likely a gift of the deal he'd made with the demon residing inside of him.

On the second day, we made good time, ending up in a northwestern direction. The Dead Lands border was still a state away in Arizona, which meant we had time to catch up, but the odds decreased the more we stopped, which we were having to do more frequently, as the need for water, food, and rest overcame us. We stopped that night about fifteen miles southwest of Roswell, if my reading of the constellations was correct.

The following day, we traveled after another four hours of sleep to end up at a more west-northwest route, avoiding cities, which we hadn't seen on our three-day trek. I wondered why Valefar did so, as the chances of other humans being out here were slim, but at least I was sure he wasn't aware that we were following him. It felt like someone was watching my spiritual presence, but it wasn't as invasive as I'd suspected it would be if he'd done so. Maybe he lacked that ability or perhaps he was just that brazen, but I was suspicious, as he had invited me to follow him. But that didn't matter now—we were closing in on him. Within an hour, we would end up behind him, meaning we had to come up with a plan or he'd hear us coming.

Before I could voice my concerns to Mara, I felt a sudden surge of pain in my left ankle and barely stopped myself from face-planting on the desert sand. I halted in place, kneeling as the pain forced itself upwards, signaling to me that I had severed a tendon or ligament from overuse. I couldn't know which without someone more skilled in medicinal invocations around, but I knew enough to realize that I was going to be in serious trouble if we didn't catch up with Valefar and Zea soon.

"You have overworked yourself," Mara said, trying not to sure her own anguish, as she bent down beside me to investigate the source of my pain.

I nodded, glad that I hadn't been carrying her at that moment in time. She didn't deserve to be punished for my weakness.

"Be still for a moment," she said. "I will do what I can for you."

Holding out her hands, she lowered my sweat-drenched sock on my left foot and then observed the affected region with the precision of a hawk. I felt a tingling sensation, as power ushered forth from her fingertips and into my ankle, slowly tethering whatever I'd torn back together. I felt a wave of relief enter me and smiled, nodding my head in thanks, bur before I could speak, I watched in horror as a sudden outpouring of red energy appeared from nowhere and surrounded Mara's fingers. Then, with incredible speed, the red energy formed into spikes and drove themselves into her skin, but didn't leave visible wounds. Mara held out her right hand to stop me from getting near as the red energy spikes disappeared as suddenly as they'd arrived, leaving no trace of their appearance besides Mara's visibly shaken face.

"I used too much power," she said, standing up and motioning for me to do the same. "It was better for me to use what little I have so that you did not. We have no time to dwell on it. My aim is still true. I will not need invocation to stop our foe."

I stood up, my ankle popping—but no worse for wear than before—and then said, "Mara, you didn't say anything."

She nodded. "I did not. Nor do I to invoke. Such is my curse."

"Invoking without a focus word or phrase is incredibly dangerous. Why can't you do so?"

"Because if I did then the cost to use my power would be higher." She sighed. "Focus on the now. How far is Zea?"

I had more questions, but every moment we wasted there would stop us from finding her, so I said, "An hour's journey ahead. Fewer if you travel on my back. Her signature's not going as fast. I think he's finally slowing down to rest."

"Good, then we must reach him before he escapes our grasp."

Sighing, I nodded, and allowed her to get back on my back. Once she was in position, I cracked my neck and ran forward at blazing speed, ready to overtake Valefar.

2

Mara and I were lying down together, surveying our foe from atop a sandy hill once we'd finally caught up with him. We watched our foe as he brought out what looked like a glowing red and black rock and ate it. He was sitting down about a hundred and fifty yards away from us. The sun was setting, but with my heightened vision I could still see perfectly fine. The moment it got dark, it would be harder for even me to see, but not to the extent a mundane would.

Zea was cradled carefully in his arms. She was still completely sedated by whatever he'd injected her with. I felt a slight stirring in her mind, but nothing came of it. Perhaps a part of her unconscious mind had registered my presence. Anger swelled in my mind, but I resisted the urge to lose control, afraid that if I leaked too much of my power out too soon that Valefar would realize that he'd been tracked down. Still, the look of smug satisfaction on Valefar's face as he mockingly offered the rock to Zea to eat made my blood burn with fury.

I had concocted an ingenious plan, one that Mara had had some reservations about for some reason. It involved Ageg and the element of surprise. Getting too close to Valefar would mean he'd hear us coming and avoid any attack we offered. However, if we had a means of suddenly appearing without using sound, then he'd never notice us. That's where Ageg came in. I could summon the bow, send a light arrow tethered to the light rope I'd also construct with it, and then propel myself forward once it had contacted a solid target. I could control its mass at will, causing it to become elastic or heavy if need be, which would send me flying at incredible speed faster than Valefar could hear. Mara would provide backup from her position, with the Winchester rifle in her possession easily able to target anything within three hundred yards. The goal wasn't to fight Valefar, but to retrieve Zea before he had a chance to react. Waiting back at Mara's position was a hastily crafted teleportation circle dialed into home at the Silver Fortress.

Aiming before I summoned the bow, I waited for Valefar to drop his guard. It came right when he went into his knapsack and tried to retrieve another one of those rocks.

"Ageg," I whispered, conjuring the bow into existence. "Silentium."

Planting the lower limb of the bow into the sand, I shot a now silenced arrow straight at my target, as Mara let out a singular shot from her rifle. The sound alerted Valefar to danger and he instantly rose from his seat with Zea clutched under his chest and dodged to his right, which was exactly where I'd imagined he'd go. He realized his mistake when my light arrow planted itself right underneath his left clavicle. At that same moment, I held onto the rope attached to the arrow and felt a rush of adrenaline as I soared forward at ludicrous speed. The panicked look of realization as my fist landed in his face would be one I treasured for the rest of my life.

As soon as I connected with him, Mara fired off another round, this time in the direction that Valefar's head was moving from the impact of my punch. The bullet hit him with such force that his left cheek flapped madly in the desert wind, having been mostly separated from his body. Blood spatter and bits of viscera landed on my clothes, but I ignored them, holding my left hand backward, summoning light into it for my next attack.

"Fiat lux!" I cried out, rushing my left hand forward as light surrounded it.

However, before I could connect with Valefar, I felt a sudden sense of dread, as a black ripple appeared around his body and he suddenly disappeared. The ripple then rushed back at me and threw me backwards as I connected with something that should have had no physical form. Landing in the desert grass behind me, I quickly recovered and planted my hands into the sand, managing to somersault backwards into a standing position. Looking around madly, I couldn't see a trace of Valefar's presence until I heard clapping from behind me. Turning around, I saw Valefar continuing to clap happily, while still holding on to Zea. Mara fired another round at him, but he simply sidestepped to his left and avoided it. Purple energy covered over his exposed left cheek, mending the damage it had taken from the rifle shot.

"Very, very clever," Valefar said, grinning. "I underestimated you, Blake Azarel. Never have I almost been caught so easily. If you hadn't had to worry about Zea's safety, I'm certain that I would have died or at the very least not in a position to concentrate on any of my magic. But I have her to thanks for my being able to do so." He opened his mouth, baring his teeth at me. "Using the gunshot to make me think that was the most direct threat, while actually using the arrow to not only hit me, but deliver yourself to me before I could react. That is exactly why I took this job. Winning so easily gets so boring after a time. Unfortunately, I can't stay. I have promises to keep after all."

He continued grinning with teeth in full display, gently playing with Zea's hair.

"All right," I said, as calmly as possible. "I'm only going to say this once: give us Zea and we leave you in peace or refuse my offer and end up a bloody smear on the desert ground."

Valefar threw back his head in laughter, disappearing after once again using the same black ripple from before to avoid another shot from Mara's rifle. When he reappeared behind me, he placed his head over my right shoulder, leaning in to put his lips next to my ear.

"Be very glad I'm not here to kill you, Blake," he whispered. "Because if I was, then this great game of ours would be over."

I whirled around to see that he was no longer there, a sulfurous smell left in his place. Charging up a light invocation in my left hand and a darkness invocation in my right, I prepared myself to speak the needed words for the combo attack, but found that he was nowhere in sight. Desperately, I gazed at Mara, who was pointing behind me. Instantaneously, I turned to examine what she'd seen, only to be greeted by a fleeing Valefar with Zea in tow, moving swiftly.

I raced towards him, the strain from three days of persistent motion making my muscles and tendons cry out in agony, but I ignored them. He was still in sight. We could still make this work.

"Oh, and Blake," I heard Valefar cry out from ahead of me, "thank you for falling into my little trap! I wondered if I'd get to use it or not!"

I stopped in place, fearing what lied ahead, only to realize that I was already in the trap's embrace when a bony hand erupted from the sand and grasped onto my leg. Crying out in terror, I accidentally released the light and darkness invocations without a word, sending them toward the hand. They clashed with it, but the unfocused nature of the invocation caused the energy to spread harmlessly on the ground, which allowed me the chance to escape the hand's grasp.

Soon, more hands erupted from the earth. Some of them still had flesh attached to them, while others were similar to the one that had first attacked me. I tried to summon the courage to run past these undead abominations and continue my pursuit, but I couldn't, especially when I heard Mara cry out for help behind me.

I ran towards to sound of her voice, seeing her about to be surrounded by a horde of zombies and skeletons.

"Ageg!" I cried out, planting the bow into the ground.

Doing the same technique with the exact precision as the first one was immensely taxing, but I had no other means of arriving there in time. I aimed the bow at the closest zombie to her and fired, propelling myself forward as soon as the arrow connected with the broken flesh of the creature. However, this time, the purchase it had gained was vastly different than if I had made contact with a living creature. The arrow sailed out of the zombie's body and flew into the night's sky. Having little time to do anything, I let go of the rope attached to the arrow, barely grabbing onto to Mara before we both flew over the undead horde.

Unfortunately for us, this meant that we were now traveling rapidly through the air without any way to stop ourselves from hitting the ground harshly.

I used what time I had to wrap my body around Mara and positioned myself to hit the sand first, feeling my skin tear itself off my face from the ferocious impact. Mara cried out in anguish as she too felt the impact of our landing, but grew silent, having been knocked out by the intense force of our fall. I cried out in pain, letting go of her to try and stand up. My legs barely responded to my desire to move, but I slowly managed to get up, only to see the various hordes of undead monsters had gathered as one unit and were moving right for us. I tried to summon the energy to invoke a light blast, but I fumbled over the words as blood entered my mouth from the various wounds on my face and I collapsed on the ground.

Looking up feebly, I watched the undead army approach me and my eyes glassed over, right as a blast of fire appeared from nowhere and rushed ahead of us to charge into the horde.

Rolling over, I barely made out the image of two people running forward, one of them veiled in intense flames.

CHAPTER 8

"Burn in Hell!" a woman's voice yelled from yards away from me. A massive vortex of purest flame descended from the sky falling in the midst of the undead horde. The skeletons and zombies alike cried out in agony as the flames purified them, incinerating their bodies from existence. Nothing escaped the blast and every single abomination in that miserable army moved no more, disintegrated by the intensity of the inferno. However, they wouldn't be the only things taken out by it if I wasn't quick enough to defend us.

I held my hand out in front of myself and uttered a weak invocation to protect Mara and myself from the heat, but in so doing I allowed the impact of the fire to get through, which sent us flying backwards. I feebly attempted to grab Mara in the air, but my arms limped out from the toll the invocation had taken and we both tumbled on the sand. I felt my teeth gnash into each other and yelled out in pain, but providentially none of them seemed to have chipped.

"Blake!" the voice cried out again, which I finally recognized. "Mara!"

I looked up to see Cinderella running over to my side. She hurriedly examined Mara and myself, looking for injuries. She was breathing heavily; the invocation having taken a lot out of her. Ignoring her tiredness, she went to the unconscious Mara first and placed hands over the more obvious wounds the older woman had.

"Cleansing Flames," Cinderella invoked.

A small stream of fire wrapped around Mara's wounds and they twisted around the cuts and lacerations, charring them just enough for them to seal up. Fire invocation's a tricky element to work with and has many utilities, but medicinal use was outside my area of expertise. Clearly, she'd been training with someone other than me in her spare time. It wasn't perfect by any definition, but it had stopped the bleeding and that was good enough for now.

Mara gasped, coming back to consciousness when Cinderella's healing invocation started rejuvenating her body. She stayed on the ground, looking up at our mutual savior with surprise.

"Initiate Young, your sight in my eyes is most welcome," Mara said.

"I'm so sorry I wasn't here sooner," Cinderella said, moving over to me and preparing the same invocation for me. "Cleansing Flames."

At that same moment, the flames she had gathered earlier wrapped themselves around my body and I felt a strengthening presence surge through my nerves and blood stream. The facial wounds I had received from hitting the sand after our initial fall were stitching themselves back together with a calming warmness, akin to the feeling you got after drinking from a cup of hot chocolate after a wintry day. I felt reenergized, but not enough to fight for Zea's return.

I looked at Cinderella, who was smiling at me. Why was she here? She was supposed to be back in Corpus Christi.

"What the hell are you doing here?" I asked, as Mara and I picked ourselves up. "I thought I ordered you to stay behind at the Fortress!"

Cinderella's smiling mouth closed and she took a step backward, looking like she was about to cry. I quickly chastised myself for losing my temper, knowing full well I had better people to be angry at. After all Zoë had done to her, here I was making her feel inadequate again. I went to her side and held her hand, as she failed to repress her tears.

"I'm sorry," I said. "I'm not mad at you, I swear, Cinderella. You saved Mara and me because you didn't listen to me. We're alive because of you. I'm a hotheaded idiot who deserves to be punched in the face. Please forgive me."

Cinderella's face scrunched up more and she cried harder as she pushed herself into my chest and hugged me.

"I was so scared," she said. "I had a dream and you were dead. I couldn't let that happen. I needed to find you. She helped me get here."

I pushed back from the hug and scanned the area, finding—to my astonishment—that the second person I'd seen earlier when

Cinderella first appeared was Sedecla.

"You brought her with you?" I asked. "Neither one of you is fit to travel. You're still wounded."

I reached my hand down to feel the spot where she had been hit earlier, only to feel the wound didn't exist anymore. Cinderella blushed and stepped backward.

"I asked Clooney to heal me," she said. "He was a little embarrassed, but he did what I wanted."

"I don't think there's anything he wouldn't do for a pretty girl."

She blushed again. "When I explained that I had seen you dying in a dream, he seemed upset and did the strangest thing." She paused, clearly confused. "He asked me if I believed in God."

I flinched. Way too much was going on at once. My mind was overloaded with questions. Minutes ago, I was about to be killed by the undead army Valefar had left behind and now this had all happened. What was I supposed to deal with first? I paused, choosing to dwell on her most recent revelation.

I had approached Clooney on the topic of belief before several times—given the religious leanings behind the origin of the Christened—but he'd evaded the answer every single time. I'd tried to teach Cinderella what I knew over the past year, but she hadn't been the most receptive to my evangelism, which she was free to do; I didn't plan on making conversion a condition to join Excelsior.

"He wouldn't tell me why it was so important," Cinderella continued, "but I remembered everything you said about it and I decided something then: I decided to believe. I don't fully understand why, but it seemed like the right thing to do."

I stood there massively confused and oddly proud at the same time. I was never the best explainer when it came to my faith, but I did believe wholeheartedly in its message and God's intention for everyone to believe in Him. I wanted to pick Cinderella up and hug her tight, welcoming her as my spiritual sister for the first time, just like the angels in Heaven were doing on her behalf, but something stopped me. Why was Clooney suddenly so adamant about his own brand of evangelism? What had he said that had gotten to her that I hadn't been able to do? Was it possible this was some fake conversion based on a geas? If that was the case, I was going to bash his skull in, friend of mine or not.

"Why are you angry?" Cinderella asked, breaking me from my thoughts. "I thought you'd be happy for me."

I calmed down and offered a smile. "I am, Cinderella," I said, beaming with pride. "I just—it's a lot to take it all at once. We're gonna be together for eternity, Red. That's a lot to celebrate."

Cinderella laughed awkwardly and smiled, not expecting my reaction, I guessed.

Mara stepped in and stood beside us. "You have made a very important decision, Initiate Young," she said, standing upright with her hands crossed behind her back. "See that you do our mutual Lord well in His service." Mara turned to Sedecla and eyed her intently. "How were you able to track us?"

"There are very few roads left that head towards the Dead Lands," Sedecla said. "We had to find you eventually. That and we encountered the caravan that you were once a part of, and they showed us which way you were going."

"And it was even easier when I felt the teleportation circle being drawn," Cinderella said. "I know it's risky to travel to a temporary circle like the one you drew, but I knew we had to get here as soon as possible, so I drew another temporary circle so we could make it here in time."

I shook my head, stunned. Traveling via temporary circles was incredibly dangerous, but Cinderella had done it almost effortlessly and had then had enough power to torch the zombies and skeletons almost without any effort. Not only that, but both temporary circles were miles apart from each other. A lesser Christener would've sent different body parts to both sites. This whole ordeal was too much to take at once. I needed some rest.

I smiled. "Very impressive, Red," I said. "Risky and brash. I like it."

Mara sighed, saying, "But be sure to learn that the lesson here is not to always act foolishly, but to be ready to make such a decision if no other option remains."

Cinderella nodded and then asked, "Were those things sent by Morior Invictus?"

"One of their agents. The same who stole Zea. We had planned to steal her away from him while his guard was down, but we were not enough to do so, despite our tactics."

"I was too slow," I said, frowning. "Even with Mara sniping him I

70

still wasn't able to stop him from leaving with her."

Mara nodded. "Your plan, while audacious, was sound. Our only failure was a lack of numbers. We have learned valuable intelligence about his abilities and have figured out what we need to make up for regarding our own inadequacies."

"Yeah, but now he's getting away! At this rate he'll reach the Dead Lands before we can stop him!"

"And what would you have us do, Guardian Azarel? He avoids my best shots, you and I are only standing now because of Initiate Young's serviceable healing, and she is far too tired to be useful in a fight as a result. We have lost this skirmish. We must rest, regroup, and see what the Almighty has in store for us."

"Even if that means Zea gets taken into the Dead Lands."

Mara bit her lip, but steeled herself. "Yes."

I sighed. She was right. Again. We were in no condition for another fight and even if we did, who was to say Valefar didn't have another undead ambush ahead? It was better to rest, do some recon, and figure things out from there.

"There is some small help I may offer," Sedecla said. "Near the border is a human-controlled town called Phoenix. I wasn't able to enter it when I escaped the Dead Lands, but I know that the people there have been repelling assaults from the undead soldiers sent to kill them. Perhaps we should ask them for aid and shelter as we figure what to do next."

I paused, mulling over what she said. Phoenix had been our original destination. If what she said was true that made them potential allies against Morior Invictus.

"All right," I said. "I don't have the strength to keep fighting today and I don't think tomorrow will be any good either." I sighed. "Let's rest for the night and head on the road to Phoenix in the morning."

CHAPTER 9

That night I dreamt of terrible outcomes, lost causes, and overwhelming failures. Many times, I ended up in a rose garden maze, only to realize that Valefar was there—Zea in tow—as he raced ahead of me, always exiting the maze before I could find my bearings. The loops would repeat, seemingly endlessly, always setting me back to the center of the maze, where I heard Zea cry out my name and Valefar cackle at my inability to find him. Every twenty-six seconds I was put back here in the center of the maze, regardless of where I'd been when the loop ended.

This particular loop, however, was one I was determined to make the last. Having gone through this scenario many times before, I could recall exactly which part of the maze the two of them would end up in the moment the loop started.

Invoking energy around my hands, I gathered it into a ball of light and pushed it outwards to the rose wall on my left, shouting out, "Ultima Mico!"

The light that had swirled in my palms ushered forwards, completely incinerating the fifteen outer edges of the left part of the maze, leaving behind an eighteen-foot-wide circle that would let me move forward and catch up to them before they got out of the maze. However, the moment that I approached the hole I'd made in the rose bushes, the plants surged with a mystical light and completely rejuvenated themselves, leaving no exit except the one that had previously existed. Valefar's cackling jests ran through my ears as he fled the maze with Zea in tow and the world reset the loop once more.

I fell down to my knees. How was I supposed to escape this? How many times had I been here? Fifty? A hundred? Was this even a dream anymore? My mind was so lucid, not that that mattered. Nothing I did here mattered.

It's hopeless, I thought, lying down on the ground as my face hit the dirt, tears forming in my eyes. I can't do this.

"And that, my young padawan, is why you fail," a familiar voice said from my right.

Looking up and barely spitting the dirt out of my face as the loop repeated itself once more, I saw Nathan-Prime with his arms crossed as he leaned back onto the rose wall. He gazed down at me, witnessed my miserable state, and took compassion on me by walking over to help pick me off the ground. I didn't resist as he stood me up and telekinetically wiped off the dirt and grass from my body and clothes.

"I was wondering when you'd finally show up in person," I said, shaking my head as I finally regained my senses.

"Well, I like to only chime in when it's the moment I'm supposed to," he said, smiling gently.

I sighed, as the loop started once more, and I heard Zea cry out my name and Valefar send another witty repartee my way for failing to catch him.

"Annoying, ain't it?" Nathan-Prime asked, watching the scene play over. "Repetition's one of my pet peeves, which is awful, especially when you're both a time traveler and a teacher." He paused. "Also when you're the one causing the loops in the first place. We're on loop sixty-six, by the way."

I grumbled. "Then why don't you stop them?" I asked. "I figured you had something to do with this once I realized how aware of everything I was."

"Then what would you learn?"

I grunted. How many times had I heard some variation of that phrase before?

"Thirty-six," Nathan-Prime stated, presenting thirty-six fingers on his right hand that returned to normal once I had counted them all. "Although you wouldn't know if that number was correct, anyways, seeing as you never bothered to count them in the first place."

"Enough games," I said. "I'm so tired. Just come out and tell me what I'm supposed to learn here."

His face grew grim. "Is that so? Well, you should be careful what you wish for, Blake."

Before I could ask what he meant by that, Nathan-Prime

teleported in front of me in a flurry of light and rose petals, driving his left hand into my chest with enough force to break out the other side. I gagged, not able to deal with the pain in time to prevent him from sending his right hand into my head, starting from my chin and ending as he wrapped his hand around my brain stem. Even though by all rights I should've been dead from either blow alone, I was still aware of myself, and I could only look at him in terror at what he would do next. My eyes were overwhelmed by a blue light that originated from somewhere inside of my head, as energy he crafted then created a radioactive surge that exploded my body from the inside out. My body was incinerated and the last word I heard was "Frei."

Instantaneously, my body reconstituted itself, mending all my wounds and removing the physical pain, but not my memory of the event. Planting one knee on the ground I looked up to see that he was counting down on his right hand from five. He was on three now, making me realize he was about to attack again in that many seconds. Was he insane? Coming up with a counterattack in that little time? There was no way I could—

—Nathan-Prime's index finger fell inward into his palm and he launched his offensive the moment his finger contacted his skin. I could only watch feebly as what looked like solidified alcohol erupted from his hands and wrapped around my body, entering every orifice it could locate. My mind swelled, as I felt the intoxication overwhelm my senses. I had never been drunk before, not that I remembered at least. Most Christeners are resistant to its effects thanks to our enhanced physiology, but, as per usual, Nathan-Prime had found a way to destroy whatever advantage I had. Still, I knew I had to do something, so I pointed a finger at him, hoping to craft a darkness invocation to blind him, possibly severing his control over whatever he did to me. However, I saw the look in his eyes and knew I'd been too slow to react again.

"Flame Invocation: Salamander's Embrace," Nathan-Prime announced.

Once again, I felt an explosion from the inside out, but this time it was due to the flames that had erupted from contact with the alcohol in my bloodstream. The fire ignited brilliantly, completely burning every molecule of my body.

I reconstituted myself in the exact same spot, once again

feeling no corporeal pain, but was able to recall my previous deaths with precise recall. Nathan-Prime was once more holding five fingers up and had gotten down to four by the time I looked up at him. Enraged from what he'd put me through, I got up, ready to make this the last death. I smiled when his middle finger fell, leaving me three seconds to come up with a plan, but the smile quickly faded when he held out his other hand palm forward and arcane runes resembling binary appeared in front of it.

"System Call: Overkill Healing Element," Nathan-Prime invoked, even though the time limit wasn't over.

The arcane runes swirled around as a pleasant wave of energy went from them and surged over my body. Expecting pain, I gritted my teeth, only to realize that I instead felt as if I'd just received the best massage of my life paired with a wondrous dinner at a five-star restaurant. I stopped in place, glad that he was stopping his assault to heal me, at least until I remembered one of the keywords of whatever invocation he'd used.

Overkill? I repeated. How can healing be overkill? I—Gah!

Numerous tumors appeared all over my skin, covering every inch of my body and sealing my eyes from seeing their surroundings. Lethargy overwhelmed me and I fell to the ground, unable to speak in order to invoke a healing word to stop the spread of this infection.

Infection? I asked myself. No, I'm not being infected. I'm healing too quickly! He gave me cancer!

My medical training was rudimentary at best, but I'd read up on the topic out of curiosity once in-between missions at the Silver Fortress. Early in Gray Forum history medical invokers were viewed as quacks, because their success rates were questionable. However, over time, we learned more about the human body and how to properly heal injuries as a result, learning that the reason so many people had died from healing invocations early on had been as a result of the invokers healing their patients too much.

Normally, when the body's cells divide into new cells for whatever functions they're intended for it has a finite number in mind to perform the task. Over time, these cells serve their purpose and then die. However, when the body creates too many of certain types of cells, they group together and overwhelm the regular cells, which are duplicating at the correct rate. I had just been hit with a healing wave that was "overkilling" my body, creating too many cells that were responding to what they thought were threats because Nathan-Prime had somehow tricked them into thinking there was a nonexistent problem.

Time passed slowly, or at least it felt that way, as eventually I stopped thinking, only to have my thoughts return moments later in a new, cancer-free body. I panted in relief, looking over to my side to see that Nathan-Prime had created a second me and the one from before was still left behind, covered in massive tumors, some of which had burst open. I looked from him to my other body, seeing him counting down once more. It wasn't fair. He hadn't even reached his original countdown when I'd attacked. What kind of rules were these that even he wouldn't follow them? What was I supposed to be learning from this?

As his index finger fell down, Nathan-Prime disappeared from sight in a flash of light and rose petals. I looked around, wondering what I could do to stop him this time.

"Sloppy!" he declared, teleporting behind me to smack me in the back of the neck.

I felt bones crack as my head was severed from my body starting at the trachea and sailed across the rose maze, landing several feet to my left. I tried looking around, but my eyes were stuck facing forward now that I no longer had the appropriate neck, muscles, or bones to turn to look in other directions. Instead, a small rose chair akin to a throne crafted itself from the ground and Nathan-Prime sat in it, counting down again in an almost bored fashion.

"Please, just stop," I said. "I can't beat you. I don't know how."

"That so?" he asked, reclining. "But of course you know how to beat Valefar, don't you?"

"I'm figuring that out as I go."

"And how's that working for you?"

"I—well, it's—a work in progress."

He looked down at me and shrugged. "Well, it's nothing to lose your head over."

I gawked at him. He had the gall to—I paused. No, everything he said had some purpose in mind. With what vision I had I looked at my current situation, realizing that, with great irony, I was the perfect metaphor for this situation, which, of course, meant that he'd planned for this exact moment in time.

I sighed. "Can I at least have my body back?" I asked.

He smiled and snapped his fingers, restoring me back to being whole. I heard a rumbling behind me and found a rosy throne made in the likeness of the one he was now sitting upright in. Taking the hint, I sat down and waited for him to speak.

"Knowing now how I've treated you, how would you have done things differently?" Nathan-Prime asked.

I mulled over the question, trying to connect whatever insane dots he'd placed in what he'd done. He had made it a point to make me watch Valefar get away from me no matter what I did, made it so that Zea was always crying out my name, and when he'd fought me, he'd made it so that I had no chances of winning in my current state. What connected all of them?

"I was alone," I said. "Here, at least. But I don't understand. I'm not alone down in my world. Mara was with me to start and now I have Cinderella and Sedecla to help."

"And what was your initial reaction to all of this?" he asked.

"I...I didn't want them there. I wanted to go by myself."

"And now, knowing what has occurred, was that the right action to take?"

I sighed. "No, it wouldn't have been. So was that it? Just learn to be a team player?"

"No, but it's a part of the whole. There is something to be said about being effective on your own, and there will be times in which you need to do so, but you would be far more useful if you were great at both. You are a leader now. Lead by example." He paused. "How could you have stopped any of my attacks?"

I placed a hand on my chin. I honestly didn't know. He'd cheated, but maybe that had been the point. Not every enemy I faced would be some honor-bound foe who would never stoop to cheap shots or subterfuge. I had no answer for stopping his initial strike, outside of learning how to use shielding invocations. Nor did I have an answer for the alcohol barrage, as I had no way to invoke a fire strong enough to burn it before it ever reached my body. As for the cancer, I was sure that was just a means to show me that while I knew some aspects of biology, it would be worthless if I didn't know how to counteract someone who controlled it, which, given that I was up against necromancers, likely meant there was someone who could mess with flesh or bones. Finally, I was certain that whole chopping my head off was just to make a stupid joke about losing it.

"I think I might know," I said, "but if I'm honest my answer is 'I don't know.'"

Nathan-Prime smiled and clapped twice. "An excellent answer!" he declared, standing up. "Nothing can ever truly be learned without acknowledging that you don't understand what you're asking about, Blake. Now, as to an actual answer that doesn't hinge on my personal philosophies, you need to ask for help. You were right to think on several strategies that might have worked if you had the necessary skills, but you, currently, do not have them."

"Well, yeah, it's not my fault that I can't invoke fire just because I was born with a talent only in light and dark invocations. No one's born with the ability to use every single kind of invocation there is."

"If that's the case, then why were you able to silence your invocations in battle with Valefar? Or why were you able to produce a small flame when you first met Zea in order to create some light in the sewers? Or, better yet, why would you bother learning healing if you weren't naturally good at it?"

"I—I don't know. I just thought it was easier to learn than others."

"Really? So simplistic. It's a shame this is what the Forum turned into. Back when I helped found it thinking like that would've been laughed at. But, alas, good things fade over time. And why? Because it was hard. It was just so much easier to tell new Christeners just to focus on their specific elements and not bother teaching them things that were harder for them to produce. In other words, laziness ran supreme." He shook his head. "Now, don't get me wrong, there will still be invocations you will never master, but just because you won't be an expert doesn't mean you just give up, now does it? You don't go into a job interview saying, 'Well I'm no good at certain tasks and have no interest in getting better,' now do you?"

I blinked twice, stunned to silence. Was he suggesting what I thought he was? It was madness. Did he really expect me to learn every single type of invocation there was in the world? I didn't even know how many there were. Not even Zea as a Psionic could use differing types of elemental invocations without wearing herself out. It just wasn't supposed to be a thing.

"Are you saying I can learn other types of invocations?" I asked, bewildered. "Sure, I can kinda do other things, but do you have any idea how long it'll take to even try to learn others when I'm still mastering what I know? It's not like I'm like you! I can't just use countless years across the multiverses to be the best at everything!"

"And?"

"And? You can't just keep doing this to me! You literally killed me several times over tonight! I felt every single death! Maybe you think you can get away with this just because it's a dream, but I won't let this go!"

Nathan-Prime folded his arms together and leaned forward so that his hands disguised his face. "Now do you honestly think I haven't done anything to you that hasn't happened to me, boy? You're angry at 'dying.' Good. Learn from it. Get better. I took it easy on you tonight. Too easy for my tastes, but I do what I am told. You would do well to learn the same."

"You—you've died too?"

He nodded. "Yes and then some. How do you think I got so powerful? Learning from my many failures. My masters over the years knew not to coddle me, because if they did, I wouldn't be able to do what needs to be done. I extend the same courtesy to you. I don't care if you don't like it. You're not supposed to like feeling like you're dying. Now focus that anger to far more productive means and figure out how to be better than yourself."

I held my head in my hands. This was too much. Why couldn't my life just be simple?

"Because you chose it to not be simple," Nathan-Prime said. "You chose to stay with the Forum, even after being given the option to leave forever. You chose to make Excelsior by announcing it to the entire world. You chose to get sloppy and not train to your fullest potential. Own up to your choices and deal with the consequences."

I glared at him, although I knew my anger wasn't truly directed at him.

"You don't think I know that?" I asked. "I know it's going to be hard, but I don't see why you have to make it harder. I just want to finish this whole ordeal and be done with it. I don't deserve this!"

Nathan-Prime rolled his eyes and sat back down, pointing to his right at an unseen figure. "S.T.G.O.H., play the world's smallest violin for me, will you?" he asked.

To my immense surprise the figure he'd been pointing at materialized, but nothing I had ever seen had prepared me for this grotesque figure. Standing at twelve feet tall was a massive plant-based monstrosity, of which I can best describe as a Meganium warped and twisted in ways that would kill an ordinary being. Part dinosaur and part eldritch abomination, the thing was covered in petals and leaves that were mostly situated at what I thought was its head. Many twisting vines wrapped around the figure, while they were also suspended in the air, ready to strike at a moment's notice. Its head looked at me and the moment its eyes locked onto mine, I could tell this creature, while hideous to the appearance, was nothing more than the kindest, friendliest being in existence. No more dangerous than a loyal Great Dane. Once it had sensed my slowly growing ease, it responded to its master's request, and the beast brought two of its vines together, crafting a tiny violin from its petals and leaves that it played magnificently.

"MUR-STAKE!" it announced, continuing to play.

Nathan-Prime chuckled and scratched the creature's forehead. "Oh, Storm the Gates of Hell, you always know how to cheer me up," he said. "Especially when I'm dealing with yet another me out there. Not, literally, mind you. Figuratively."

"MUR-STAKE!"

"Yes, I always am cursed to deal with myself, aren't I? Eloquently put."

I couldn't hold it in anymore and pointed at the creature with the ridiculous name, shouting out, "Is that a freaking stand?"

The two looked at one another and both offered a hearty laugh.

"Resolve, actually," Nathan-Prime said, wiping tears from his eyes, only to turn to his companion. "All right, the preview's over, ya loveable lug. Time to go back to being unseen because he shouldn't be able to see you right now anyways. We both like to cheat, yes we do."

The creature with too long a name nuzzled Nathan-Prime's head and disappeared from view with no discernable means of doing so. My rage had slowly died; I just couldn't focus on that after what I'd just witnessed. Seeing my quizzical look, Nathan-Prime turned to me, still smiling.

"Like I said, the preview's over," he said. "Now onto other matters at hand. The undead you'll be facing can be worn down with light and dark invocations, but it would be far more effective to utilize fire. Providentially, you have just been gifted with a companion who is both willing to teach you and completely devoted to you as a leader. But I warn you, Blake, be gentle on the poor girl. She's heading towards dark times. Not now, but in the future. She will need you to continue as you have before. All of them will. Now learn how to use fire invocations or die."

"What does that mean?" I asked.

"Eh, you'll figure it out at some point," Nathan-Prime said, as he flashed in front of me to poke me in the nose, waking me up.

CHAPTER 10

I woke up in a foul mood, still feeling Nathan-Prime pressing my nose even though logically I knew he couldn't manifest physically on my world yet. Shaking my head, I looked around, seeing Mara keeping watch as the sun slowly rose on the horizon. Sensing movement, Mara turned to see me and nodded in acknowledgement.

"Good morning, Guardian Azarel," she said. "Although from your expression I can tell you did not have a restful night's sleep."

I sighed. "That obvious, eh?" I asked.

"Well, you also talk while you sleep, so I gleaned from that as well. Do you wish to talk?"

"No, but I need to."

I looked over to my right side, seeing a slumbering Cinderella and a still Sedecla lying in sleeping bags. Careful not to disturb them, I slowly walked over to Mara and sat down in the sand with her. The fire she had maintained to safeguard us from the desert night's cold was almost in cinders now, no longer serving its primary purpose.

"He spoke with you, did he not?" Mara asked.

I nodded.

"I suspected he would appear soon enough, ever since his earlier warning," she noted. "A most strange man you have gained the attention of, I would say."

"You can say that again," I said. "I don't think I could describe just how infuriating it is to constantly be in his sights and his 'lessons.'"

"I certainly do not envy your being taught in such a manner, Blake, but even you must realize the value of such training. It is most unique. Very few members of the Forum could say that they were in contact with the founder."

82

A sudden thought entered my mind. "Mara, do the Archives mention anything about earlier visits from Nathan-Prime?"

She paused for a moment, as I witnessed her eyes grow solid white, while she accessed the entirety of the Forum's library. The Archivist's main responsibility was to remember and preserve what others would forget. Every single of information ever written down by a member of the Forum was automatically known to the Archivist, no matter how small or worthless to discerning eyes.

"Yes, there have been several reports of members having made contact with the founder," Mara said, her eyes returning to normal. "Most of them unsubstantiated." She paused. "I have found one story of note from someone you knew."

"From my time?" I asked. "Who else had to suffer like me?"

"Lucien Azarel."

"Dad? When did this happen?"

"According to him, he was seeking to stop a raiding party of Aluxob from engaging in war with archeologists who had penetrated their temples at Monte Alban in Mexico in the 1980s. No specific date is given. He claims that during this the founder appeared to him along with an individual identified as Requiem and two women he has refrained from naming, citing personal matters involved with both."

I paused. Dad had met Nathan-Prime? Poor guy must've been in over his head, much as our apparently mutual teacher liked to talk. Mom would've been a better match for Nathan-Prime to work with.

"Did either of your parents bring this up to you?" Mara asked, breaking me away from my thoughts.

"I...don't know much about my parent's past," I admitted, wondering why I had never come to such a realization earlier. "That feels so strange to say. I was a curious kid. How did they ever satisfy my questions about themselves? Heck, I don't even know how old they were. They both looked like they were in their late forties, but you and I both know that means nothing when it comes to Christeners."

"There is information in the Archives about their origins, as it is for every member of the Gray Forum. I can look it up and tell you what they contain right now, given that I am always connected with the Archives."

I paused for a moment. Nane and Lucien Azarel were the best parents I could ever have asked for. Every single time I'd ever had a problem I could always trust them to lead me in the right direction. My mother was the wisest person I knew. My father was the most easygoing man in the history of the world. But neither of them had ever told me where they had come from. I had always assumed that they were just first-generation Christeners, given how importantly we upheld our genealogies. I knew my mother was Armenian and that my father had a mix of Scotch and Irish in his background, but that was about it. I'd never met a grandparent from either side of the family and when I'd questioned them about this, they had told me that their parents had died before I was born, as they were not Christeners. Thus, they were able to die of old age, unlike us, who really didn't have a timer when it came to death.

I was lying if I said I didn't want to know more about them, but it felt wrong to ask for some reason. I couldn't shake the idea away. Had they told me something in the years lost to my memory? That made sense. Perhaps there was something that they had told me in that time that I simply could not know right now. I trusted Nathan-Prime's judgment, because he had never done anything to purposefully harm me, psychic dream deaths notwithstanding. Maybe if I continued in that trust it would be rewarded with answers later.

"No," I said, finally. "Maybe later, but I think I'm okay with not knowing right now. My parents were always terribly practical people. If they didn't tell me something, then I must not have been ready for it."

Mara nodded solemnly. "You surprise me with your restraint, Guardian Azarel," she said. "To be perfectly honest the information I accessed would not have been useful to you anyways, as most of it would've been common knowledge to you."

"I do, however, have another question to ask."

"Ask it at your pleasure."

I paused, feeling the ridiculousness of the question almost prevent me from speaking, before I asked, "Why do we not teach other people to use elements and invocations they're not naturally good at?"

Mara flinched. "That…was not what I thought you would ask."

84

She paused. "It is my understanding that the Forum wishes to have its Sentinels and Psionics be better-equipped at what they're best at. Since there were so many of them around, it was just easier for them to focus teaching students in fields they specialized in innately."

"I see." I nodded. "Mara, do you think I'd be crazy to ask for help in using a particular invocation I'm not skilled with?"

"You would if you sought out my help on such a matter, but I imagine that I am not the one you are referring to." She turned to gaze at Cinderella. "She is quite talented, but still just a novice, even with your teaching. Is this what you and the founder discussed?"

"He was quite…adamant about it. Deathly so."

"Then if this is his teaching for you, you would do well to follow through with it."

I scoffed. "But you know how hard it is to learn invocations that have nothing to do with what comes naturally."

"True, but I also know that even your natural skills still took time to sharpen to the point of usefulness. So it is with anything that you seek to learn. Simply because something is easy to perform does not create worth in and of itself. Most of what we learn in this life is meant to be hard to undergo, for that is what makes it worthwhile."

Shaking my head, I groaned. "Why do I bring these things on myself?"

"Because you," Mara said, placing a hand on my left shoulder, "whether you like it or not, want to solve problems. It is an admirable trait. Many see problems in life and society and think to themselves that it would be good if someone solved them. Few are willing to go and do what must be done to change the world. But, as you've noticed, it does tend to draw problems to you, because people see that you are willing to fix matters and that will cause those who wish for things to remain as they are to lash out at you. Know this, Blake: you are not alone in this fight. Nor would I wish you to be. I believe in you."

I looked up at her and smiled. "Thanks, Mara. I needed that."

She nodded and the pointed away from her, revealing that Cinderella was starting to wake up. I shook my head and mustered my courage.

Shivering as she woke, Cinderella opened her eyes and pushed herself upright. Yawning, she raised her hands in the air and let her joints pop. Cracking her neck afterwards, she realized we were watching her and froze in place.

"Is something wrong?" she asked.

"No, not really," I said, rubbing the back of my neck. "I, um, have a question for you, Red."

"You do? I will answer if I am able."

"Well, this is gonna sound weird, but…can you teach me to use fire invocations?"

Cinderella's jaw dropped and she looked from me to Mara and then back when she saw that Mara wasn't in on whatever joke she thought I'd prepared.

"That's a good one, Blake," Cinderella said, laughing. "If anything, you should be teaching me how to use mine better."

"Well, funny story, Red," I said, laughing without confidence. "See, Nathan-Prime came to me in my dreams last night and said to learn fire invocation or I'd die."

Cinderella opened her mouth to speak, thinking I was continuing the joke, but when she saw the solemn expression on Mara's face and my unsure smile she stopped, only to say, "Oh."

Standing up, Cinderella shook her head and then placed her right hand in a fist and smacked it into her left hand, trying to look confident. I stood with her and held out my hand, which she took and shook.

"All right, kiddo, we've got a lot to figure out in little time," I said. "Please teach me everything you know."

CHAPTER 11

I had always known this about myself, but it was a different thing to say it out loud.

"I am a terrible student," I said.

"No, don't say that about yourself," Cinderella said, trying to console me. "It's just—"

I started coughing as the smoke I had accidentally conjured in my mouth exited. Trying not to throw up, I groaned and bemoaned my many recent failures.

"How?" I asked, once I regained the ability to speak. "I tried invoking that flame two minutes ago—on my hands! Not my mouth!"

Cinderella bit her lip and paused, trying not to look upset and failing miserably. "Well," she said, "maybe it's because you're thinking too much. Or not at all. It's hard to tell sometimes with you, Blake. Um, I think, well—why don't you tell me what you were doing?"

I sighed. It had been four days since I'd had my dream and we had made little progress westward. My new training regimen was holding us back tremendously, forcing Mara and Sedecla to wait four hours each day as I failed to so much as set a single bit of kindling on fire. Not even when I tried transferring flame from a match onto my fingertips and then to the wood. Every time I tried I would inevitably either lose focus or cause the flames to grow larger and burn myself because I couldn't control their size. It was a waste of matches and time. We were barely a day's walk to Phoenix when we should've made it there much sooner.

"Fine," I said, grumbling. "I was trying to imagine the flame appearing on my left hand, just right above my skin, like you

87

asked. But when I thought about it, I got frustrated when it didn't appear right away and then my stomach growled, which made me think of eating and—that's why it ended up in my mouth."

"That's okay," she said. "At least nothing got burned this time. Now just focus for me, okay? Think of the flame and think of how fire spreads once it makes contact with oxygen, but just localize it on your ring finger this time. Maybe I'm asking too much of you too early."

"If you say so."

I held out my left hand and extended my ring finger further than the others. I felt a slight jostling and inwardly groaned as I noticed the dragon skeleton ring had twisted itself around once more to face me. I'd been continually shifting it to where I wouldn't be looking at it by placing it on the side of my hand that I couldn't see, but whenever I looked away it would inevitably keep looking right back at me. The ring had always been creepy, but I had moved it to not be seen fully in the first place because it kept distracting me whenever I tried concentrating on my flame invocations. Shrugging it off, I turned the ring over again, sighed, and did as instructed.

"Intentoque Scintilla," I invoked.

Flame appeared from nowhere, gathering around the tip of my ring finger. However, the moment it made further contact with the air, it grew massively in size and I blew on my hand to prevent it from spreading, extinguishing the flame before it could burn me again.

"I'm so hopeless," I said, whining.

Falling to my knees, I hit the sand with my fists, both of which hadn't fully healed from my last failed attempt to produce flames over them, making the harsh sand hurt even more than it would have from the impact. My arms trembled from the strain of forcing myself not to let out a string of creative expletives.

"Blake, stand up," Cinderella said.

I looked up wearily, only to flinch when I saw the angry look in her face, which was complemented by her hands now being on her hips. Contrary to her normally sweet, demure self, I was now facing down a disappointed and slighted woman. I didn't know how to respond to this part of Cinderella's self. I could count on one hand the amount of times I'd seen that expression and the one that came to mind immediately was her passionate anger at Zoë Slinden during the Feast.

"Now, I'm very sorry, but I'm very mad at you, Blake," Cinderella said, wagging a finger at me. "You've done nothing but complain the whole time I've tried to teach you and it's getting annoying. I know you're working hard with little results, but that's no excuse to give up so easily. You're better than that."

Sound resembling confused grunts left my mouth. She was scolding me? And with all the sweetness of a freshly baked apple pie? A part of me wished she'd just slapped me in the face or shouted at me instead, but this was a new beast I wasn't used to. How was I even supposed to respond to her without simultaneously laughing at how pure her concern was and then hiding myself in shame for disappointing her?

"I'm sorry, Cinderella," I said, standing back up while dusting off the sand. "I guess it's been a while since I've hit so many brick walls when it came to being good at something."

"That's okay, because you won't get any better by complaining," Cinderella said, as her face softened. "Now I'm sorry I yelled at you."

I couldn't help it. I burst out laughing immediately after she finished. That was supposed to be her yelling voice? It was barely a single pitch higher than her normal voice.

Cinderella stared at me, confused at my sudden change in behavior and looked over to Mara and Sedecla for help. Neither woman offered an opinion, nearly as bewildered as her at my sudden change.

"Sorry, Red," I said, composing myself a moment later. "I needed that laugh. Okay, I'm good now. We can keep going."

"Oh, well, I guess if that's okay with you," Cinderella said, all animosity having left her voice.

Before I could speak, Sedecla's voice rang out from behind us, saying, "I don't pretend to understand how any of this works, sir, but I think I know what's wrong."

I turned to face her. Sedecla had been a bit of an oddity among oddities this entire trip. Her path to Phoenix had saved us a little time, but she wasn't much of a conversationalist. My attempts to probe her about information regarding the insides of the Dead Lands was met with reserved words that told me nothing I didn't already know, but even someone as dense as me could see the reason was for how terrible it had been for her in there. I couldn't imagine living in an area constantly overwhelmed by the undead. The fact that she'd made it out of there alive was nothing less than a miracle.

"Go ahead," I said.

"Well, like I said, I don't really understand all you're trying to do," Sedecla stated, "but there's always some kind of weird light on your left hand whenever you try to make the fire magic."

"Invocation," Mara corrected. "Magic is for blasphemers and the arrogant."

"Oh, my mistake."

"Weird light?" I repeated. "Cinderella, have you seen this light?"

She shook her head. "Try it again," she said. "I'll watch for the light instead of the fire this time."

I nodded, growling when I noticed my ring had turned to face me again, so I switched it back. Holding out my hands, I repeated the invocation, only to end up with the same result.

"I saw it!" Cinderella exclaimed, pointing at my left hand. "It's your ring! It glowed with a weird purple light. It was so small I almost didn't notice."

I looked down at my left hand, seeing that the ring had once more positioned itself to face me. I paused, gazing at it intently. The bony dragon ring had saved my life back in Vice City, but was too powerful to use wantonly. I had experimented with it behind closed doors, but hadn't been very effective in using whatever powers it held within it, nor had I heard the voice of the person who supposedly resided within it. Once I had even asked Nathan-Prime about it, but he'd given his usual spiel about it not being time to learn about it.

Was it somehow interfering with my invocations? Where did it come from? I had never seen a design like this before, although I obviously wouldn't remember where I'd gotten it from given that I had no memory of it before I'd come to the future. I had checked the skin around its placement and there was a noticeable line around it and my skin wasn't as tanned where it was resting, which meant it had to have been there for some time.

I opened my mouth to speak as I heard a gunshot ring out from in front of us, as a bullet fell right at my feet. Instantly, I entered a defensive stance, seeing two hundred yards in front of us was a group of people who'd appeared from seemingly nowhere. Although, given the terrain it would've been easy for them to have hidden behind one of the many dunes in the area. There was six of them there with three horses it seemed. However, movement to my right alerted me to the presence of another, just as I saw three more individuals garbed in clothing designed to obscure their bodies, while simultaneously protecting them from the heat. All three of them were aiming rifles at us from the top of the nearest dune to us.

I cursed inwardly. I'd gotten too distracted with everything that had been going on. I should've been at least doing a momentary psychic sweep of the area to know we weren't alone anymore.

"They got the drop on us!" I exclaimed and turned to Mara. "How did they get the drop on us?"

"Perhaps if you had been focusing yourself on your surroundings and not on another petty emotional crisis then you'd have sensed them before they came here," Mara said, shaking her head.

"Enough talk, you two," a man said, stepping forth, his gun trained on my head.

I held up my hands and motioned for the others to do the same, as they followed suit. No need to start a firefight at such a disadvantage. I could definitely start a fight, but I had no way of guaranteeing that the others would get out of it unscathed. Cinderella stood the best chance, but Mara was too slow and Sedecla seemed to have no combat experience. A cursory exam of the outsider's thoughts revealed that none of them seemed to be Christened or vampire, so at least we had that going for us.

Any advice? I asked.

Bullet wounds hurt, Nathan-Prime offered. I'd advise you to avoid getting shot.

I gripped my fists and fumed, but forced myself to calm down. I needed a cool head.

"My name is Blake Azarel," I said. "From Corpus Christi. We're hunting down a fugitive from the Dead Lands who stole our friend. We mean you no harm. We're just trying to find a place to gather supplies so that we can plan our infiltration into the Dead

Lands."

The man looked from me to his companions then to those ahead of us. A lone figure moved his horse forward and then held out a small coin that gleamed in the sunlight, using some sort of signal to give orders to the man, who nodded and looked back at me.

"Drop your weapons and follow us," the man said. "We'll verify whether you're telling the truth or not once we get to Phoenix. Resist and we shoot."

I turned to the others. "You heard the man," I said. "Drop them." I looked at Mara. "All of them."

Mara sighed and placed down her rifle, two pistols from their holsters, a silver dagger, and then lifted her socks to reveal five more of the same type of dagger and two small pistols strapped to her ankles that offered a single shot. I resisted the urge to laugh at her thoroughness and dropped my Jericho 941 pistol and silver knife, while Cinderella and Sedecla remained still, as they had no weapons on hand.

I remained as calm as possible. I had sensed no hostile intent from any of them; rather, they seemed to have all had a singular sigh of relief at our compliance, which made sense to me. I highly doubted these were the kinds of people who were used to common decency.

The man who'd been the go-between motioned for his fellows to go down the dunes and they did so in a tight formation, while he kept his rifle trained on me. His two companions grabbed our weapons and placed them in a duffle bag for safekeeping.

"Thank you for your compliance," the man said, strapping his rifle on his back. "Now march forward with your hands on your heads." He paused. "Oh, and welcome to Phoenix."

CHAPTER 12

No one spoke during our trip into Phoenix, not even our apparent captors. The best I got from them was several knowing glances between them as we approached what appeared to be an old governmental building. I sensed the presences of more people inside the building, but was having a hard time to focus on numbers at present, too paranoid about our escorts to leave my spiritual senses away from them for too long.

The others in my group had likewise remained silent. Mara had maintained her stoic demeanor, while Cinderella and Sedecla were her polar opposites with the obvious wariness on their faces. I had locked eyes with Cinderella once to attempt to calm her down, but that hadn't been good enough.

"Go inside," the man who'd captured us earlier stated, motioning forward with his rifle pointed to the ground. "No funny business."

"Understood," I said, turning to my fellows. "You heard the man."

They nodded and joined me by stepping inside the building. Once fully in there, I noticed that—opposed to buildings around it—this one seemed to have been repaired more. Obvious signs of reconstructing stairways, filling holes in the tiles, and other signs of restorative work told me that they'd been there for some time.

The building itself seemed to have once been a courthouse and was three stories tall. The main hallway led into an open room with space for all of us and what I assumed to be the rest of this group to meet in.

Our hands were still on top of our heads, never once leaving them for fear of agitating our captors. I was most interested in two of them: the man who'd taken us and the one who'd used a coin to signal with him earlier. After careful glances I had noticed that their gait was feminine, and she seemed to be the shortest in their ragtag bunch. She had never once let her eyes off me and my attempts to probe into her mind had been met with intense resistance, which wasn't out of the ordinary, but still weirded me out. There were many mundanes in the world who were just naturally able to fight back against mental probing without even being aware that they were doing so. But hers seemed concentrated, taught, and highly practiced. Clearly whoever'd taught her was a genius.

After a short walk inside the open room, my group went to the center and waited for the others to make the first move.

The man who'd talked to us first took off his facemask and goggles, revealing an older man in his early fifties. He had black hair in a buzzcut, somber brown eyes, and burnt amber skin. He placed his rifle down on a table and crossed his arms. I gazed into his eyes and a sudden warmness hit me, as if this man had been my friend his entire life. I saw vague memories of a wife and child laughing at a joke he'd made, which was suddenly replaced by a dark sense of reality when a burning home replaced the previous image. I shuddered in solidarity, feeling the pain with him.

Beside him the woman I'd failed to psychically link with took off her helmet, revealing a slender Japanese woman with black hair. She kept her goggles over her eyes—likely designed to prevent sand from hitting them during their desert excursions—but the fact that she hadn't taken them off inside made me immediately suspicious. I'd be able to vet her by looking into her eyes as I had her companion, but I couldn't see past the tinted goggles.

"Travelers," the older man said, "I am very sorry for the way we've treated you, but I'm sure you can understand our predicament. Now, before we begin, I would like you to tell me once more why you have come this way and who you are. You are free to take your hands off of your heads, but know that we are still capable of shooting you before you try anything."

I nodded. "My name is Blake Azarel, leader of Excelsior," I said. "My companions and I are going to the Dead Lands to retrieve our friend, Zea. She was kidnapped in Corpus Christi by an individual working with Morior Invictus. We had no previous contact with any of them before this moment. We came this way because we heard there were humans nearby who weren't affiliated with the Sanguine Collective and hoped to gather intel and supplies before we went into the Dead Lands. I give you my Word."

He nodded, not noticing the importance of the latter half of what I'd said. He instead looked over to the Japanese woman and waited for her to nod back, which she did.

"We have heard of Excelsior and their resistance to the Collective," the man said, sizing me up. "You claim to be its leader and yet you left that all behind to find one person in such a dangerous location?"

"Was it not Jesus who taught us the importance of saving one sheep while the ninety-nine were safe?" I asked.

He grinned. "And so He did. In which gospels?"

"Matthew and Luke," Mara and I said in unison.

He turned to look at her and his companion nodded once more. "Very well. Very few have access to those in what's left of the States. Either you're who you say you are or you're gifted liars."

"Aren't we all?" I asked. "I mean, it's quite easy for us to lie even to our Savior about who we truly are."

His smile grew and he laughed. "Very true, Mr. Azarel. It would seem that you at the very least have some sort of philosophical background, which's more than what I can say for most people who try to infiltrate our city." He paused. "Were I to say that I was a preacher, what would that mean to you?"

I paused to think. "Hmm, well, for one, I'd be extremely happy, because we need people like you back home. I don't really have the time to maintain a city, teach the next generation of Psionics and Sentinels, while also holding service on Sundays. Especially since I still don't understand it all myself. Frankly, I'd have to have a further discussion with you on the all the particulars of what you actually believe in to prevent heresy from spreading in the city. You get ruled by vampires for a hundred years and people start believing weird things, similar in a way to the *Kakure Kirishitans* of Japan."

"A philosopher, apologist, and historian? Well, I believe I have everything I need from this discussion."

The man took off his black coat and cracked his neck, as a silver cross necklace dangled above his clavicle. He placed his coat on a nearby chair and approached me. The rest of the group bowed slowly out of reverence.

He stopped in front of me and held out a hand, saying, "Mr. Azarel, my name is Aiden Delacroix, pastor and leader of our band of misfits and escapees from the Dead Lands. I must say it's a pleasure to meet the leader of the resistance out here. We've been stuck here in Phoenix since before the barrier went down."

I accepted his hand only to hear a tutting of scoffing come from Sedecla's lips. We let go of each other's hands to look at her.

"Impossible," Sedecla said. "No one could've gotten through the barrier before the Collective brought it down."

Aiden smiled at the woman to his right and gave her a thumbs up. I looked at her intently as she took off her goggles, allowing me to look into them for the first time. The short glance we shared with one another held an air of familiarity and my heart skipped without knowing why. She had short black hair, glassy blue eyes, and had to be about forty years old, but the shared look we had told me she was older.

My suspicions were proven correct when she crafted a perfect hexagon out of what appeared to be some sort of gem manipulation-based invocation, this one looking like a ruby. I whistled approvingly. I hadn't seen anyone do that in a very long time.

"That's perfect," I said, examining the structure closely, sliding a finger down the sides. "With the proper study of geometric states, it'd be a cinch for a gem invoker to figure out the structure inherent in every protective barrier. I remember reading up on it once in class. I don't pretend to understand all of its intricacies, but the way it was explained to me makes this all come together. You have a very unique talent, Ms....?"

"Tamayo Yamaguchi," she said, bowing slightly.

I studied her closely. "Far be it for me to ask a woman her age, but...how old are you?"

She paused for a moment before saying, "One hundred and eighteen."

"What?" Cinderella asked. "You look so young."

Tamayo smiled. "It's amazing, isn't it?"

"It's a result of the Christening," I explained. "It's what gives you your powers."

"I already know that."

I paused. "And who told you that?"

She looked at me, a little confused. "You did. Many years ago. I was eleven when you saved my life from The Horde and Sanguine Collective, Guardian Azarel."

I almost spat in her face from surprise. The whole room grew quiet. I felt a trembling in my mind as I witnessed a vision of a group of twenty children huddling in the darkness, fearing that their next visitor would be there to feed on them. But when I walked into the room, their expressions all changed into hope. I was garbed entirely in black clothing that was indiscernible to my eyes, even though I should've been able to recall it perfectly. In the present I smacked my face with my right hand, trying to recover from what I'd seen. Another memory recovered, but I still had no context for it. Why was I dressed in all black? I hated wearing black.

Aiden broke the silence first, asking, "You are the very same Blake Azarel who saved Tamayo a hundred years ago?"

"Yes," I said, rubbing the back of my neck.

"You don't remember me," Tamayo said.

"I do, but I don't. Something happened to my memory when I made the jump into the future."

"The future?" Aiden repeated. "How old are you, Guardian Azarel?"

"Twenty-eight."

"Unbelievable, yet here you are."

"It's a long story, but I'm more interested in you, Tamayo. Can you tell me what happened to you? Everything, it might help jog my memory."

Tamayo looked sad for a moment, but spoke up, saying, "I was ten years old when The Horde kidnapped me off the street. My parents were junkies and had both died of an overdose, leaving me alone. I had no idea that I had these powers; I just wanted somewhere to sleep and eat. These men came to me one day and promised me all the food and water I could ever want if I joined them. My parents had never cared enough to warn me about strangers. I told them yes and before I knew it, I was imprisoned along with several other young Christeners, those who had fallen out of sight of the Gray Forum."

I bit my lip. It was true enough. Even as widespread as we

were, we couldn't scan every single city to find those who had the Christening in them. I'd always thrown out the idea of training someone to be our version of the Jedi Watchman, but very few people had seriously considered the idea. Tradition dictated that all members were either born into the Forum or found by the providence of God.

"I stayed with them for a year, as vampires would feed on us, coveting the power we held inside ourselves," Tamayo continued. "But then...you came."

I perked up, hoping my memories would return, but nothing did.

"But...it was odd," she said, frowning. "I remember you freeing us, but it wasn't the night you first came there. We were all too drained by the vampires to fully understand what was going on. I'm sorry, I wish I had more to say about that."

"That's fine," I said, nodding. "What happened after that?"

"You were worried about something, but you wouldn't tell us about it. You took one of us under your wing as an apprentice, even though you weren't supposed to. In fact, you didn't even tell the Forum about us at all."

"I didn't? That's...highly irregular. Did I suspect that there was a mole in the Gray Forum? Had I been betrayed by them? Why was I acting so suspiciously?"

"I cannot say, but I do know that the next six years of my life were the best I'd ever had. You took care of us, but couldn't stay with us long, so you had a friend take care of us. His name was Atanasio."

"But the Archives say he was suffering from *Anima Sola* at the time. Had he made a recovery? Or were the Archives changed? Did I have that kind of power?"

"I wish I could answer your questions, Guardian Azarel, but you never shared that information with us," Tamayo said. "You said that if we knew what you knew then the enemy would get stronger."

I nodded, although I had no clue why I'd ever order such a thing.

"It's not your fault," I said. "If anything, I was the problem with this scenario."

"It certainly seems like you wanted to protect them from the

98

High Court's eyes," Mara said, breaking her silence. "I suspect that you were right to say that there was a mole in the Forum. Knowing you, though, I must admit that it feels out-of-character for you not to have confronted this head on."

"I was just thinking the same thing. Maybe I didn't have proof. Then again that's never stopped me before. No, something had to make me not want to tell anyone else. Is it possible I even hid this from Mom and Dad?" I clenched my fist. "I'm so close, but I have no answers."

"I do remember one other thing," Tamayo said, turning my attention to her.

"And what was that?" I asked.

"Atanasio was getting sick one day and he told us to run away from him. That was a little before the Gray Forum fell. I don't know why he did it, but he forbade us from telling him where we were going, only that we should find you and tell you what happened to him."

"Atanasio…said that?"

I frowned. Atanasio was my best friend and a member of my team, which we'd dubbed the Dream Team. It included Akemi Tyson, Brian Poole, Rica Sturm, Atanasio Mortis, and myself. Because of information I'd learned last year I suspected that a new member, Meredith, was also involved with us, but I had no definitive proof of that. I knew it was likely that all of them were dead, but to hear that something was wrong with Atanasio even before all of this had happened was devastating.

"What happened next?" I asked.

"I don't know what happened to the others," Tamayo admitted. "I remember briefly sensing your arrival in the safe house, but I had run away by then. The building exploded not long after you arrived. I broke my ankle while we were running away and they left me behind. I managed to make it to a Gray Forum safe house in Oregon that you had told me about. I got there right before the area around it became a part of the Dead Lands. I lived there for years off the supplies in the safe house, but left to find other humans, only to see the Dead Lands for what they truly were. I spent many years fighting them with the training you had offered me and managed to find some other survivors. Eventually I helped them break out of the barrier and we made our way here."

"Amazing. Well done, Tamayo. A lesser Psionic would've buckled under the pressure, but you, you came out of this golden."

"I'm a Psionic?"

"By the definitions we have anyone who is capable of gem generation is a Psionic, due to it not being something that's easy to form from your hands without the use of teleportation. The specific gems you use could be halfway across the earth, but your powers inherently locate them, although the drawback is that you need to power them up, hence you being a Psionic and not a Sentinel like me."

"I see. As always you have proved an excellent teacher, Guardian Azarel. Were it not for your past instruction I would have been unable to save everyone here. In fact, because of that very training I was able to sense your spiritual self before you arrived, although I was confused by what this meant, so I asked Aiden to ambush you just in case I was being misled."

"Praise be to God," Aiden said, smiling. "And to think I was going to shoot you all on sight. Oh, I've never been happier to be wrong. Mostly we've been forced to kill vampires, bandits, and the occasional undead escapees from the Dead Lands."

I chuckled. "Wouldn't be the first time I've had bullets shot at me from all directions," I said. "But since we're on the topic, what can you tell us about the Dead Lands?"

"They are a dark and terrible place. The sun rarely shines. I know not why. Morior Invictus holds immense power. There are very few human settlements in the Dead Lands. If they exist, they are underground and hiding, so as not to attract the covetous eyes of Morior Invictus. Those necromancers are unforgiving and hate that humans remain alive in their territory. I was not alive then, but those of that generation who were alive when I was a boy said that during the upheaval following the reveal of the supernatural, that the necromancers seized power before the Collective could arrive in the West Coast. Cities fell overnight as they were overwhelmed with the growing forces of the recently raised dead summoned by their dark masters. They were ruthless, caring not for anything but destruction. Very few groups managed to survive the initial onslaught, forming what cities they could to keep the undead at bay. However, whenever these cities were identified, they were always marked for destruction by the necromancers. All of us do not originate from the same city or village, but are survivors who fled when their homes were overwhelmed by the undead.

"Over these past hundred years, Morior Invictus has created new monstrosities to deal with the living in their realm. They do nothing but grow with power as they experiment with what is not theirs to meddle with. I know only the name of their leader, but not what they are capable of. Their leader is a madman called Abraxas and it is rumored that he alone controls the undead horde that surrounds the Dead Lands, while the others focus on other means of spiting the living. They are said to be based in what was once a large city in California known as San Francisco, but not in the city proper. They are said to reside in an impregnable fortress in the sea that cannot be reached by conventional means, much less escaped from should you be brought there to be experimented on."

"Wait a second," I said, mulling over what he said and then turning to Mara. "You wouldn't happen to be thinking what I am, would you?"

"I am no expert on Californian cities," Mara said, "but I do think we share suspicions on this location in question."

"Alcatraz. This just got a lot harder."

"How so?" Cinderella asked.

"Aiden's descriptions are pretty on point if they're true. Alcatraz used to be a large prison in the ocean designed to prevent the worst types of criminals from ever escaping its walls. Many terrible things happened there, and the Forum marked it as a dark place, one that no member was ever supposed to go to alone for fear of being attack by whatever lingered there. Ghosts, demons, undead, you mention it and they were probably there at some point."

"But this is unconfirmed as of now," Mara said. "Perhaps we should wait to speculate."

"True enough," I said, turning to Aiden. "So now that we're friends and all, how about we get our weapons back."

"Oh, of course," Aiden said. "Fred, please return their weapons to them."

A burly man nodded and unzipped the bags that contained our varied weapons, handing them out to their original owners.

"Well, now that that is all taken care of, we must allow you time to rest," Aiden said. "Please, we have some spare rooms upstairs. Use them and recuperate for tonight I think I won't make anyone upset by having a feast worthy of this moment. I will guide you to the rooms myself."

"Wait, Tamayo, I have one last question before we go," I said, staring at my ring.

"Yes, Guardian Azarel," she said.

"Was I wearing this ring when I rescued you?"

"Yes, sir. You said it was your wedding ring. To be honest it always made me feel a little scared of you, but I know that wasn't really true. You were always the nicest man I ever met."

I nodded. "Thank you, Tamayo. I may not fully remember you, but I am so very happy to see you again." I turned to Aiden. "Pastor Delacroix, please lead the way. I haven't had a bath in weeks."

CHAPTER 13

Phoenix, Arizona was beautiful at night. Even with the empty streets and lack of care given to the other buildings, I could tell how great it had once been. I'd never been there before that I could recall, but it was hard not to imagine it in its heyday.

I was sitting on a sniper's nest on top of the courthouse, having volunteered to take the night watchman job so that others could rest. I hadn't felt tired the whole day, not even after the bountiful feast we'd had for dinner to celebrate our newfound alliance with the survivors of the Dead Lands. They had welcomed us all with open arms and were now making plans to leave Phoenix behind to make the long journey to Corpus Christi in order to rejoin society, or whatever passed for it these days.

Tamayo had spent most of the feast talking with me, regaling me with stories of moments I should have remembered, but literally couldn't now. Stories of how I had taken the time to teach each child I'd rescued individually in whatever invocations they were proficient with, while making sure that no one could ever find them. I had demanded utmost secrecy and the only contact they'd had with another human being had been a recovering Atanasio, who would guard them in my stead while I kept doing my normal duties for the Gray Forum. It all seemed like a ton of work, but the way that Tamayo smiled while she regaled me with the details told me that it had all been worth it, even if she was the only survivor of the group as we were aware.

Sighing, I wiped some sweat off of my neck. I'd long since taken off my shirt. Even though it was nighttime there was still plenty of heat left over from the day before to make me sweaty. Eventually, it would cool down significantly, but I was fine for now. But then I saw a purple flash appear and I looked down at my chest. Purple pulsations greeted me every other minute whenever I looked down at my body. Even though I had first learned about them a year ago, it was still unsettling to see them all over me. They ran all over my body in some sort of geometric pattern that I had yet to decipher.

According to Nathan-Prime they were some sort of protective seal designed for my defense. What precisely they were supposed to keep out he hadn't specified, and despite my efforts to learn on my own in the Archives of the Gray Forum I had found nothing useful about them.

I turned to aim the scope of my rifle to the left, seeing a lone armadillo investigating an upturned trashcan whose contents would've long rotted. Movement to its right made me turn the rifle and scope again, only to be greeted by the left side profile of a girl with blonde hair wearing a black yet somehow bright sundress. I moved upward to look away from the scope and with my eyes instead, only to see that she was gone. I expanded my awareness, hoping to sense her presence, but nothing but the occasional animal minds registered to my thoughts.

Pushing myself up out of my sniper position, I placed the rifle on the floor and gazed out, enhancing my vision to see what normal humans couldn't make out. However, no matter how much I zoomed in I couldn't see any trace of the mystery girl, physical or spiritual. As if in response to my questions, the pulses on my body grew in number and brightness, only to settle down moments later.

I placed my right hand over my mouth, thinking hard. I'd seen the blonde woman before, but I could never remember her name. I had an inkling that she wasn't someone I was very familiar with, but that she had done something to me to help protect me. If she was tied into these strange marks or not was a matter open to debate, but no matter how much time I spent thinking about it I never got any closer to an answer. For now she was as much an anomaly as a fair percentage of my past.

Before I could pursue the thoughts further, I felt an odd sensation in my chest. Almost like something was burying into my heart so that it could stay there forever. I clutched my chest, but the feeling soon disappeared. A brief flash of a memory appeared in my mind and I saw an outline of a woman who was holding my hand and laughing with me.

"Was that her?" I asked. "My wife..."

I clenched my fist. It wasn't fair. Who was she? How had I ever fallen in love with her? Why would I ever propose to her so that I could wear a ring like the one I had now?

I sighed, knowing I wouldn't be any closer to the answers I wanted. It was easy to say that I was willing to be patient to wait on the right time to remember them, but it was another thing entirely to be forced to live it out.

However, my thoughts were interrupted by my mind sensing someone approaching from below the courthouse, heading up the stairs to reach me. I felt no hostile intent and a short mental probe let me know that I was in no danger, as Cinderella ascended the stairs to the sniper's nest, wearing some covers around herself that she'd taken from her bed. She eyed me oddly upon noticing my lack of a shirt, but chose to focus on something else.

"Aren't you going to sleep?" Cinderella asked, rubbing her eyes.

"Can't," I admitted, staring out at the night sky. "Too much going on up here." I pointed to my head. "Besides, I can skip one day and be all right. I generate and gather more power than you do. If I wanted to, I could go a week without sleep. Granted, I'd have to sleep for at least a day after, so it's a win-lose kinda thing. Also the next person on night watch isn't due for another hour."

She didn't say anything, but sat beside me, watching the night sky, slowly waking herself back up to eventually talk with me.

"It's a lot prettier now that we're not polluting it as much," I said. "This'll be hard for you to believe, but in a city like this you could only see little bits of the stars, because of all the pollution in the air. Nature finds a way, eh, kiddo?"

"I'm not a kid," she said, breaking her silence. "I'm only four years younger than you."

I turned to look at her, finding that her lips were pursed and her eyes were narrowed. "Is everything okay?"

"You don't call Zea a kid and I'm older than her."

"Well, I—well. It's complicated."

"Then explain if you have all night."

I sighed and turned the rest of my body to face her. "I don't mean it as an insult," I said. "It's just something I've always kinda

105

done with people with less experience than me. I get how that could sound patronizing, but I don't intend to do that."

"What about Nathan? I haven't heard you call him a kid in a while."

"Well, I did at first, but that was before I found out about how much experience he'd had."

"And I don't have any?"

"No! That's not what I'm saying. You do have experience, but when you look at it objectively, they have more than you. Zea's been training her whole life and Nathan's been fighting God knows what whenever he has to sleep at night." I paused. "That's not to say you didn't have to deal with a lot. Lord help I couldn't imagine going through what you did, but it's not the same kind—I'm sorry. Let me start over. I'm really not helping, am I?"

"I'm withholding judgment."

"Thanks." I scratched the back of my head. "I think of you all as family. I know, I'm a sucker, but we really came together, didn't we? Nathan's like my little brother. Zea was the first friend I ever made on this godforsaken world and she saved my life way too many times than I care to admit. Clooney…well, he's there. But then we get to you. I felt your pain inside the dream when we talked to you for the first time. My heart broke when I realized all that Zoë had done to you. None of that should have been possible. Not when we were around. Yet it had and I knew I had to do everything I could to save you."

"But you didn't even know me."

"And? You were in trouble. I could help. So I did. And when we finally got you out of that hell, I was so happy. You smiled for the first time in what had to have been years. I wanted to make sure you could smile for the rest of your life." I paused. "You're like…you're like the sister I never had. When I saw you smile, I swore to protect you from harm. I know, it's stupid and a bit sexist, but I never wanted to see you hurt again. That's why sometimes in my mind when I think about you, I think about that smiling girl from a year ago and, mentally, it makes me devolve into that protective state of mind. I know you can handle yourself. Heck, you've saved my life several times over since then, but old habits die hard, I guess. So…that's why I call you 'kiddo', Cinderella. I'm not trying to be mean or patronizing. I swear."

To my surprise she smiled. "I like it when you explain yourself," she said, still smiling. "You get so defensive. It's kinda cute."

"I...what?"

She laughed. "I'm sorry. I shouldn't be playing with you like that. What you said...that was sweet. I've never had anyone who cared so much about me before. I've never had someone who cared so much that they almost died to make sure I could smile." She paused, her face growing grimmer. "I've never told anyone else this before, but Zoë would often read bedtime stories to me."

I flinched.

"Upsetting, I know," Cinderella said. "But it was always so she could break me further. She'd tell me stories like *Sleeping Beauty* or *Cinderella*. That's where I got my name. I don't even know the one my parents gave me. Zoë saw how much I loved that one and to further torment me she would call me Cinderella to mock my idealistic hopes of escape. I couldn't help it. I would always feel this happiness when the stories were told and this hope would swell inside of me. But Zoë knew exactly what she was doing. Whenever she would finish reading the stories she'd feed on me, because—even though I knew what would happen—I would dwell on those thoughts. I would pray that a brave prince would rescue me from her. I spent days locked in my room after she had forced me to locate a Christener and just pray for help, but it never came and I lost all hope of rescue. Until that day when you and Nathan appeared to me in that dream. I saw the fire in your eyes. It was stronger than anything I could ever hope to invoke. Here you were, this man who knew nothing about me other than that I needed help and you were there to rescue me. You weren't in love with me like the imaginary princes were, but you loved me like no one else ever had before."

I stopped listening when a throbbing pain entered my right hand. I saw Zea in my mind, strapped down to some forsaken stone slab. She was hurt and dark figures were torturing her further. My mind screamed as I realized I couldn't do anything to help her. I felt that burrowing once more in my heart and I snapped back to reality.

Cinderella tried to talk to me, but I held up a hand. I didn't know how to feel. There were so many thoughts trying to piece themselves together in my mind that it was impossible to keep track of them all. I saw Zea laughing at me when I'd fallen down during training, I felt the warmness of her touch as we practiced our hand-to-hand fighting, and I remembered watching her fall to sleep on one of the benches in the garden of the Silver Fortress, as I picked her up to take her back to her room.

Was I...in love with her? Is that what my mind was trying to tell me? That was such a crazy thought. Zea was my friend. I had to be more fatigued than I thought. All of that constant worrying about her safety was making me focus on conjuring some illusory romance to make me further emboldened to find her. The whole thing was ludicrous. I had better things to think about, let alone the fact that I was being incredibly rude to Cinderella, who was patiently waiting for me to finish whatever was going on in my head.

"I'm sorry," I said, shaking my head. "I just felt her. They're hurting her." I punched the floor. "And there's nothing I can do about it here."

"You...can feel her?" Cinderella asked.

"It's the strangest thing. Ever since Zea and I shared our senses together the first time we met we've always been able to kinda pick up on each other, no matter how far apart we are. I know it drives her crazy, because of her empathic sensibilities and especially when she's stuck dealing with my mental processes."

"You two must really be close then."

"I guess you could say we're closer to each other than to anyone else."

"I see."

Cinderella sighed and looked back at the night sky. She yawned and pulled her covers tighter around herself, closing her eyes for a moment before shaking herself awake. She held out her right hand and invoked a small flame that warmed us both as it lay suspended in the air. Then, realizing what she'd done, she frowned and looked at me.

"I'm sorry," she said, simply.

"For what?" I asked.

She grimaced. "I—It's hard to put into words. I didn't want to make you feel like a failure right now by making the fire so easily. I'm sorry."

108

"Don't be. Don't ever apologize for being good at something so beneficial. It's not your fault I suck at it."

"But that's just it—I want to help you use flame invocations, but I haven't been any good at it. I don't know if that's because I'm a bad teacher or if I don't know how to explain what I do. It just seems impossible."

"It's not impossible, kiddo. I'm just a slow learner. Teaching, I've learned in the past year, isn't something that comes to me naturally either. (Amnesia years aside, apparently.) I've always been more of a doer kinda guy. I've second guessed myself every single time I've had the opportunity to teach Clooney and you. I don't know if what I'm doing is helping or hindering your progress, but I do it anyways, because who else will? Zea when she has time, but she has other duties to perform, so you're stuck with me until someone more competent comes along."

"But I don't think that's enough. When I think about trying to get you to do something you don't understand or grasp easily, I get upset and can't focus. I just start thinking that it's impossible and can't ever be done."

I nodded and looked up at the moon. It was about a day away from becoming a supermoon. There was an old legend that said that on such a day the passage between worlds was thinner and you could jump in the air and suddenly be in Álfheim, home of Fair Folk. Of course, this was ridiculous, as few Fae had any sort of connection to the moon, but that did make me think of something else.

I smiled. "Have you ever heard of the Lake Like Glass?" I asked.

"No, I haven't," Cinderella said.

"It's this amazing lake in Álfheim. That's where the fairies live. It's made entirely of glass, but you can swim through it like it was water if you know what to do. There's some real weird magical and metaphysical properties going on there involving Fae enchantments that make it like that. Anyways, my point in bringing it up is that I had to deal with it as part of my training."

"But wouldn't the glass still cut you, even if it was some kind of liquid?" She paused, confused by her own question. "Does that make any sense?"

I laughed. "I'm trying to think of how to describe what I went

109

through. Álfheim is very different from Earth. Things that wouldn't work here are perfectly logical there. Lake Like Glass is a beautiful area, but like I said it's made of liquid glass. The light shines off of it in this really cool way that refracts it into these rainbows built of colors you can't see on Earth. Now, like I said, I had to go there at some point in my trials as a prospective Sentinel to see if I could deal with it. Now imagine, if you will, you have been taught everything you have about how science works here and now you're being told that not only is that false, but you are supposed to sacrifice your body to prove that what is true is false.

"Now, I went there with four of my friends: Brian Poole, Akemi Tyson, Atanasio Mortis, and Rica Sturm. I don't know if I ever told you this, but we had this little name for ourselves: the Dream Team. Later, once we had graduated we worked together as one unit, but, at that moment in our lives, we didn't know if we'd ever pass our tests.

"So we're there, standing as our testing instructor, Naomi Vivas, starts reciting the usual things we did, like how there was someone trapped on the other side of the lake and that they would die if we didn't manage to save them in the next five minutes. She told us about how dangerous it was to swim in the lake, because you wouldn't know whether you'd be swimming in glass or water, or both at the same time. But before she had even finished explaining it, I had jumped right into the lake."

"You didn't," Cinderella said, shivering.

"Oh, yes I did. Everyone nearly died of a heart attack as they watched me swimming through it all. I remember feeling my skin breaking off as I pushed through glass and I really should've died from all the blood I lost, but I was determined to make it to the other side. I casted every healing invocation I could think of, even though the water was canceling most of it out, given what it does to people like us. No matter how much I lost I kept swimming forward, eventually seeing the other side and the person who was acting as the one we were supposed to save. Well, little did I know that that same person was actually a member of the Fair Folk and the one whose job it was to protect that lake. He watched me swimming where logically no one should be able to swim and started cursing at me for my stupidity, but I ignored him. Eventually, through a lot of sheer willpower, I made it to the other side of the lake and 'rescued' the fairy there. I honestly was dying, but I still had enough strength to draw a teleportation circle, which was what my friends were busy drawing on the other side of the lake, as all of them frantically tried to think of a way to save me. So I grab the fairy and activate the circle, bringing us back to the other side where I kinda collapsed from the strain.

"I woke up back in the Silver Fortress, where I saw the medical invokers doing their best to keep me alive. I asked them if I'd passed the test and they looked at me like I was insane. Next to my bed were my mother and father, both of whom were consoling the other. When they found out that I was still alive they rushed to my side. My mother scolded me for doing something so impulsively stupid, while my father was doing everything in his power to not laugh, because he thought the whole thing was brilliant."

"I don't understand," Cinderella said.

I laughed. "What I did there was impossible, even by Álfheim standards," I said. "That glass should've ripped me apart the moment I jumped into that lake, but it didn't, because I didn't think it could, because I couldn't let it do that to me. I needed to save someone's life. It was my belief that kept me alive there. I believed I could reach the other side of the lake and because it was so stubbornly strong, I ended up being completely right. I was simply too ignorant of the fact that what I was doing was impossible to bother thinking that it was possible that what I was doing shouldn't be happening. The whole point of that exercise was to try to get us to work as a team, so that we could figure out the best way to counteract the resistance of the water to our invocations. Once that was settled, we needed to develop a one-way teleportation circle that then would allow its user to craft a second on the other side.

"But because I was too focused on the idea of saving the person on the other side, we never got a chance to do that. No one in the history of the Gray Forum had ever done anything except that until I found my way there. I was awarded several academic credits for my 'out of the box thinking.' In fact, it helped me make a new friend. Remember the fairy I 'saved?' His name was Puck. He was so impressed by what I'd done he had saved my life at no cost to himself—which, if you know the Fair Folk, goes against their very nature—and asked if he could teach me for a while."

Cinderella stared at me for a moment, equally impressed and

distressed at the decisions I had made in the past. I enjoyed watching her reaction. This was always one of my favorite stories to tell.

"So why tell me this?" Cinderella asked, having finally come to terms with it all.

"Because no matter how many times I have to jump into a lake filled with glass to save someone, I'll do it every single time," I said. "Zea is my friend. If the only way to save her life was to travel straight to Hell with only a water pistol as support, I'd make every shot count. Even if she weren't my friend; even if she hated my guts and wanted me dead, I'd jump straight into that lake to save her life. I know that even if I can only make it to one side, I have people backing me up who'll adjust their plans for my stupid nobility, and they'll help me get back to safety. Belief, kiddo. Belief is the strongest thing you have in your arsenal. Never let anyone tell you something is impossible, especially if you have us at your back."

"Are you saying you have the power to warp reality?"

"You're missing the point, Red. Yes, my belief was able to do that in Álfheim, but that's beside the point. My point is that your belief factors into how powerful you become. I should've died several times over by now, but here I am, still kicking, because in those times of need, I was willing to kick reason to the curb and go beyond the impossible. Did it always work? No, but I at least went out there attempting to do more than I was told was possible. Now am I saying to make stupid, reckless, kneejerk reactions? Absolutely not. And yes, I know, hypocritical humor at its finest, but I am saying that a part of this job is the ability to defy logic and do whatever it takes to protect people.

"Think of it this way. Do you know what our plan was to save you?"

"Nathan told me in the dream, but I'd like to hear what you have to say about it," she said.

"There we were, four of us with all these extraordinary powers, but no real clue as to how to use them to save you. But one of us had the ability to enter dreams. No one in the history of the world that I know of has ever done this before Nathan, yet our entire plan to go and save you hinged on the fact that we needed to enter your dreams to talk to you. If I had ever gone forward with such an idea

112

when the Forum was still active, they would've locked me up, because, to them, the idea was ludicrous. People just couldn't enter the dream of another. And yet, we did. Not only that, but I had to learn how to interact with the dream, while still dealing with the fact that all of this was uncharted territory to me. But I knew that you were hurting. I knew that you would kill all of those people at the Feast if we didn't try to save you. So I ignored my doubts. I wrung the neck of any dissenting opinion that entered my mind. It was simple, really. You needed help and I needed to go do the impossible to save you. That's all the motivation I required."

"You really are a simple man."

"What?"

"I'm sorry. It's something Zea says about you all the time. I think she means it as kind of an endearing insult. Like you're a really selfless man, but you also make a lot of stupid decisions because you want to help people."

"I'll take that as a compliment."

"Good, it was meant as such."

I laughed. "Tell you what, why don't I work one more time to make something with fire just to help prove my point?"

I held out my left hand and focused on my pinky finger.

"You don't have to, Blake," Cinderella said. "I know it's hard for you. It might be better to do after some rest."

"No, I just inspired myself, so I'm gonna do it," I said, smirking. "If I expect you to do the impossible, I might as well do the same. Here goes nothing, Cinderella. *Pinky Ignis.*"

A small blue flame ignited around my pinky finger. It stayed exactly where I'd placed it and made no attempts to move further. The two of us marveled at it. In truth, I had done this small invocation before, but had failed to maintain it for long periods of time. My mind was remarkably calm and easy to keep my focus on this singular flame without burning my finger.

"It worked!" Cinderella exclaimed, smiling.

"Baby steps," I said.

Holding out my right hand, I summoned the willpower to move the flame further out, removing it completely from my pinky and then into the air. The small, blue flame remained suspended inches away from its origin point and flickered softly as a slight breeze passed by in the air.

"Wow, I think this is the longest you've done it," Cinderella said, holding out her hand to place the flame on her hand.

The fire did so and she giggled as passed it between fingers on opposing hands, while I maintained concentration on it. She then handed it back to me, but when she did so the flame snuffed out and the smoke glided upwards into the night sky.

"Well, it was nice while it lasted," I noted.

"That's very good, though, Blake," Cinderella said, yawning once more. "I think that you've made some real progress tonight."

"It helps when you have someone cheering you on and when you really want to impress them while you're at it."

"Even still. It is far better than what you've done before. I can't wait to see how you progress." She paused. "Or wait—I just had an idea."

"Have at it."

"You've had a hard time maintaining control over the flame and it gets out of hand quickly. What if we embraced that idea?"

"I'm not following."

"Instead of trying to make a concentrated ball of fire, why don't you just invoke the small flame on something and then pour more energy inside of it to make the fire grow stronger? You have too much power to control flames larger than what you've made so far, but the reason you're learning fire invocation is to destroy the undead. You don't need to control the flames that well—you need to make it so that they grow out of control, so that they travel farther and to more targets rapidly."

My jaw fell agape. "Cinderella—you're a genius! There's something to say for learning how to control the flames in an environment like Corpus Christi, but out there in the Dead Lands? It all needs to burn anyways! My dumb, brute force is perfect for this! And I wouldn't have figured it out without you!"

Her head slumped a little and she shook it to try and stay awake. She smiled at me in a dopey, sleep-deprived manner.

"Thanks for the talk, Cinderella," I said, smiling, turning to the right to think. "I think I needed that a lot. You're a good friend."

I turned to look at her to say more, but found that she had fallen asleep in place, letting out almost silent moans of tiredness. I smiled again and said nothing else.

An hour later, when I was relieved of duty, I picked Cinderella

114

up and put her back in her bed, although this time I did so as a newly-invoked flame was sitting on top of my head, acting as a candle in the blackness of the courthouse.

CHAPTER 14

Several days later, Mara, Sedecla, Cinderella, and I departed from Phoenix, setting out on a route that both Sedecla and Aiden had worked on using their mutual knowledge of the area. The Phoenix Force—as I'd grown to calling our new friends—had agreed to accompany us to where the barrier to the Dead Lands had once been before its mysterious vanishing. However, they were staying hidden, fearing potential ambushes from prior patrolling of the area, so they had done their best to mix into the desert, while we marched onward with purposeful visibility.

The plan now was to get inside the Dead Lands and make our way to where the Fort Yuma Reservation was, wherein we would infiltrate the Quechan Casino Resort. I knew that there was a teleportation circle hidden on the reservation in the casino, having previously used it during my younger years as a student in the Forum. Most Native American reservations had one on them, given the Forum's secret ties to them, as they had helped the Forum many times in fighting against the supernatural beings that had ravaged the land. I knew that people like my father had been appalled with how the Forum had done nothing to help our allies once westward expansion had forced most of them onto reservations, but it had also been people like him who'd helped to salvage the Forum's relationship with the tribes. In exchange for their continued help in hunting down menaces like wendigos and newer threats like boo hags, the Forum would then clandestinely use invokers with plant-based invocations to help with crop growth on reservations allied with us, as well as offer healing when needed. It hadn't been perfect or ideal, but it was more than the Forum had been willing to offer before my parents had openly rebelled and taken likeminded Christeners to offer this deal to the reservations against the High Court's regulations.

But now most of those reservations would be empty, especially if they were within the Dead Lands. While that would make it easier to infiltrate, it didn't make their loss any less significant.

Our plan from then was to see if the teleportation circle there could contact another circle which was inside of Mission San Rafael Arcángel, an old Spanish mission that we'd converted into a teleportation hub. While it wouldn't land us in San Francisco proper, it would get us much closer than traveling by foot. We had no such circles in the city itself, as it had resisted our many attempts to establish a foothold there. Some places were just born bad, as my mother would say.

We had debated making one of our own in Phoenix, but I'd vetoed it, as such impromptu circles could get less accurate, especially since I was the only one accomplished in making and utilizing them. Plus, since that generated too much power, it would signal to anyone with the proper training that we were barging in through the front gates. Premade circles, however, were less likely to spark such interest as they relied not on the user's abilities and spiritual strength, but that of the original caster's, which couldn't be detected without specific invocations in place. If Morior Invictus were as powerful as people said they were then we had every right to be cautious. We were on an infiltration mission, so the less we drew attention the better, and even I could do that if properly motivated.

"Blake, I just got a headache," Cinderella said, breaking me from my thoughts.

"Are you okay?" I asked, stopping to look at her. "What happened?"

Cinderella shook her head, placing a hand on her forehead. "I just got a bad feeling, I guess, but it made my head hurt to experience it."

"Oh, it's just your danger sense. Kinda like Spider—you don't even know who that is." I sighed. "Basically, it's warning you that trouble's coming. We Christened have such heightened spiritual awareness because we—"

I stopped, feeling a tingle of danger myself. Instantly, I turned to face forward, barely dodging out of the way as a contingent of arrows fell down where I'd once been. Zooming in with my enhanced eyes, I saw that four hundred yards ahead of us was a group of skeletal warriors armed with bows similar to the ones we'd fought in Corpus Christi.

"Seek cover!" I ordered, demonstrating by diving behind a sandstone formation on my left. "Weapons out and ready to fire once you can line up a shot! Cinderella, wait until they get closer to hit them with fire! I'll draw their attention and you finish them off!"

"Got it!" Cinderella replied, invoking flames in her hands as she hid behind a large silver sage plant.

Mara covered Sedecla as the latter went to another sandstone formation to avoid the newest set of arrows sent our way. I poked my head out of my hiding spot and gauged their strength. There were at least a hundred of them, all in tight formation resembling a phalanx without the necessary shields, though, given that they didn't have a body to protect anymore I gave them a pass this time. These skeletons, however, were different from the ones I'd seen before, as they were garbed in what appeared to be centurion armor, which confused me all the more, since the Romans were notorious for destroying Greek phalanx divisions, not using those formations themselves. Obviously, whoever I was fighting wasn't a great student of history.

But before I could think any further on them, the skeletons moved forward, walking in unison to about a hundred yards ahead of us when they suddenly stopped, apparently waiting for orders of some kind. The skeletons seemed to have no individual thoughts of their own, at least while in this state, and were all looking with their empty eye sockets ahead at our location. I almost walked out to draw their fire, but a sudden rupturing in the earth about fifty feet ahead of me stopped me. The cracking moved rapidly, creating a hole about ten feet wide and twenty feet long. From the hole came a display so ridiculous I almost fell backward in incredulousness.

A lone man garbed in different bones from various humans and animals was hoisted in the air on top of a palanquin with no ceiling by four skeletons that were larger than their bony brethren. The bones on the man's legs and hands were all sharpened like spears, jutting out at least six inches from where his skin and were colored in garish versions of pink and blue. On his chest were two large elephant tusks and a rhino's horn in the middle of them that were also jutting out, albeit forward instead of towards the sky. The man seemed to be in his late fifties and had salt and pepper hair that edged more toward the salt. He stood about six foot two, but was dwarfed by the four skeletons holding him up in the air, which seemed to have been made by some sort of chimeric assortment of human and animal bones to make them taller.

"Ah, what a fine day for battle!" he proclaimed. "I know not how you avoided the first volley, but you have proven yourselves a great foe to fight! You must be the ones who escaped from our clutches and now cloister yourselves futilely in Phoenix! Face me on these open fields and prove your might against mine! Prove yourself against the mighty Exosso!"

"Exosso?" I repeated, stepping out to get a better look at our foe. "More like a *flaccidos mentula*."

To my utter surprise, I heard Mara suddenly bark out in laughter, only to quickly hold a hand over her mouth, suppressing further laughter from erupting out of her mouth. I smirked, tallying that one as a victory to taunt her about when we got out of this mess.

"What did he call me?" Exosso asked, his face racked with confusion. "Are you making fun of me?"

We stared at him confusedly.

I spoke first, asking, "You do understand Latin, right? I mean, that's where your name comes from, after all."

He shook his head to remove the confusion he felt. "Of course, I do," Exosso said, defiantly. "I hail from Rome."

"A necromancer from Rome? How the hell have you lived this long?"

He threw back his head in laughter, recovering from his earlier confusion to grandstand. "Once you understand magic as I do, time is merely for those who don't understand it!"

I shook my head, it now being my turn to be confused. This was what we were now up against? I hadn't exactly been expecting the showboating. Most necromancers I'd known had been the hammy sort, but more Emperor Palpatine than Mashmyre Cello.

"Ah, screw it," I said, tried of not understanding anything anymore as I raised my hands. *"Fiat lux*!"

Twin beams of light left my hands and formed a singular beam several feet in front of me as it raced towards my foe. Surprise filled my opponent's face, but it was swiftly replaced with anger when the light beam made contact with his left elephant tusk. The radiant display then ricocheted into his face, knocking him backward on the end of the palanquin.

"Fire!" I ordered.

Cinderella pointed out to the nearest contingent of skeletons and shouted out, "Rain of Fire!"

A cloud of flames appeared from above twenty of the skeleton archers and fire rushed out from it, incinerating all in its path. Some of the archers managed to get a shot off at the cloud before they were destroyed, but it did nothing to stop the flame's assault.

Mara, meanwhile, laid down suppressing fire with her rifle, hitting the skeletons on the left side of the phalanx.

Hastily getting back up from my attack, Exosso snarled and glared at me, as a small wisp of smoke left from the wound he'd received from my attack. His skin had been charred, but he was still more than ready to fight, surprising me, as I'd poured a lot of energy into that attack.

"He's strong," I said, thinking out loud.

"You ruined my elephant tusk!" Exosso cried out in a rage. "Do you have any idea how many elephants I had to kill and raise back up to perfect this look? You'll pay for this!"

I ran to my left, drawing his attention away from the others, as a rain of arrows fell behind me, too slow to catch up to my enhanced speed. I frowned, noting his distinct lack of surprise at my also being an invoker. I wondered why this was, but the looks he gave me as I ran told me everything I needed to know.

As if in answer to these thoughts, Exosso pointed at me and grinned, saying, "Ah, you must be him. The leader of Excelsior. The light user. Blake Azarel." He cackled madly. "Well this will certainly save me the trouble of finding you and better yet I don't have to pay that fool demon."

I grunted, trying to ignore the reminder of Zea's capture and that they'd originally been after me for the ring I possessed. Exosso was staring at the ring with avarice.

Exosso opened his mouth to continue speaking, but barely avoided a bullet Mara had sent his way, obviously hoping to kill him before he could fight me or use his final release, the last resort of every Christener. However, all it had really done was draw his attention to her.

Rushing ahead before he could do anything, I focused on the idea of crafting a small flame above him, like a lesser version of what Cinderella had done. I would then pour as much power as possible into this flame and make it light him and his entourage up.

"*Ignis ultionis!*" I cried out.

True to form, a small flame appeared right above Exosso's head, causing him to cry out in surprise. It then descended towards his face and grew in size as I added more of my spiritual power into it. He groaned in pain and smacked his face to smother the flames, which he needn't have bothered doing, as my control over the invocation had failed when I felt a sharp pain in my abdomen. Looking down, I saw an arrow protruding from my body. I'd been too focused on him; I'd forgotten all about his backup.

I looked over at the skeleton archers aiming at me and knew I'd screwed myself over by standing too long in one spot. Acting swiftly, I kept the arrow in place and ran in a zig-zag pattern away from them, preventing myself from getting hit again. I couldn't dislodge the arrow without opening the wound further, which was always a terrible idea, despite every action movie I'd ever watched encouraging its use. It may look cool, but only a fool takes the very thing that's stopping the blood from gushing out of their body out of them. I vaguely heard Cinderella's voice invoke more flames as those same archers fell victim to her newest attack, but I knew that even with them gone I wasn't out of the clear yet.

Exosso had recovered once more, his face singed, but not heavily damaged since the fire had disappeared once my concentration had been diverted elsewhere. "Scion of Death!" he roared out, pointing at me.

I felt a rumbling in the ground and barely jumped out of the way when a new fissure appeared, this one heralding the arrival of several skeletons of immense size, similar to the ones carrying around Exosso's palanquin. Despite my pain, I continued dodging them, as they used their lengthy arms to try and swat me to the ground. There were six in total and it occurred to me that they weren't the only ones burrowing through the dirt. Even though Exosso hadn't chosen this battlefield he was still the one with the most to win from its use, given that his undead army was perfect at using our surroundings against ourselves. Our danger sense could warn us about potential threats, but if every step we took was dangerous because of what was underneath, then we were never going to take the initiative back in this fight, especially with such low numbers. Clearly, I'd misjudged his intelligence.

"Fall back!" I ordered, running away from my assailants. "We've got no advantages in this fight! He's got more of his skeletons underneath us!"

Behind me, one of the giant skeletons detached his arm and sent it flying at me. I ducked to avoid it, unintentionally driving the arrow deeper into my abdomen. I gritted my teeth and forced myself to roll to the right, avoiding the giant's second arm as it planted itself in the dirt next to me. As I stood up, I watched as a storm of fire surrounded my assailants, incinerating them as I offered a weak thumbs up to Cinderella, who was now covering my escape. Behind her I saw movement as several people appeared over a nearby dune.

Feeling a wave of relief, I smiled, realizing what was about to happen next. Several shots rang out as the Phoenix Force had finally managed to reach an advantageous firing position and were wiping out anything in their path. Exosso roared with anger as his creations were mowed down by guns that had more range than their weapons. I wondered why he hadn't supplied these with firearms like he had in the assault on Corpus Christi, but something told me that this had been Valefar's idea and perhaps this necromancer was too archaic for his own good. Either way I was grateful that we finally had an advantage here.

Reaching Cinderella, I took her outstretched hand and we ran in unison away from Exosso, as she slowed her gait to match mine.

"Are you okay?" she asked.

"No," I said, "but I will be as soon as we get somewhere safe. I can heal this wound, but we need to get to it quickly. Even for us an injury like this could kill us if we're not careful."

"Come back and face me!" Exosso demanded. "Are you cowards? I'll—"

I looked back to see what had made him stop mid-rant when I was then blessed with the wondrous sight of a giant emerald that had appeared from nowhere and flung itself forward by rolling on the sand. The emerald increased in size as it sped forward, trampling over anything in its path. Seeing that he was losing more soldiers, Exosso snarled and ordered his giant skeletons to fall back, taking the time with me to look at a confidant Tamayo, who was standing beside an armed and shooting Aiden far away from us, and was now busy sending her summoned emerald into more skeletons.

"You win this round, Blake Azarel!" Exosso declared. "But the next shall go to me and Morior Invictus! Come into the Dead Lands if you will, but death is all you shall find!"

I shook my head, too tired to offer a half-hearted retort as Cinderella and I reached the others. Mara and Sedecla had made it there first, with the latter now wheezing and hunched over. I groaned in pain and looked down at my wound. Because of my constant movement, blood was rapidly seeping from it, even with the arrowhead blocking most of it.

"Master Azarel!" Tamayo cried out, running to my side. "Don't worry—I'll take care of it! Just like you taught me!"

Tamayo placed her hands over my wound and touched right above it with both hands pressed down, causing me to wince in pain.

"Jade Invigoration," Tamayo invoked.

A lump of uncut jade appeared in the air and six beams of green light surrounded my wound. I felt a force pushing the arrow out of me and I grunted in pain, but felt that as soon as the arrow was being taken away that my wound was sealing up behind it and that I felt a sort of new freshness akin to spending time in a hot spring. I patted the area down where the arrow had been and then smiled at Tamayo.

"That was amazing!" I declared. "Using gem invocation to heal? Who'd have thought of that?"

Tamayo giggled. "Well, you did, of course, Master Azarel," she said. "You said it was simple for people like me and you were absolutely right."

"But on to more important matters," Mara said. "Our expedition has been repulsed, but Exosso's has also been. I doubt for long. We cannot hope to reach the casino in this state."

I sighed. "You're right," I said.

"However, we do have a certain advantage now. Exosso will

likely retreat to gather his strength, perhaps even to Alcatraz itself. While he is en route there, we create a teleportation circle here and risk being discovered so that we reach it before him. I would also suggest that our friends here leave Phoenix behind and go to Corpus Christi."

"Just in case Exosso doesn't go to Alcatraz and instead comes back for us," Aiden said.

"Correct. You have proven yourselves invaluable in backing us up, but the fewer people we take the better, especially for a reconnaissance mission. There should be several wards in place in the mission that will prevent undead or evokers from entering it. We will have time to organize there even if they discover our arrival."

I nodded. "All right," I said. "Guess we'll just have to risk it then."

CHAPTER 15

1

Once we had returned to Phoenix and sent the Force off to Corpus Christi, Cinderella and I spent the next few hours prepping the teleportation circle there. Normally, we wouldn't need to take so long to make it, but with Morior Invictus out there we had to take as many precautions as possible, especially if they were waiting for us to forcibly invade their realm. Besides, we didn't know if the circle inside the mission was active either. Circles could permanently be placed at a single location, but if the buildings they were housed in were destroyed or damaged the circles wouldn't be too far behind. Since we also needed to avoid detection, I was instructing Cinderella on how to properly ward the circle with extra engravings that would disrupt any early warning systems the necromancers had in place.

Finally, after our preparations were done, Cinderella and I kneeled on opposite sides of the circle, while Mara and Sedecla stood in the middle of it. The older woman seemed uneasy, which was only natural given this would be her first time teleporting.

"This is safe, is it not?" Sedecla asked, staring down at the circle we drew.

"This circle shall be more than satisfactory for our needs," Mara stated simply. "Guardian Azarel has instructed Initiate Young well in how to properly craft this. Fear not."

Sedecla nodded wearily and avoided our eyes, looking instead to the ground.

I looked over at Cinderella and nodded. "Ready, Red?" I asked.

"Ready!" she replied, pumping her fist.

"Then let's do this!"

Placing our hands on the circle, Cinderella and I channeled our power into the circle as it started glowing with a bright, white light. Energy invoked from our inner supplies flashed around us like lightning as we continued concentrating on our destination. Feeling a connection to our intended target, I smirked, knowing that at the very least we would reach it without issues.

Finally, the white light enveloped the four of us, transporting us to the insides of what was left of the Mission San Rafael Arcángel. We stood up together and checked the surroundings to see if we were safe.

The building we were in was serviceable for now, having stood up well with no one living around it for a hundred years. The mission itself hadn't been in use for many years and, in fact, the one we were standing in now was merely a replica of the original, which had been created after the first one had stopped being used thanks to the church built next to it. At least, that was the official story. In truth, the Forum had made a deal with the Archbishop of the Archdiocese of San Francisco to use the replica as a base of operations that had been used to try and stop the human trafficking propagated by The Horde within the region, from which they would take their victims across the Pacific to their strongholds in Asia and Africa.

I sniffed the air, sensing the presence of mold and mildew and then a musty smell similar to the mildew, which meant we had termites to worry about, but it wasn't like we were planning on renovating this place and selling it for a profit anyways. I shrugged and looked over to see Cinderella, offering her a thumbs up for a job well done. She smiled sweetly in response.

"What is our next course of action?" Sedecla asked.

"We recon the island with our telescopic vision as best we can in the dark," I said, "and figure it out from there. The prison's not terribly far from where we are, even on foot. Of course, we'll also need to locate a serviceable boat that'll be silent enough to get us to the jail and back."

2

Over the next few hours, we snuck out of the mission and onto the streets of San Rafael, careful to stick together and not make a sound, for fear of alerting whatever undead guardians were posted

126

around the city. It had been near eight once we'd teleported to the city, but now it was closer to midnight. It was difficult to see in darkness, because, unlike Zea, none of us had night vision, although our sight was better than a mundane's. Sedecla acted as our guide, showing us which streets to take and which to avoid, so I was glad we'd dragged her along.

About two hours in, Sedecla had stopped us, having discovered a group of zombies chaotically moving as a group without direction, merely waiting for the next sound they heard until they would go investigate it. I sent a darkness blast into a building far away from us. They immediately skulked in the direction of the noise, making them easy to sneak past.

Then, right before midnight, we had managed to locate a dock to see if there were any salvageable ships to use to bring us to Alcatraz. However, most of them had taken too much damage from the elements without anyone to look after them, leaving us to break into a locker near the dock's office, wherein we found one paddleboat that would at the very least ferry two people in without making too much noise to attract attention. Just in case, I also took two of the sturdier remaining oars around to use to help propel us in the water if need be.

I needed to be as careful as possible to get us there. Alcatraz hadn't just been chosen as a prison on a whim—the island was a fortress, one designed to keep its occupants there without a means of escape. The Spanish hadn't used Alcatraz much outside of setting a few buildings there for various needs. Once California had gained its independence and later statehood, the island had been converted into a military fort that would eventually be used to house Confederate prisoners. It was only in 1933, when the Department of Justice had acquired the island, that it would become the Alcatraz people only spoke of in hushed whispers.

Alcatraz was intended to be used as the prison to kill the wills of the hardest prisoners, who wouldn't let their sentences stifle their true natures. Robert Stroud, "Machine Gun" Kelly, and Al Capone were only a sampling of the men who would spend their time on the island, and every single one of them had been broken by its unforgiving shores. In its history, not a single prisoner who had attempted an escape had done so successfully. It was entirely possible for an adult human male to jump into the freezing waters of the San Francisco Bay and make his way to shore, but the effort alone had killed or fatigued anyone dumb enough to try it, outside of the chosen few who would later participate in better conditions for the Escape From Alcatraz Triathlon. But the cold wasn't the only obstacle: the fast currents could pull a man under so quickly that he could drown within moments without knowing which way was up anymore. Simply put, we wouldn't be getting there without immense effort.

All that was left was to scope out the island proper. Cinderella and I took turns, using what enhanced vision we could utilize in order to see despite the darkness. It was incredibly taxing, both because of the darkness and because the human eye isn't meant to be used as a telescope for long periods of time, invocation-powered or not.

"I see two of those larger skeletons Exosso used against us in the desert," Cinderella said. "They're patrolling the west section of the island. At least the parts I see."

"I also see two zombie-like beasts with what look like broken-down cement walls in their hands on the east side," I noted.

"Our options grow shorter by the minute," Mara stated. "We need to get on the island while its evoker occupants are sleeping. We have six to seven hours before the sun rises."

"I'm aware. The problem is we only have the one paddleboat and it's not meant for speed or stealth or more than two occupants."

I waited for Mara to offer something else, but she was too lost in thought to say anything. I turned to Cinderella, but she had no more answers than I did. I groaned. This was possible; we just had to figure out how.

Sedecla sighed and looked right at me. "I have a confession to make," she said. "I have not been entirely truthful with you about my origins."

I furrowed an eyebrow and instinctively went into a defensive stance, placing my body in front of Mara and Cinderella. Now that she had admitted it, I suddenly felt a stirring of the purest Christening in her, but it was akin to Mara's, weak and subdued. I marveled at how well she had hidden her true self from all of us. Most people had never received the training to do so and then there were people like me who were especially terrible at it with how

128

much power we leaked simply for existing.

"I am from the Dead Lands, but I lied about how I escaped them," Sedecla said. "I didn't escape while traveling with others, only to be left for dead. I was once a prisoner—one who was imprisoned here by Morior Invictus. They found me living in the Dead Lands in a community hidden underground. My village was slaughtered and I was one of the few they let live. They brought those of us they were interested in here and experimented on us. Their reason for doing so was because we had the Christening within us. Most of us were too weak to be called proper Christeners, but we were in tune with it enough for their purposes."

I eased up a bit, but kept my hand out, ready to invoke if needed. "Why did you lie about this?" I asked.

"Fear. When I learned about your powers, I thought you might do the same to me. You don't understand what it was like in there. I can still hear the screams." She paused. "It is my understanding that when Christeners mean to tell the truth, they look into another's eyes. Would it please you to do this with me?"

I paused. I had deliberately avoided doing that just in case I saw more than what I was meant to. I could look into someone's eyes and not instantly start a spiritual connection with them, but it was harder to do the more you gazed at them. Christeners were able to see past events and the truth of recent statements made by those who they locked eyes with. But there were ways around it. Illusion invocations that projected the image of the caster's eyes would look just like the real thing and fool the other person's eyes to think they were real and were even capable of producing a link that provided false information.

But was she capable of this? She was certainly able to fool us into not believing she possessed the Christening, but was this merely for survival's sake? It made sense. If I had spent all that time used for that very thing, I would want no one else to know I was capable of even the simplest invocation. I looked at Mara, who was most certainly thinking the very same things I was. She simply nodded and awaited my decision.

"I'll look," I said.

Sedecla and I shared a brief exchange and the moment our eyes locked I was instantly swept into her past. I saw a young woman in her early twenties passing a potato to her husband as they held a feast in the center of their underground town. I then viewed a contingent of spirits flood the caverns the woman lived in, as the ghosts somehow became solid enough to kill all in their path, save for the woman, who was spared once her Christening was felt by another. I was then shown a dark, destitute cell where the woman was forced into and only taken out whenever it was her turn for experimentation.

Breaking away to reality, I shook my head. There had been more that I saw, but it was more of the same. It was horrible. I didn't want to think about them anymore. I thanked God more than ever that I didn't have an eidetic memory.

"Okay, but I don't see how that helps us get there," I said, trying to recover.

Sedecla nodded nervously. "Well, I think I can get us there if you and I were to take the boat," she said. "There is a secret way into the jail." She pointed to the west side of the island. "After the Dead Lands were made, one of Morior Invictus' number experimented with a spell that had never been used before. The resulting explosion opened a hole on the island, but had serendipitously crafted a cave and harbor that they then used to travel to shore. It is invisible to sight unless you are near it. That is what I used to escape the prison proper."

"But how?" Mara asked. "Especially alone."

"I don't understand the specifics, but to help themselves not be bothered by the currents, the three necromancers would use a specific path that they had made that was not bound to the normal rules of the ocean that would allow them to travel unhindered. I simply stole their boat, which automatically followed that very same path and ended up in the city, wherein I hid until I was able to escape my undead pursuers."

I looked out into the waters. "So you can lead us to this path?" I asked.

"Yes, but there are some limits. It only allows two living people at a time to enter the harbor once we reach it. So you and I would need to go alone before someone came back for the others. There were no guards posted there, because no one had even been foolish enough to escape or try to infiltrate the island."

I nodded and walked over to Mara. "Okay," I said. "Mara, you and Cinderella wait here while Sedecla and I get to the island on

130

the boat. While we're there, we'll scout it out and plant a circle for you to use to reach us. Make a circle here and go back to the mission. That way you can make one that's more stable than a hastily made one here, especially with all that water out there in the bay messing with our invocations." I leaned in and whispered in her ear, while pretending to crack my neck. "Stay here and make a circle anyways, just in case she's lying. You don't hear from us for fifteen minutes after you can't see us in the boat anymore and you make a circle to get there and back me up."

"Understood, Blake," Mara whispered back.

"Good!" I shouted, turning back to smile at the others. "Let's go, Sedecla! We have a jail to break into!"

CHAPTER 16

I held up a hand to command Sedecla to stop paddling with me. We waited in silence for two full minutes before we watched as a hulking, decaying undead corpse of a great white shark leapt up out of the water and swallowed a pelican that had flown above the water at the wrong time. I waited another minute before I allowed us to push forward again. I wished Clooney was with us, as he'd be more than able to offer us a favorable wind that wouldn't blow our cover, but this was the best we had.

We paddled in unison, fighting the tough current to make our way to the west side of Alcatraz Island. I kept a constant spiritual surveillance of our surroundings up with my mind, which had providentially stopped us from being detected by the zombie shark. I hadn't sensed the beast itself, but had merely felt a foreign threat, which had caused me to listen to my instincts and stop in place.

I looked up, feeling uneasy. The night sky was filled with cloud cover, with the moon barely managing to pass through it to light what little we could see. We weren't completely blind. My enhanced sight could see passably in the night, but I didn't want to judge our future safety solely on that. Despite the current, the waters made little noise and even our fervent paddling wasn't making any loud sounds. I didn't know how long it was taking us, but we were almost to the location Sedecla had specified on the western side of the island that would allow us to simply let the "path" as she had called it bring us to the harbor.

Sensing danger again, I held up a hand again. I looked around the water, but felt a stirring ahead of us and looked to see a lone, tall figure staring in our direction from the island. This was one of the beasts I'd seen earlier during my scan of the island. It hadn't noticed us, but it had seemed to sense something out of the ordinary where we were. But its curiosity didn't last long, and it simply turned to its right and returned to its single-minded pursuit of protecting the jail, as the cement block that had once belonged to the prison's walls dragged behind it.

"Oh, thank God," I said, shaking my head. "The last thing we need is to have that ersatz Laestrygonian sink us."

My companion was silent, instead waiting for us to paddle again, which I did moments later. We continued on the path until Sedecla pointed to a section of water ahead of us. I stared at it, seeing seafoam around the borders of a line of water formed in a rectangular pattern that was unaffected by the tides of the bay. Not understanding how this particular brand of evocation worked, I decided to just be grateful for its presence and we paddled into it, our boat somehow able to break whatever barriers it had. The moment the whole boat was inside this section of water, the boat suddenly turned towards the island and moved forward without our doing anything. The boat continued forward slowly and we rested our feet.

"This is what it was like when I escaped," Sedecla said. "Only in the opposite direction."

"Funky evocation," I noted. "Doesn't really fit their M.O."

"Their what?"

"Modus operandi. Their usual habits or way of doing things."

"I see. As I said, I do not understand how it works, only that it does. I suspect Morior Invictus is merely incredibly-skilled in many unnatural things."

"So they're all skilled in some form of entropic evocation," I noted, nodding my head. "That must be what this is—it perverts the natural order of the physics of motions to cause a different effect. That's not good for the environment. It could permanently warp this entire area if left alone."

"You know much of the necromantic arts," Sedecla said. "You surprise me."

"I only know so much because my best friend was a natural when it came to entropy, although he used invocation."

"A member of the Gray Forum used necromancy?"

I shook my head. "You misunderstand. Entropic invocation is a blanket term we used for anything that revolved around degrading life or violating natural laws of science. Necromancy, spirit summoning, forcing an object to erode quickly, or control over the human body are all subsets of this. Atanasio would've been stellar at doing any of them. He, however, focused solely on eroding objects and, when the need arose, on people. Many people in the Forum thought that he was a danger to us, because of what they saw as entropic invocation's inherent evil. But wiser and cooler minds managed to convince them that it was not our job to condemn the natural gifts that God had offered one of our own, so long as they used them to further His glory. Atanasio was one of the most gifted people I've ever fought beside. I wish he were here right now to help us out."

A dark shadow covered the faint moonlight, forcing me to look upwards out of fear of attack. What I saw defied my expectations, as the moonlight slowly returned to view, just as a large tail of some sort faded into the higher clouds. I didn't get a good look at the creature I assumed it belonged to, but I knew based solely on its ability to blot out the moon from sight and the swiftness of its movements that I wanted nothing to do with it.

"You wouldn't happen to know anything about that now, would you?" I asked without looking back to her.

"Only rumors," Sedecla said, her voice barely above a whisper. "It would not surprise me if someone like Exosso crafted such a beast or if Abraxas or En-dor managed to summon it from an ethereal plane. I would suggest staying out of its sight whatever it is."

"Duly noted."

I grunted. I didn't understand most of what was going on here or exactly what my plan was once I got the others here, but there was no turning back now. We either retrieved Zea or died fighting. I felt a twinge of familiarity at the thought of her name and I briefly brushed her thoughts, feeling a sudden darkness envelop my mind as I felt her pain, obviously from some sort of torture inflicted on her by the inhabitants of the island.

I shivered, sending out as many positive encouragements as I could to her, not knowing if they would reach her.

"You are afraid," Sedecla said. "This is wise. Morior Invictus are powerful beyond our imaginations.

I turned to look at her. "I'm not afraid of them," I said, smiling

134

to reassure her. "I've got God on my side. It's in the name."

"I don't understand."

"Azarel. It means 'aided by God'."

"In this cruel world you dare believe in God?"

I chuckled. "Hard not to when He's the one supplying your power. You're not as trained as I am, so you don't really know the differences between invoking something and evoking it. Evoking requires you to pour all of yourself into your attacks and takes a little of you with it every time. But invoking an ability into being? That's where it's at. You're asking for help. Your body's supplying the energy necessary for it to be made, but there's something else to it—you feel that you're not alone in making it reality. Another force is guiding what you create, helping you not strain yourself by offering apart of what they have at their disposal to aid you."

Sedecla scoffed. "And this makes you believe in God?"

"Hardly; it just helps. Look, I wasn't exactly planning on starting an apologetics course on our way to Alcatraz, so you've caught me a little off guard, but I do believe in Him. Sure, the world sucks as it is now, but the world before this all happened wasn't much better. Things like this were just hidden in a convenient manner."

"What a ridiculous thing to say. Surely this is better than what was before. People know the truth of reality now—that they are nothing before the chaos of the world. Before this all happened, people were fools—dragged around by their folly to say that they cared about others, but this new world has brought their true natures to life. The strong control the weak who were never meant for greatness. This is why people like Morior Invictus thrive while others died like dogs. Exosso deals in evil spells that can control the bones of the living and the dead, Abraxas studies the anatomy of living beings and tortures them to death only to raise them as undead thralls, and En-dor summons the shades of the dead to infect the living. They are stronger than us, so they are right."

"*Argumentum ab auctoritate.*"

"What?" Sedecla asked, turning to look at me.

"'Appeal to authority' or an 'argument from authority,'" I said, smiling. "Just because they're in charge here doesn't make them right, no matter how talented they are with whatever necromantic arts they use. That's a fallacious argument to make. Truth is truth. It doesn't care who's the strongest person in mind, voice, or deed. It will simply speak for itself. We're also way off target on what started this conversation."

"You talk much of things I don't understand."

I chuckled. "I like learning. Part of that's figuring out whether or not you can trust the information being offered to you. You should always question what you're told, but also be willing to realize you won't understand everything. But just because you question things doesn't make you smarter than other people." I paused. "Look, I know what this is really about. You don't know if we can pull this off. Let me let you in on a little secret: neither do I."

Sedecla flinched as if I'd slapped her in the face. "Then why embark on this trip?"

"Because Zea is my friend and I want her to be safe."

"That is all?"

"Do I really need more of a reason than that?" I chuckled when she flinched again. "It's my job to do the impossible. Why else was I given these powers? To use them for myself? What a waste! No, I have them because they're meant for others—to give them what they can't have for themselves. Maybe one day you'll understand that, Sedecla. For now, we're about to enter that harbor up there, so let's be quiet."

Looking ahead, we watched as our boat was pushed by unseen forces into the harbor and into the right side of the docks crafted some time after this cave had been created by the spell Morior Invictus had abused years ago. I grabbed some rope on the dock and tied the paddleboat on one of the wooden supports. Helping Sedecla out, I scanned our surroundings, knowing that we were one step closer to finding Zea.

CHAPTER 17

Sedecla and I were alone. I sensed nothing out of the ordinary around us, but I wasn't wholly convinced of that, feeling a tugging in my mind to be on constant alert.

I found myself shivering and the fingers on my right hand started trembling. Grabbing them with my left hand, I managed to stop them from shaking, only to feel a new sensation, as I felt blood trickle down from my right eye. I hurriedly wiped the blood away and frowned. I then grabbed a mirror from a pouch on my belt and studied the area in order to see the damage and be able to properly seal the wound with a healing invocation. I gazed at the affected area, finding that my right eye was oozing out blood from the lacrimal caruncle. I fixed it with a healing invocation, stopping the blood flow. I then gazed at the eye, seeing that everything worked perfectly normal, aside from the fact that it my iris was a darker shade of red than it had been before. From birth I'd had two hazel-colored eyes, but sometime in-between the beginning of my amnesia and my jump to the future the color of my right eye had turned red. But not this red. Only the iris had been affected, while the sclera was pristine.

Grunting, I shook my head and put the mirror back in the pouch.

I knew exactly why my eye was acting up. It had happened before when I had used the ring on my left hand in Vice City, only not nearly as pronounced as now, but I suspected I knew why it was doing so now too.

It was the island. Alcatraz was bad. In every possible way. I felt the lingering deaths of its former residents as if I were going through the same process repeatedly with them. I felt a prayer of thanks leave my thoughts due to realizing how glad I was that none of them seemed to have been Christeners, at least on this part of

137

the island. When mundanes died, they left something akin to the death mark of a Christener, but nowhere near as powerful. But those, I knew, would be closer to the center of the island in the prison, based on Sedecla's tales of the experiments done on Christeners.

But even if nothing had been done by Morior Invictus, I knew that I would feel the same way I felt now. Many terrible things had been done here in the name of safety and order. All Morior Invictus had done was exacerbate an already terrible place to become a bastion of dread and lifelessness.

I shook my head. I couldn't focus on this. I needed to charge myself up and prepare for a reconnaissance mission. My usual antics would do me no good in this scenario. I needed capable backup to assist me once the actual fighting broke out.

Turning to Sedecla, I saw that she was mindlessly staring at the doors that would lead into the lower sections of the prison.

"Sedecla," I said, snapping my fingers in front of her face.

She shook her head and looked at me. "I am sorry," she said. "I was distracted."

I nodded. "I'm sorry too. Coming back here can't be easy for you, given what happened here. I appreciate everything you've done for us, but I need to know you can do this well. A lot is riding on this excursion."

"Of course. I will do as requested."

"Will you be able to break out of that weird current thing and head their way?"

"I haven't tried before, but I think I will be able to."

I nodded. "Stay safe and aware of your surroundings. If you sense anything out of the ordinary, then you stay still and avoid getting caught. Don't move to get the others unless you feel safe. Understood?"

She flinched, not expecting my protective warnings. "I—yes, of course I will."

"Good. Now go get them now before anything finds us here. I'll establish this as our beachhead for the invasion in the interim."

Sedecla turned around to do as told, only to stop in place and point to an area above us. Looking up, I saw on the leftmost wall of the cave was a small opening that led to the surface. Several dark silhouettes appeared from the surface and then jumped down

138

to a metal platform. I watched as several more followed suit. I recognized them as zombies once they got closer to what was left of the moonlight and that they were descending the platform to head straight to us.

"How?" I asked. "How did they know we were here?"

Grumbling, I held out my hands and brought to my mind the image of a blazing inferno, but this one sized like a basketball. Then I imagined that basketball exploding outwards, creating a formidable firebomb.

"*Sphaera ignis!*" I invoked.

The small orb appeared right above the nearest cluster of zombies and then swiftly grew in size thanks to the spiritual energy I poured into it, completely incinerating them all and then momentarily stopping the group behind them. I pumped my fist, glad that my brute force was working in my favor for once. But when I heard Sedecla cry out in horror, I knew things were going to get worse. Looking for her, I found her running away from the paddleboat, as a group of previously submerged zombies were rising from the water and heading our way. I stepped in front of Sedecla to act as a shield.

I held out my left hand shouted out, "*Fiat lux!*" and then ushered my right hand forward, yelling, "*Tenebris regni!*"

Two beams of light and darkness emanated from my invocations, rushing onward into the newest horde. The beams impacted the closest zombies, but were too small to envelop the others.

I shivered again, feeling pulsations of fear enter my mind from an unknown source. Something was trying to mess with my mind and put me off balance. I hurriedly looked around for the source, but could see nothing, only noting that more zombies were piling in from the sea and from above the cave.

My hands trembled, as that foreign fear broke down any mental walls I made to shut it out. I was panicking. I'd been backed into a corner too soon and wasn't ready to fight properly. No wonder my invocations were so weak.

A brief red flash alerted me to light on my left hand. Looking down, I saw the eyes of the dragon on the ring turn red again. I grunted and returned my gaze to the advancing zombies. They would be right on me within moments. I looked back down at the ring. I had no choice. I needed to use it again. I gritted my teeth and cursed myself in my thoughts, but I knew I was right.

"Lend me your power," I said, almost in a whisper, my voice cracking from terror.

The ring pulsed with a purple-black light as a rush of energy swept out from it and then overwhelmed the closest zombie, rendering the creature's withering flesh as it blasted the undead being into chunks of decayed meat. A surge of frenzied madness swept aside the fear that had been implanted in my mind and I started laughing. I felt no resistance as the superior force of the madness overtook both myself and the fear at once. Pointing the ring at the zombies behind the others that had risen from the depths, I cackled and sent out a swirling vortex of energy from the ring and watched as it swallowed them up in a dark cloud of negative force. The cloud swept itself into a frenzy as it reduced everything inside of it to ashes.

Icy swelling filled my veins and I felt the muscles in my back contract as the energy from the ring also entered my body. I had a brief moment of clarity and tried to look back at Sedecla and warn her to run, but before I could see her, my eyes saw the zombies falling from above the cave and all rationality was lost to the ring again.

I pointed the ring at them and the dragon's eyes grew even redder and almost seemed to be bleeding as it summoned more chaotic energy to strike with. I sent another chaotic strike at them, but this one was slower and unwieldy, causing a kickback that almost knocked me off my feet.

Please control yourself, the voice emanating from within the ring begged. *You are getting overwhelmed. You need to return control to your mind swiftly.*

I had heard the voice before during my use of it when Zea and I escaped from the Slinden mansion in Vice City. It was male and definitely an older one, but other than this I had no clue of the voice's true identity. It was silent unless the ring was in use or when the original user had enough power to try to contact me it seemed. They had claimed that they were in penance for their past misdeeds and wanted to work with me, but had dodged any questions I had sent their way. The ring was clearly meant for evil, but I had used it successfully to protect others, so I had chosen to ignore its darker leanings in favor of limited use, just in case its powers were addictive.

I'm fighting, but I need help, I sent. *Help me.*

Suddenly, I felt a new force enter my mind, albeit momentarily. The force sent a strong pulsation akin to electricity through my nerves, causing my mind to snap back into control. Fearing this wouldn't last, I tried to wrench the ring from my fingers, but failed just as I always had before. Instead, I held my right hand into a fist, charging up an invocation to threaten it.

"*Fiat lux!*" I commanded, as light swelled around my fist and then rushed forward to hit the ring.

Instantaneously, I felt the darker presence forced out of my mind and back into the ring, as a small purple bubble appeared over the ring, protecting it from my light blast. The light was instead deflected to my right, hitting the last zombies remaining and removing them from the fight. Too consumed with turmoil to be impressed at the unlikelihood of that event, I charged up another attack, but I was hit in the back of the head with something dense and metal, which knocked me unconscious.

CHAPTER 18

I woke up later with an immense pain in the back of my head and I felt dried blood on what felt like stone from where my head was resting. Opening my eyes, I saw that I was in what appeared to have once been an operating room. Trying to stand up, I found that my hands and feet were bound by chains. Struggling against them, I felt further pain throughout my body and stopped fighting, afraid I'd open a wound I hadn't repaired with my innate healing abilities while I was out. I was strong enough to break them, but I needed to recharge and get my bearings. I was lying down on some sort of stone table that extended just beneath my feet.

"So, you finally awaken," a woman's voice said, mockingly. "Less than an hour at that. Quite impressive."

I knew that voice, which did nothing to make me feel any better. I turned over to face it, finding an older woman garbed now in black robes that covered her entire body and a hood that obscured the upper half of her face. Grinning at me with decrepit teeth, she removed her hood and I found that I shared my current prison with Sedecla. I would've smacked the back of my head on the stone table out of despair at my own stupidity, but the pain I felt there reminded me not to be even dumber than I already was.

"All right, listen," I said. "My head hurts. Just get it over with, Jadis."

"What?" Sedecla asked.

"The table. The stone table. You're killing me for something, so, just go ahead. After what I pulled today, I deserve it. I just warn you that if you strike me down, I shall become more powerful than you can possibly imagine."

Sedecla cackled. "I see that your resolve has returned at the very least. No, Blake Azarel, we don't intend to kill you yet. Or turn into you into a Force ghost. We have higher priorities this night."

"Is that supposed to make afraid? Good luck with that. I think I got over that earlier tonight."

"Well, I must admit it was hard getting you to feel the magic I placed on your mind. You resisted it well, at first."

"That fear in my mind—that was you?" I asked.

"Yes," Sedecla said, "I implanted the fear there—made you feel an unnatural sense of terror so that you wouldn't be fully in control of your mind. Although I must admit I had merely hoped that you would submit to the fear and cower, but you proved resilient enough to seek out help in the ring, which surprised me, so I had to improvise by hitting you in the back of a head with a crowbar I found in the harbor."

"You hit me with a crowbar? Are you insane? If I wasn't Christened that could've caused some serious brain damage! You think that you can just knock someone out and that they'll be perfectly fine when they wake up? If the least of my problems is a concussion that's still nothing to downplay!"

"Oh, please. Of course I knew you would awaken. I only hit you with a crowbar. Even a mundane would've sprung back up."

"No, they wouldn't! I thought you people understood human anatomy to do your little necromancy schtick! If I didn't have an enhanced healing factor, I could've been a vegetable!"

Sedecla seemed genuinely confused, making my anger rise. Where had she gotten her medical license from? The Acme Corporation?

"Whatever," I said, shaking my head despite the pain. "I don't care right now."

"Oh, but you will," Sedecla said. "You must have some questions remaining. We have time before Abraxas and Exosso arrive. Don't be shy. I will answer them."

I sighed. "What's your real name?" I asked, not expecting an answer, since Christeners knew better.

"Why it's En-dor, of course."

"En-dor? As in the forest moon or…the Canaanite city?"

"The latter, my dear. The city is named after me. How else do you believe I got this strong so as to fool you? I am quite ancient."

I turned to look at her, but she avoided my gaze. "You were the one Saul went to? You rose Samuel from the dead?"

"Why of course I was. It is my specialty—the raising of the shades of the deceased."

"Yeah, except you're full of crap. Only God would've been able to raise a righteous soul like Samuel's. You were surprised that it happened. My guess is you were planning on just scamming that fool of a king until you got put in your place by the Almighty."

"So narrow your viewpoints, young one. If I could not overcome the powers of God, then how was I able to fool you if you claim to have His power?"

I paused. It was a fair question. We weren't infallible, but our abilities were channeled through us from the divine.

"Okay, I'll bite—how were you able to lie to my sight?" I asked. "I looked right into your eyes and I felt no illusion invocations from you."

She sneered and smirked. "Why of course, because what I was saying was the truth, from a certain point of view. It's what the spirit inhabiting my eyes at the time believed at least."

As if in reply to my future round of questioning, En-dor's eyes grew white and I could only watch in horror as I saw an ethereal spirit cry out in agony as it was forcibly removed from her body and placed beside its past host. The ghost was a young woman who was screaming without making a sound, obviously reliving the last moments of her life repeatedly without pause.

"This is the ghost of a dear, young woman who we found possessed the Christening," En-dor stated, with faux sweetness. "We experimented on her for a time and then she was given to me. So before I left here to fool you into following me here, I placed her spirit in my body so that I could utilize her to fake out your inner sight." She gently stroked the ghost's hair, even though her hands should've passed right through the specter. "I see you're confused about this as well. I can touch the souls of those who've departed, because I've studied immensely on how to bind them here to the mortal coil, wherein they are controlled by me and forced to do my bidding here. Now depart from me, shade. I have no more use of you for now."

The spirit descended beneath the floor, leaving us alone.

144

I nodded, too stubborn to admit out loud just how clever her plan had been. I hadn't once considered the idea that I was looking into a ghost's eyes instead of Sedecla's when we'd shared our visions with one another. It was a ludicrous idea, but I of all people should've been more open-minded about the impossible being true.

"But why me specifically?" I asked. "What do I give three powerful necromancers that they don't already have?"

"Power in its truest form," En-dor stated. "It is true that we are strong and old, but even we can't hope to overcome the Collective by ourselves. That is why we have sought out many artifacts of great power, hoping to add them to our arsenal. Your ring, for instance."

"What's so important about my ring?" I asked, not bothering to look at it out of fear of what it would do next. "What do you know about it?"

"Only that Abraxas lusts for it more than anything on this earth," En-dor said. "Other than that powerful body of yours, of course."

I shivered. "I don't like where this is going."

En-dor cackled. "Of course, we won't need your consent to use it once we're done. You will be an undead thrall used on the frontlines of our coming war on the Collective. All the time we spent messing with Christeners of lesser power will be worthwhile once we control you to do our bidding. Pure power. Oh, it took everything within me to not cradle up to it the entire time we were together. I've never felt so alive."

"I need an adult," I whispered.

En-dor stepped up from her seat and approached me, placing a hand on my chest, making me cringe when her eyes rolled back from pleasure. Finally, she stopped and cackled some more.

"There is nothing that can be done to stop us," Sedecla said, mirthfully. "We even possess a weapon unearthed from a vault where it had been sealed years before by those who feared its power."

"What kind of weapon would that be?" I asked, glad we were on a different subject.

She leered at me and grinned. "Dionysus' Thyrsus."

I tried not to let the shock show up on my face. Every Gray Forum member knew that most of the gods of old had been very real and active on the earth. Most of them were humans brainwashed by demons into believing they were divine so that men would worship them and fall into sin, while others were demons themselves who fed off the power of men who praised and sacrificed to them so that they would grow in strength. But they had either all been killed by Forum members or had fallen into infighting once the revelations of their true origins were exposed to those who had once worshipped them. The Gray Forum had taken great pains to ensure that none of the gods' artifacts fell into use by mundanes or other supernatural beings, but we were spread too thin to have found everything.

But how had a Greek god's staff ended up on the west coast of America? There were dozens of ways it could've come here, but I surmised it didn't really matter now. The point was that if Sedecla was telling the truth they had a terrifying weapon at their disposal.

"You can't use that thing," I said. "It drove people mad with whatever Dionysus desired. Lust, anger, greed, you name it—he could overwhelm someone's mind and force them to do things they never would. The Maenads who accompanied him became violent, hedonistic brutes. They were quite literally out of their minds. No one should have that kind of corrupting power."

"And that is precisely why we intend to use it," Sedecla said. "It has only recently come into our possession, but now that you're here perhaps we should use you to test it out. See just how far we can go in driving someone mad and forcing them into our service." She opened her mouth to speak some more, but she sensed something else and turned around. "Ah, they're both here. They can tell you what I cannot, Blake Azarel. I hope we can satisfy your curiosity before we kill you."

CHAPTER 19

I looked over to the door that opened out to a larger hallway outside, right as two men walked inside, one of which I recognized instantly. Exosso was garbed in the attire that he'd possessed during our initial fight and he seemed less than pleased to see me there. I wondered how he'd gotten there so quickly, but these necromancers were mysterious, so they obviously had some means of travel I wasn't privy to yet.

Beside him stood a much taller man, whose very presence demanded respect, or so he'd like to think. He was covered head to toe with garments crafted from what appeared to be human skin of various colors. His face was mostly hidden by a mask filled with black and white spirals with the number 365 etched on it. He wielded a staff in his right hand that had a gem of some sort affixed to the center of the top, which was a collection of spindly branches. Upon closer inspection I saw that the gem was jasper, which I knew had been used in Gnostic circles for jewelry that would showcase their heretical beliefs.

Exosso and En-dor stepped out of the way and allowed Abraxas to leer down at me. I felt anger at his approach, but said nothing then.

"So, Blake Azarel, we meet," Abraxas said, his voice sonorously traveling throughout the room with a deep baritone. "You have caused much mischief in the Dead Lands, but all for naught, it would seem. You are now ours to use as we please."

There was menace and venom in every word he spoke, but there was something wrong with it that I couldn't explain at the time. Regardless, I didn't respond.

"Ah, so the boy's finally learned to shut up," En-dor said,

cackling once more.

"Nah, I was just wondering if anyone would offer the big bad over here a breath mint," I said.

Abraxas flinched, but swiftly recovered and laughed. "Yes, this is exactly what we desire from you, Blake Azarel," he said. "That fiery spirit and power. The Collective will fall." He turned to Exosso. "I see now why you failed in your initial assault on Phoenix, Exosso. You are forgiven. It was only natural. En-dor's plan was necessary after all."

"So it was her idea to bring me here like this?" I asked.

"Only if Valefar failed to take as you as planned. We sent her in the guise of Sedecla, a reference to a potential name given to her by the church, so that we could find you."

"All right, so you have me, now what?"

"Why now we explain ourselves. It's only sporting."

"Here it comes."

Abraxas, ignoring me, gesticulated wildly with his hands, pointing out to the bay and then to San Francisco proper. "Years ago, before the rise of the Collective, we dwelt here in this city, gathering the artifacts necessary to gain the power needed to rule the world! I had gathered my comrades from distant lands here, because it was suited for my designs! For too long had humans ruined this world—polluting it with their filth! They needed direction, so I came down from my form as an archon so that I could guide them to the truth of pure knowledge! Can you imagine it, being forced into such a lowly form, because your great evil wouldn't affect the natural world if you remained the high being you truly are? So because I had to become lesser, I sought out those whose hearts were filled with the purest of evils, creating Morior Invictus to let the sins of humanity become known! Working together, we could do what they could not do by themselves! We learned of a truly, powerful artifact that aligned with our goals and waited for it to appear here, thanks to the guidance of a trusted ally, who promised that should we remain here, no matter what, we would gain what we sought!"

"And what was it you were after?"

"Why, we're after the Bone Ring, of course," Abraxas stated.

I frowned. "That's it?" I asked. "That's its name? How underwhelming."

"For one who knows of its power, you besmirch its true name with a jest unbefitting of its grandness! The Bone Ring is no mere trinket! The Bone Ring was crafted by one of the greatest necromantic geniuses of the ancient age—Cnámh of the Isles."

I felt a psychic backlash in my mind. I knew that name. I had heard it many times before in the time I couldn't remember. Was that the name of the necromancer sealed within the ring? It had to be. I couldn't let them gain access to it. I looked down to my left hand and gasped, not knowing what to do when I found it no longer on my ring finger.

"Are you all right?" Abraxas asked, leaning down to look me over. "Were you even listening to me?"

"Where is it?" I asked. "I've been trying to get rid of that thing for over a year and it's gone like that?"

"Why, because Valefar already stole it from you," En-dor noted. "He was quite adamant that he remain here in our employ in order to fulfill his obligation to steal it from you. In fact, I was meeting him before this, which delayed my introduction to you."

That made sense. Valefar was every bit the extraordinary thief he presented himself as. In fact, he'd almost stolen the ring in our first fight. This was bad. If these people were as strong as they seemed to be, a ring like that in their hands was a disaster, especially if they already had weapons like the Thyrsus in their arsenal. Now if only they would stop monologuing so I could focus and break out of these chains.

Looking over to the right, I saw a small glass box that had once held a fire extinguisher was wide open and now held my gun and regular attire inside. I paused, pretending not to have seen it, and bided my time to strike.

"Look at him squirm!" Exosso shouted, laughing. "He knows now just how evil our desires are!"

"Oh, for the love of God, shut up," I said, groaning. "I can't take the Saturday morning cartoon villain spiel! Who taught you how to deliver your villainous speeches? Dr. Evil? Cobra Commander? Kio Asuno?"

"Enough of this! I tire of your insolence, boy! You will bow at the feet of your betters!" He pointed at me with his bony fingers. "Enforced Servitude!"

I waited for something to happen and looked down at my body.

To our mutual surprise moments passed by with no changes. Exosso quickly grew flustered and looked to the other two necromancers with a failed bid for aid.

"What is this?" Exosso demanded. "My ossification evocation is useless on you! How can this be? What have you done to protect yourself from my powers?"

"I did what now?" I asked, my confusion only growing. "Wait—you use evocation to control bones in people? I thought you were just a discount grave robber! What kind of freak does that?" I paused, feeling uneasy about something that I couldn't remember. "Well, I suppose someone who knows enough Latin to try and sound edgy by naming themselves 'I debone' would do that. Real imaginative work there, son."

"Silence! I have been alive for hundreds of years! I know not what has given you the ability to resist me, but I will overcome you and—"

"Silence, Exosso!" Abraxas commanded. "He merely wishes to get under your skin. We are above such matters."

"Says the guy who named himself after a concept from a pathetically-developed heresy like Gnosticism," I said, smirking. "I mean, why not something a bit more interesting like Pelagianism or Triclavianism? At least then you'd be worth talking to. But no, you had to be a Gnostic, like every other pitiful, basement-dwelling thirty-year-old neckbeard with a discount katana hanging over their gaming rig looked over by their unclean body pillow of Lacus Clyne and Rei Ayanami."

What I could see of Abraxas' face under the mask looked like he'd been stung by a dozen bees and was now suffering from a total allergic reaction. The skin of his cheeks grew blood red.

"Silence, the both of you!" En-dor counseled. "I have just consulted with my knowledge of the arcane and found that Capricorn has told me to tell you to calm down."

"No, there's no way in hell you people actually believe in horoscopes," I said, cackling madly.

"Well, of course I do. The stars guide us and tell us our fortunes. It is only natural. Do you doubt them so even with your power?"

"Well, the thing is I knew the great sage Yankovic, who wrote a song about people like you. So go ahead and tell me your signs."

"Well I'm a Pisces, Exosso is a Taurus, and Abraxas is a Scorpio."

I laughed again, remembering the lyrics well for each sign, but decided for succinctness over precision.

"Okay then." I said. "I'll just paraphrase: 'the stars all predict you'll wake up, do some stuff, and then go back to sleep.'"

"What kind of nonsense is that?" Exosso demanded.

"I know, right? You'd think stellar objects that have absolutely nothing to do with the destinies and lives of humans would be a bit more accurate in their forecasts. Especially since they should've told you that I'd be killing you today so there is no tomorrow for any of you."

"I'll kill you!" En-dor declared, grabbing a knife and raising it to plant in my chest.

"Quit giving him fuel for the fire!" Abraxas demanded, grabbing her hand and stopping Exosso from moving forward. "He seeks to divide us, you cretins!"

The three of them squabbled between themselves, lost in the moment completely. I gawked at them in disbelief, wondering if everything I'd seen before now had been an act. It was true that I felt the Christening within all of them, but if they were as powerful as they said they were, then how could they let my schoolyard jests divide them this easily? I'd had more of a problem destabilizing an entire room of squabbling fairies than this.

Not only that, but none of them had noticed that I'd broken out of all my bonds, having gathered the strength I'd needed while they'd been talking with me. A competent Christener would've called me out a long time ago. Something wasn't adding up and I needed to know the truth, so I cracked my neck and swerved my body to the right so that I was sitting upright with my legs crossed.

"Ahem," I said, clearing my throat. "I have a question."

The three of them turned in unison, locking their gazes with my eyes, which they realized too late was exactly what I'd wanted.

Three separate visions of past lives entered my mind simultaneously. I had almost never used my spiritual sight on more than one target before, as it could be overwhelming, but there had been a gentle nudging in my thoughts that had told me to do it this way, so I had chosen not to ignore it.

I saw a young man crying as a much taller one stood over him,

151

his fist raised for another strike. Later, the young man was stalking a squirrel that had fallen into a trap that he had made. He watched the helpless animal struggle to release itself from the bonds, but it was suddenly stopped by his hands grabbing it around the throat, as he squeezed the life out of it. Once it was dead, the young man tore open its body and took the bones as a souvenir. The young man was now older, going to college at the University of California, San Francisco, meeting with two other students in a dark room where they practiced summoning spells and other witchcraft with no regard to their safety.

From another's eyes, I witnessed a young woman with dark, spindly black hair that covered her face hand a note to a boy wearing a varsity football jacket. The boy laughed in her face and tore the note in two, causing the vision to transition to a dark bedroom lit only by five candles placed in the form of a pentagram. The young woman was crafting a doll from string and now stabbing it repeatedly with malice, only for a new scene to appear the next day where the object of her hate was alive and well. I then watched her reading up on magic, culminating to the vision I had seen earlier.

In the last round, I saw another young man watching a coffin wherein the man's mother lay in, beautiful even in death. The same young man was later in another room, writing down a list of names in his self-titled "Death Note," only for its existence to be discovered by a fellow classmate and reported to their teacher. The young man's life flashed further, as I witnessed him researching the possibility of controlling life and death, once more returning to the room wherein all three of them were studying.

I watched as they managed to locate a book hidden away in the dark libraries owned by an agent of the Sanguine Collective. They poured over the book, finding that they were all gifted in various forms of necromancies. En-dor found herself visiting graveyards to talk to the shades left behind and then bind them to her will. Exosso broke into the San Francisco Zoo and took its animal occupants apart with his evocations, binding their bones to use as armor or weapons as he then turned his attention to living humans. Abraxas used his credentials as a medical student to study the dead bodies under his care and infused them with chaotic energy, causing them to rise again and kill under his command.

The three joined together, vowing to get back at a world that had wronged them. They had done more researching in the book, finding an evocation that could control large swathes of land and cause its inhabitants to become the undead, which would be an army under their rule that would conquer the world. But then the fall of the Gray Forum had come, and the armies of the Sanguine Collective were swarming the continent. Desperate, they had turned to a man surrounded by shadow who had offered them a spell he'd prepared that would save them from death. Working with him, they had casted it over the west coast, killing millions in an instant as others watched in horror as their loved ones tried to eat them alive.

More thoughts and past moments converged in my mind, as they stood there in shocked silence, not only at my brazen attempt to enter their minds, but also at my freeing myself. When the visions stopped, I held a hand to my face and failed to stop myself from grinning.

"No way," I said, laughing madly. "It's so stupid. Please tell me it's not true."

"That what's not true?" En-dor asked.

"That you're not just a bunch of magical weaboos who have no clue what you're doing!"

The room grew silent. Abraxas looked as if I had slapped his dead mother in the face, while En-dor and Exosso's jaws were agape. Then they made a fatal mistake and looked me right in the eyes, confirming what I had seen earlier when they replayed in my mind.

I let out a slight chuckle, too overwhelmed by being right that words escaped me for a moment. Looking up to the ceiling, a sweeping, serene feeling overwhelmed me. Sure, I was still in massive danger, but I now had a massive arsenal of information to throw right back at them if they tried anything funny. Nobody liked being reminded of their past, and with the idiots all in one room all I had to do was turn them against each other.

"*It's true!*" I shouted out, cackling uncontrollably, causing them all to cringe in a mixture of fear, confusion, and a sudden awareness of what they'd done. "You idiots have no idea what you're doing! You're the ones the Sanguine Collective's so afraid of? Oh, if they only knew! They're gonna be so pissed! I kinda want to deliver this bit of news myself! Look, look, we'll call this whole business off right now if you let me go, so I can free Zea, and then just so I can tell the Collective this! I don't care how dangerous it'd end up being, I just want to see the stupid looks on their faces when they find out they were afraid of a bunch of nerdy college dropouts!"

The three stared at me in horror, their deepest, darkest secrets now brought into the light. All three trembled in terror, but then their gazes moved from me to each other.

"It's your fault this happened, Spencer!" En-dor cried out.

"Shut up, Velma!" Abraxas countered.

"No, you shut up!"

"Both of you shut up!" Exosso demanded.

"No, you shut up, Mervin!" the other two shouted back.

"Mervin?" I repeated. "What kind of Latin name is that? I thought you were from Rome."

"Of course he's from Rome—Rome, Georgia!" En-dor declared.

I almost fell backwards off the stone table as I kept howling with laughter. In any other situation, I would've bolted out of the room in the confusion, but I knew they were too far gone in embarrassment and anger to worry about me right now.

They ignored me and started attacking each other. En-dor swatted Exosso in the face, earning herself a cut palm from one of his bones. Abraxas tried to get a blow in, but he got hit by En-dor's elbow when she recoiled in pain. Abraxas' mask fell from his face and crashed into the ground, revealing a ginger-haired man who looked no older than twenty. It took everything in me not to laugh as I saw the pimple-laden minefield that he called a face staring back at his attacker. One hundred years at this and he hadn't done anything about that?

I paused, looking at them with genuine curiosity. Abraxas being the exception, they had all aged far too much in such a short amount of time. As Christeners, if they had been born as young as they had to have once been contemporaries to myself, they shouldn't have aged as poorly.

"You're old, because you abused evocations you didn't understand!" I announced, gleefully. "No one's that stupid, I thought, but thank you for proving me wrong!"

154

This drew their attention back to me and I reveled in what I had to offer to my audience, as growing rage burned in me. I was done laughing. I was outnumbered by all of them, but I wasn't going to leave this fight until I'd had my say. Then I would take Zea and get out of here, but first they needed to understand what they'd done.

"This is why the Dead Lands exist?" I asked, clenching my fists. "Militant stupidity! The greatest single force of change in the world! I honestly thought you three were ancient and strong necromancers from the past who had bided your time to rule over the ashes that remained after the end of the world! I should've known better! It's so much easier to pretend that this was one great elaborate plan crafted by a brilliant mastermind, but it's way more realistic to realize that everything that's happened here's the result of a bunch of pathetic, dropout, wannabe LARPer, basement-dwelling losers!

"The entire West Coast gets thrown into darkness because you incompetent morons tried to use powers you didn't understand! Millions of people are dead, because you just had to feel special! To justify your pathetic attempts at a life! Don't make me laugh! Incompetence or not, you three are going to pay for what you've done!"

I held out my hands and roared with anger. Unseen force emanated from my fingertips as I sent more power into the invocation.

"*Rudis vis!*" I invoked, as that unseen force ushered forth from me and out into the three of them.

The blast knocked them back and into the glass windows of the operating room. Quickly, I got up and went to the glass case, taking out my gear while they were winded from the blow. I was about to shoot one of them when Exosso recovered first and sent a bone spear right at me. I ducked to avoid it and gathered the rest of my gear. I heard him grunt out in pain and saw that, because of my earlier attack, he'd been impaled on a broken pipe and had just died, his last act to try to kill me with him. I silently praised God that the fool knew nothing of final releases and gripped my fist to see my other opponents recovering to fight me. Abraxas held his hand out over Exosso's body and evoked something I couldn't hear, but got the gist of when I saw Exosso's reanimated corpse rising. Figuring I was outnumbered three to one, I then slid out of the room as I placed my hat on my head.

"Get him!" Abraxas ordered.

Running as swiftly as possible, I raced down the hallways, not knowing which direction to go until I heard the sound of an explosion nearby, but in the opposite direction of where I'd been. Curious, I figured it was better than the alternative and headed towards it, hoping it was less hazardous.

CHAPTER 20

I rushed forward swiftly towards the source of the blast. I felt a stirring in my mind, one familiar and pleasant to my thoughts. A warmness of spirit and refreshing understanding washed over my mind and I smiled without fully knowing why.

Passing into a new corridor, I turned back around and pointed my hands to face the entryway.

"*Rudis vis!*" I invoked, sending the unseen force I'd conjured straight into what had once been an exit sign.

The force collided with the top of the wall, causing the ceiling to fall down with it, but only where my invocation had struck. The rubble left behind completely blocked off where I'd come from and I fist-pumped. Now what was left of Morior Invictus would need to find another way to follow me, as I knew they couldn't be too far behind me.

I heard a voice cry out something I couldn't decipher, and I heard another blast shake the foundations of the jail. A new emotion replaced the warmth and familiarity from before and was now attuned to feel righteous anger.

Sensing that I was close to whatever this was, I pressed forward and almost got hit by a barrage of water that was propelling a severed zombie's head my way. I ducked underneath the water and slid on my knees, scratching them up, but preventing myself from getting pulverized as the water gushed forward in the air above me. I stopped sliding a moment later and pushed myself back up, seeing the rest of the zombie was moving forward aimlessly at a target hunched down in front of it. I powered up a darkness invocation, but before I could say anything, I was interrupted by a welcome voice.

"Earth Tremor!" Zea cried out.

The cement floor underneath the zombie swiftly opened up and the zombie flailed around helplessly as the earth swallowed it whole and then crushed him when Zea forced the open floor to repair itself.

I stared at her in wonder. She hadn't noticed my arrival yet, seemingly too tired then to be aware of her surroundings. My hands trembled in excitement. How long had it been since I'd chased after her? I could barely contain myself as I gazed at her, having wondered if I'd ever be able to see her alive again ever since her capture.

She was wearing her senior Psionic robes, but they were covered with dust and soot. Her normally neat, well-maintained hair was obscuring half of her face and she was covered in dirt, looking as if she hadn't bathed in weeks. She was breathing heavily, having used more power than she'd intended in her last attack.

Sensing something, Zea quickly stood up and went into a defensive stance, only to stare at me with her jaw agape. We stood in silence, neither able to process what we were witnessing, or—perhaps cynically—wondering if this was some trick to fool us into complacency. But all thoughts of being swindled left my mind when my feet started moving before I knew what I was doing. I ran up to Zea and hugged her fiercely, trying to speak, but failing utterly when I started crying uncontrollably. Zea, feeling my weariness in conjunction with hers, wrapped her arms around me behind my shoulder blades and proceeded to cry with me.

"Zea!" I exclaimed. "You're alive!"

She laughed once and said, "Of course I am, Blake." She pushed me back to let us look into each other's eyes. "I—"

But she stopped when I started crying even harder and slumped forward, leaving her to help keep me upright in her embrace. She said nothing and nodded, rubbing my back as I tried to stop sobbing further and compose myself.

"I'm sorry," I said, moments later, letting go of her to wipe my eyes clean. "I just—I felt—I thought I was going to lose you."

Zea continued nodding. "I saw what you did when we looked at each other's eyes," she said. "You worked so hard, Blake. I'm sorry that I couldn't do anything until now to help. It's my fault this happened how it did."

"How is this your fault? I'm the one who got distracted when you needed me most and you got taken because of me!"

"Because I was too slow while fighting Valefar. I wasn't fast enough to stay out of his range and paid the price. I'm sorry for the trouble I caused."

I bit my lip. This wasn't fair. This was my fault and she was blaming herself? I wouldn't stand for it, but then I felt her sincerity in my mind thanks to our link. We both paused, realizing that we were both assigning blame at ourselves instead of compromising with mutual failure. We nodded in unison, silently agreeing to work this out at a better time and place.

"How did you escape?" I asked, as eager as her to change the subject.

"It was so strange," Zea said, pointing back to where she'd come from. "I woke up here not too long ago in restraints, but they were so easy to break out of that I thought that I was being tested as some kind of trap or sick fantasy on Morior Invictus' part."

"They did the same to me. My bonds were extraordinarily weak to break free from."

"For such fearsome and ancient evokers, they seem to know very little about keeping those like them imprisoned."

I started chuckling and she eyed my weirdly. "Oh, you didn't see that part with your spiritual sight?" I asked. "Yeah, turns out that they're not quite as ancient as they want us to think they are."

Zea furrowed an eyebrow. "Not as ancient as we believed? Then what are they?"

I kept laughing, now crying from mirth. "So it turns out that the big bad evil magic guys the Sanguine Collective are terrified of—so much that they erected a giant magical barrier just to keep them out—are a bunch of pre-med morons who started a magic club in-between *Vampire: the Masquerade* sessions."

Zea blinked twice. "I thought that I was more able to figure out when you were joking or not, Blake, but it would seem I have failed yet again."

"No, no, no—it's true! Ten billion percent true! Look in my eyes again!"

Doing as instructed, Zea gazed into my eyes and the memories were relayed to her with perfect recall. For a moment she stayed still, until her face sunk, and she scratched her left cheek, trying to process what she'd seen. Then, without warning, she started laughing heartily and threw back her head. Flushed at first, I could only watch as she kept laughing, until I couldn't help it and joined in with her. It felt so good to do something so simple in that moment.

"Ah, it does my heart good to see you two together again," Valefar's voice said from in front of us.

Instantaneously, I summoned Ageg into my hands and aimed it at the direction of the voice as Zea's hands glowed with fire as she invoked it around them. We looked ahead, seeing Valefar sitting on a window ledge whose iron bars had long rusted off and fallen out. He smiled at us as he regally reclined with one leg swaying in the air, while the remainder of his body was leaning against the right wall of the window ledge. In his right hand was a saucer that contained a hot cup of tea, which he then picked up with his left hand to examine its aroma. Laying across his waist was some sort of staff similar to a branch with vines hanging from it.

"I was worried you two wouldn't be able to find each other when you got here," Valefar continued, "but as always it seems you must keep proving me wrong, which I must say is a new feeling that I've grown accustomed to."

"Where's the Bone Ring?" I demanded.

"Bone Ring?" Zea asked, as I pointed to my ringless ring finger and she flinched. "That's its name?"

"Real anticlimactic, right? I mean, it looks like a bunch of bones, but it has a dragon on it. Why not the Bone Dragon Ring or something cooler like that?"

"Because that's not its name," Valefar said. "Although, I do believe that you know its true origins, or, rather, you did." We turned to look at him and he grinned. "But to answer your question, Abraxas owns it now."

"Then why didn't he use it on me when we talked earlier?"

"That I cannot answer, but if I had to offer a guess, well, it's probably because he's not strong enough to use it to its full effectiveness. Obviously, necromancer he may be, he is no match for your invocative might."

"I don't use necromancy."

"Of course not, but you still clearly possess the power and will necessary to use the Bone Ring when it's convenient for you."

I clenched my fists. He was right. How many times had I used something so obviously evil just to suit my interests?

"Although, I'm not one to judge," Valefar said, sipping his tea. "After all, that's God's purview and we see how well that ended up for demons like me. Not that I bear a grudge, mind you. It is His job after all to punish rebellion. Frankly, I'd be mad if He didn't."

"Why work with Morior Invictus?" Zea asked. "If you're with The Thirteen, then why care about what they do?"

"Well, to be honest, I don't really care about anyone in either group. I'm just up for a good challenge is all. I merely worked with them because it aligned with my interests."

"And what were those?" I asked.

"To steal the Thyrsus of course."

He placed his saucer and teacup on the windowsill and grabbed the wooden staff with both hands, idly pointing it at us. I rushed in front of Zea and powered up an attack, but he interrupted me.

"Oh, I'm not what you have to worry about at the moment," Valefar said, pointing with the staff to our right. "Abraxas has called for one of his experiments to sniff you out and, well, to be honest, I made the tea for a reason. Creatures like this one are attracted to the smell of gold, and I laced my tea with many such gold flakes for such a time as this."

"Gold doesn't have a scent!" I protested. "It's inert, which makes it odorless!"

Valefar chuckled. "Maybe to beings such as you and I, but to what is heading your way, the gold in my tea might as well be blood in the water calling to every shark in the vicinity."

He snapped his fingers and a small stack of gold dust appeared at our feet standing about five inches tall. Before I could ask how he'd done so, Zea and I stood at attention when a strong, unholy shriek made the hairs on the back of our necks stand up in primal fear. The harsh sound pierced our ears sharply, making us grab them and drop our focus on my bow and her prepared fire invocation, respectively.

We looked around to find the source as Valefar grinned sadistically at our predicament. The flapping of what almost sounded like wings traveled into the prison from outside, but there was something wrong with the noise that just didn't sit right with me. It wasn't like the sound a condor or eagle might make when they flapped their wings. This was wrong, as if there was no flesh or feathers attached to the bones that allowed this creature to fly.

"Uh, what's that noise?" I asked, hearing the sounds originated where Valefar had been pointing with the Thyrsus.

Sensing danger, Zea and I moved as one to dodge to the right, barely avoiding the falling concrete that had been destroyed by the large figure that was smashing into the jail. A swirling of dirt, rubble, and gold dust almost blinded us as it filled the hallway. We barely managed to avoid what seemed to be some sort of enormous maw that snapped violently at where we had been and was chomping down on the gold dust Valefar had placed at our feet that was still on the ground in the aftermath of the creature's attack.

Zea helped me up and we waited for the dust to settle, only to be stunned into silence at what we saw in front of us.

Standing at over seventeen feet tall was a giant monstrosity that was thirty-five feet long from the front of its bony snout to its withered tail. Its eyes were hollow, but still seemed capable of a sight I didn't want to understand as it glared at us. Two horns protruded from the top of the creature's head, curving to the opposing sides of where they originated. Its four clawed feet methodically played with the gold dust on the floor, sinking its talons deeper into the dust as if it was in rapturous pleasure. In the center of its exposed ribcage was a black gemstone that radiated with chaotic energies that rippled from the creature's body and sent out something that appeared to be black fire from the beast's gaping, toothy mouth. The fire poured over the gold dust and made it travel into the air and into the corrupted gemstone, which glowed with an ebony hue.

I shivered with fear, trying to rationalize what I was seeing. Never in my life had I seen a flesh and blood dragon, nor had I ever expected to see such a creature due to their rarity and hatred for meddling in human affairs, mundane and Christened alike. But this wasn't that same creature I only had seen before in textbooks. No, this monstrosity had died and had been forced back into a cruel undeath, reduced only to its base instincts to hoard treasure and protect what it owned. Worse still, by standing in the gold dust Valefar had placed on Alcatraz, we had made ourselves enemies of the state.

162

I steeled myself and felt Zea doing the same. There was no way out of this without a fight.

The skeletal dragon bared its teeth at us and let out a tremendous roar as it rushed towards us, intent to protect its territory.

CHAPTER 21

"Is that what I think it is?" I asked, dodging to the left.

"Of course it is!" Zea protested, rolling over to go underneath the dragon's open maw as it tried to bite into her. "It's a walking dragon skeleton!"

"How did these idiots find a dragon skeleton? And then make it a dracolich?"

"Does that really matter? It's right here in front of us! Wondering how they found it isn't going to help us kill it for good!"

"I just like having answers to my questions, so sue me for expecting at least one of them to actually have some closure for once!"

Valefar chuckled, having decided to recline further on the windowsill with the Thyrsus laying on his lap. "So casual in the face of danger," he mused. "It has been some time since I have had so much continual fun with my targets."

I grumbled and summoned Ageg, firing off a shot at the dragon's empty right eye socket. The arrow of light penetrated the void and cracked some of the bones. However, before I could fire another shot, there was a pulsation of energy from the black gemstone in the beast's exposed ribcage and the broken bones regenerated themselves.

Zea, seeing this, fired off a blast of fire at the dragon's ribs, but its bony wings flapped thrice, canceling out the attack.

"I'm open to ideas!" Zea announced, rolling underneath the dracolich's front right claws as it swiped at her.

"Give me a break—this is my first dragon!" I yelled back. "That I can recall, at least! I wasn't expecting to fight one here, let alone an undead one!"

"Where is everyone else? Don't tell me you came here alone!"

I fired twin shots of light at the dracolich, hitting it square in the right horn, which was chipped off by the attack and fell to the ground. The same pulsation from before erupted from the gemstone and caused the horn to rise from the ground and restore itself to its original location.

"Of course not!" I yelled. "Not from lack of trying, though! Mara and Cinderella should have been here by now!"

"You left Clooney alone with Nathan?" Zea snapped.

"I had to leave someone there! Cinderella was supposed to stay too, but she didn't listen to me, just like Mara did!"

"You let Mara come? She's too frail!"

"I think we both know better than that, sweetheart! Lady knows how to use a gun!"

I produced my own gun as Zea brought out her spatha and parried another attack from one of the dragon's claws. Firing twice, I aimed at the ribcage again, knowing this would solve a lot of problems if it got hit. My first shot missed the gem and crashed off a floating rib, breaking the bone it impacted with. Before the corrupted gemstone could repair the damage, my second bullet hit it on the bottom. The bullet shattered on impact, but had served its purpose. I hadn't gotten close to shattering the gem, but it had caused some damage, forcing the gem to focus on repairing itself, rather than the dragon skeleton.

"I have a plan!" I announced, avoiding a wave of black fire that erupted from the dragon's wide-open mouth by dodging to my left.

"Listening!" Zea replied, sending several bolts of lightning from her fingertips.

However, her target hadn't only been the dragon, as three bolts landed into the skeleton, charring the bones they connected with. At the same time, four more bolts had suddenly changed direction and gone for Valefar, who'd reacted with genuine surprise and disappeared, only to reappear at another windowsill, this one closer to ground level. He laughed mirthfully at the unexpected attack and clapped playfully. I, however, grinned, as Zea had felt a thought I'd been toying with but hadn't come out to say yet. She'd used that attack to confirm to me that our link was secure without me ever once asking for it.

"Nice one!" I shouted. "But let's not worry about the thief right now! The dragon's our priority right now!"

Screw that, I sent her way. *If we can find a way to deal with the dragon skeleton and our demon friend, I say we go for it.*

"You're welcome!" Zea shouted back. "That was more for me, though! I had to look at that smug grin a lot more than you did!"

Okay, it seems he can't sense our thoughts like I feared, Zea sent back. *Now how do we kill this dragon and him too?*

Whatever happens we can't let him know about the link, I thought. *But as for the dragon it seems that Abraxas implanted that gem there as some sort of conduit to keep it alive. They may be a bunch of screwups, but they did have a hundred years to improve their evocations. We need to damage the gemstone as much as possible to stop it from regenerating the dragon skeleton.*

And what about Valefar?

He'll see any attack we send his way. We need to be sneaky. Make him focus on our fight with the dragon so much he loses his sense of awareness.

Okay. Whatever you want to do I'll follow suit. We'll fight as one.

I grinned. Zea and I didn't have to speak with each other out loud to plan our strategies. Our minds were more in sync than with others, so our thoughts poured easily from one to the other. There was a margin for error, so we preferred speaking aloud to one another just in case what one was thinking wasn't what they really wanted to do. However, in circumstances like this, when an opponent could react almost before we could, we needed absolute silence in the physical realm. Our minds would need to act as one to dispatch not only the dragon, but also our demonic foe, who was enjoying every moment of this battle.

The gemstone finished repairing itself and a fresh pulsation erupted from the corruption, allowing the dragon to once more breathe its black fire. I dashed to Zea's side, knowing I didn't have the power to erect a barrier to protect myself.

"Perfect Shield!" Zea cried out.

A cerulean-colored shield appeared from nowhere, forcing back the black fire that attempted to get past it, not even allowing the heat of the flames to pass through it either. Using the brief respite she'd offered, I jumped to the right and conjured up the image of the small ball again.

"Two can play at this game, ya dracolich freak!" I taunted. *"Sphaera ignis!"*

The small fire ball appeared near the gemstone and soon rushed out to become a large, sweltering blaze of pure fire. The dragon skeleton shrieked in pain and wrapped its large tail around itself as it used both its tail and wings to use the gale force winds it created to snuff out the flames. I'd managed to hit the gemstone dead on, but it hadn't been strong enough to cause too much harm.

Precious gems for the most part have a high melting point and I highly doubted any of the flames I'd invoked had gone above the lowest range of a deep red-colored fire. I had witnessed Cinderella craft flames that had almost turned blue, but I was nowhere close to that intensity. I couldn't tell what type of gem the corrupted gemstone had once been before Abraxas had done whatever he'd performed to make it like it was now, but I knew that chances were that even before it had been changed it could easily shake off my low heat flames.

"You can invoke fire now?" Zea asked, incredulous.

"Stay with me, sweetheart, you might learn a thing or two," I said, laughing.

Emergency training with Cinderella, I sent. *Can't control it, so I learned not to. Makes a big boom.*

I expect nothing less, Zea sent. *Though, I must admit you've done well in such a short time.*

I grinned and then raced to my right as Zea went left. The dracolich roared out, trying to decide which one of us to go after. It chose me and rushed to gnash its teeth at me. I grabbed the top of its jaw and flung myself upward to get onto the beast's back. I didn't have a plan, so much as a distraction, knowing Zea was deliberately charging up an attack that would do more damage than if she'd simply invoked it like I would.

The dracolich, however, decided that he didn't like being mounted and was now shaking wildly to try and buck me off of it. Raising my right fist while I used my left hand to maintain my questionable hold on the dragon, I yelled as my fist started to be covered with a dark field of energy.

"Percutiens tenebris!" I declared, striking my darkness-shrouded fist into the back of the dragon's head.

167

The sounds of bones cracking filled my heart with flee as I saw the hole I'd made into the back of the beast's skull. Had it been alive I would've killed it then and there, but owing to its undead nature I had merely hurt the shell of the dracolich. Crying out in pain, the dracolich flailed about wildly, causing me to lose my grip as I fell to the floor. The dracolich fell as well, hitting its already broken head against the wall and it slumped flatly, as the corrupted gemstone attempted to repair the damage that it had just taken. Grunting, I picked myself up just as Zea finished preparing her invocation.

"Rock Fist Volley!" Zea commanded, pointing her hands to the cement underneath the fallen dracolich.

A series of stone-shaped fists emerged from the cement, punching upwards and into the dracolich's bones repeatedly. The undead creature roared out in defiance, but the continued shower of stone fists prevented it from healing itself from the damage. Zea kept summoning more fists, continually striking the dracolich, but she hadn't permanently damaged the gemstone yet, even though it was now exposed for an easy strike. We had other plans.

"Bravo!" Valefar exclaimed, applauding with reckless abandon. "This is precisely what I came here for! This is a battle for the ages! The cool fight I've been wanting to see for a long time!"

"Oh, yeah?" I replied, smiling madly. "You want to see something cool, then watch me, Valefar!"

Valefar idly played with the Thyrsus with the fingers on his right hand, as he followed me with interest because of my recent boast. I locked eyes with Zea and grinned.

"Now!" I ordered.

Our combined strike was instantaneous, but would never have registered to the eyesight of a mundane. At the exact moment I gave my order, Zea rushed to her left, aiming her spatha not at the dragon's exposed gem in its chest, but at Valefar's right arm, which was severed the instant her clean blade contacted the demon's skin. Valefar reacted with surprise and was about to evoke something when his eyes were drawn to the white beam of light I'd invoked to ricochet off of Zea's spatha. The three of us watched in unison as the beam's path was then redirected at a forty-five-degree angle straight into the dragon's ribs, where it continued to bounce back and forth until it made its way into the corrupted gemstone at the center, hitting it with far more force than if I'd hit it with a straight shot. The dragon roared in pure agony as its bones started to disconnect from the others, causing it to crumple onto the ground into ash. Using that brief respite, I then lunged forward to grab Valefar's severed arm and take possession of the Thyrsus, while Zea used her free hand to craft an ice invocation straight at the demon's face.

However, before either of us could reach our target, Valefar grinned and flash-stepped forward to the end of the hallway ahead of us. He then held out his left hand and mentally-compelled the severed arm to return to him, leading Zea's invocation to shatter the window he'd been sitting near moments before and for me to hit chin first into the cement floor of the hallway. The severed arm attached itself to Valefar without incident and he placed his left hand on his right shoulder and then moved his shoulder rhythmically to make sure it was still in one piece.

"Really?" I cried out, barely able to muster anything else.

Valefar chuckled. "I see your surprise and will assure you that it is not your fault you failed," he said. "You simply don't have the *resolve* I do."

I flinched in response, making him smile and let out a short laugh.

"Ah, I see you are familiar with the term," Valefar noted. "But judging by your lack of knowledge about the existence of my resolve before I mentioned it, I would surmise that you don't have one of your own, which means you cannot see mine unless I wish it to be viewed by those who possess none."

I nodded, realizing now exactly why Nathan-Prime had shown me his resolve. If he hadn't, I would've had no real-world applications on how to understand what I had just seen. Valefar was nigh unbeatable in this state. If he chose to use the Thyrsus now, we were goners.

"I see in your eyes that you know you cannot win as of now," Valefar stated simply. "But fear not, as I have said before your demise is not what I'm after. If anything, you've provided what I desired and more with your masterful and stubborn refusal to give up on killing me or at the very least," he chuckled, "disarming me. Albeit momentarily."

169

"Blake, what is he talking about?" Zea asked. "What's a resolve?"

"It's some sort of guardian that's based on your soul and it has special abilities," I said. "I've only ever experienced one other before today, at least that I can recall. I had no idea that he had one before now."

"It's not your fault you didn't know about all of my powers," Valefar continued. "But in the interest of making things more stimulating I'll explain how it works, although I believe that you've started to understand some of the basics at least. My resolve, Phantom Thief, allows me to 'escape' from anything I am aware of, as well as allow me to steal anything I am aware of, if I am swift enough to do so. So, if I need to avoid an attack I can see or hear, then Phantom Thief helps me 'escape' from it by allowing me to move faster or perhaps to dodge at just the right time. Since I was fooled by your attempt to make me look at you, Blake, I was unable to pay attention to Zea, who deftly took my arm from me and my access to the Thyrsus. However, since the arm is still part of me, I can make it 'escape' with the rest of my body and, if need be, I can also detach limbs or flatten myself in order to be free from imprisonment. It's the perfect ally of an accomplished rogue. Now, the time for fun is over. I do need to bring this Thyrsus back to its rightful owners. They are paying me after all. I look forward to our next meeting, my friends. Ta-ta!"

Valefar took off his hat, bowed, and then disappeared in an instant.

I looked at where he'd been and groaned, hitting my head on the concrete multiple times in anguish. What was it going to take to beat him? We'd done everything right. Perfect precision, immense trust in each other's abilities, a skillful deception, and it still wasn't enough. I was grateful now more than ever that he wasn't interested in killing us.

"Blake, are you okay?" Zea asked me, having moved beside me.

I looked up at her and sighed. "No, but I'll make it, sweetheart," I said.

Zea extended her hand I accepted it, as we picked myself off the floor. She placed a hand on my head and offered a healing invocation to stop the bleeding I'd caused from my puerile antics on the floor.

"There's a lot in this world we still don't understand even after all this time," Zea said. "It's only natural we'd end up fighting something we couldn't beat yet."

"You're right," I said, nodding. "I'm not mad at that. I'm just mad that right now we're going 0-3 against him."

"We only need to win once, Blake."

"Then let's win next time, Zea."

I held out my fist at her and she grinned, offering back a fist bump, something it had taken over a year for her to learn properly. We nodded at each other and surveyed the remnants of the fight. The dracolich had indeed turned to ash, taking the gold dust with it as they flew out the wall that the dragon had originally forced itself into to get at us.

"You said that Mara and Cinderella were here," Zea said.

"Yeah, but they should've made it here by now," I said. "I instructed her to make a temporary circle to force themselves here if need be, but Morior Invictus doesn't seem to be dealing with them right now. I wonder what's keeping them."

"We have to trust in them. They'll find us. Now let's figure out a way off of this island."

I shook my head. "Not yet. We need to stop this while we're here. Morior Invictus needs to die tonight. If we escape from here all they're going to do is exactly what the Collective wanted them to: overwhelm us and kill us before we can do anything about them. Besides, they have the Bone Ring too. We can't let an artifact like that stay in their hands."

Zea sighed. "You're right. Then let's explore this place. Hopefully we can divide them and take them out individually."

"Then let's go kill some necromancers, sweetheart."

CHAPTER 22

Zea and I trudged further into the prison, our lack of knowing the layout of the old jail working against us immensely. I'd originally planned to skulk about and explore the penitentiary while Sedecla had gone off to collect Cinderella and Mara, but her betrayal had killed that idea before I'd even gotten a chance to move past the cave harbor.

We had gone in an eastern direction across the hallways, finding ourselves in one of the prison blocks. Sensing no danger, we went inside, seeing the broken and open cells that had once housed several of the most notorious criminals in the history of the United States. We were currently on the first floor and this particular wing of the jail was two stories in height. In all there were sixty cells on the right side of the room and another sixty on the left.

Zea stopped in place, making me stop too when I sensed her apprehension through our link. I looked back at her and saw her staring hypnotically at something to the left of us in one of the open cells. When I followed the source of what had drawn her attention, I found myself also mesmerized by the appearance of a broken, chaotic orb of energy colored in various shades of red, black, and purple.

A voice called out from it, asking for help and it took everything in me to ignore it, as I shook my head and forced myself to look away from the death mark. I grumbled and gripped my hands into fists, knowing that this had to have been the site of the death of the many Christeners that Morior Invictus had experimented on in Alcatraz.

Instinctively, I reached out my left hand and grabbed Zea's hand, surprising both of us when she found herself drawn back to reality. Realizing what she'd almost done, she shook her head and

I let go of her hand.

"I'm sorry," she said. "I sensed the power and—"

"—wanted to add it to your own," I said. "I know. It's okay. It's always going to tempt people like us."

Zea nodded, avoiding the sight of the death mark as much as possible. "It's not the only one in this room."

"No, I sense more too, but we can't get distracted by them. We need to get out of here and meet up with Mara and Cinderella."

"You're right. Let's—"

But she was interrupted by sinister cackling emanating from directly in front of us. Looking forward, we found En-dor holding out her hands so that her palms faced upwards as she continued laughing. Her face had seemed to have aged further, which I chalked up to her having used more of the evocations that she barely understood the dangers of utilizing.

"You could not have picked a worse spot for you to enter here!" En-dor declared, further descending into maniacal laughter. "This is my chosen room of study! I can summon every single shade that has ever died in this room and make them fight for me! You will both become my newest spirits in my undead, spectral army!"

"How did she catch up with us?" I asked. "I blew up the only entryway that led me to you!"

"That's what you're concerned about?" Zea asked, disapprovingly.

Black and white pulsations traveled from out in front of En-dor's body, crafting a circle of immaculate design to appear in front of her. Zea brought out her spatha, while I prepared a light invocation to fight back once the summoning had been completed.

"Come forth, Al Capone!" En-dor commanded.

Zea and I watched as a spirit ascended from the summoning circle that En-dor had placed. He stood beside her, wearing a dark checkered three-piece suit with a fedora to rival my own. In his right hand was an enormous machinegun that was laying backward on his shoulder in a clear ploy to look menacing. He was smoking an ethereal cigar that somehow was also emitting a smoke trail that extended upwards. I stared at him in confusion, knowing that something was missing from this equation, but not how to articulate how I felt.

"You're doomed!" En-dor declared. "The deadliest crime lord of the Depression-era is gunning for your lives!"

"Yeah, see," Al Capone said, adopting as stereotypical a gangster accent as possible. "You're gonna gets what's coming to yous guys!"

"That's not Al Capone!" I yelled, incredulously. "He's way too thin! That's no Brooklyn accent! Not to mention this idiot doesn't look anything like him!"

"What are you talking about?" En-dor demanded. "He told me he was Al Capone when I summoned his specter from the beyond!"

"And you just believed him? Al Capone didn't die at Alcatraz! He served his time and went to live the rest of his miserable life in Florida! I don't know who this conman is, but he clearly isn't who you thought he was!"

En-dor gazed suspiciously at "Al Capone," who smiled sheepishly as his machinegun disappeared along with the rest of his ridiculous getup. I didn't pretend to understand how ghosts worked, but I knew enough about spiritual beings to be aware that they could make things appear if they believed in them, which I'd shattered without even realizing it. Crying out in anger, En-dor rushed at the fake gangster and grasped his ectoplasmic form, shaking the ghost violently.

"How do you know so much about the people who were imprisoned here?" Zea asked, while the necromancer and her shade were working out their differences.

"I used to watch a bunch of noir films with my dad," I said. "He'd tell me all about how he used to be involved in preventing the mob from gaining access to Christeners to use in their schemes back in the day. He liked watching the movies because it made him feel nostalgic."

Zea nodded in fascination, but her stance quickly shifted to a defensive one as we both sensed approaching power. En-dor had destroyed the fake Al Capone, severing her control over his spectral self and releasing his soul from this mortal coil. She was huffing angrily and pointing in our direction.

"I want them dead," she said, coldly.

Zea and I looked around, wondering who she was directing this proclamation to, as we stood side-by-side, ready to defend the other as needed. The power we'd sensed earlier seemed to emanate originally from En-dor, but had now spread to almost everywhere in the vicinity besides where we currently stood.

Sensing danger, I dodged backward, unknowingly avoiding two sets of ethereal hands that had erupted from the ground without disturbing it physically that had attempted to lock me in place. Zea, likewise, had done the same, as three sets of hands had gone for her.

At that same moment, we witnessed more disembodied spirits appear from the jail cells on both sides of the prison block. Their reveal was furthered by a ceaseless, communal moaning and wailing as they continued to reach out for us. The sound of the wailing sent shivers down our spines, as we tried to ignore it, focusing instead to size up our new foes. Most of them seemed to have attire like what the people of my time had worn before the Gray Forum's destruction, which made a certain amount of sense to me since few prisoners had died in Alcatraz. I surmised that most of them had to have been people who'd survived the initial turmoil that had created the Dead Lands and had been brought here to be experimented on by Morior Invictus.

"Kill them, my shades of the deceased!" En-dor commanded, gesticulating wildly with her hands in our direction. "Bind their souls to this island so that they may service me, even in death!"

I ran to my right, unleashing several short volleys of light beams to discourage any of them from following me, as Zea swung and made contact with three of the shades that had tried to attack her. Normally, weapons would fail to hit something that had no physical body, but with the right invocations and spread of the Christening, even mundane weapons could hit a ghost. Zea had spent many years pouring pieces of her Christenings over her sword, which allowed her to fight back in a manner that the ghosts hadn't been prepared for, so they retreated from the both of us. Spirits of the dead could assume a quasi-physical form long enough to make an impact on the world of the living, but it required a lot of power.

"Don't falter, my shades!" En-dor ordered. "Do as I command!"

A strange rippling erupted from every single ghost there, as they seemed to have tried to resist the orders, only to then head

175

straight for us. Zea held out her left hand and crafted a vortex of water that ripped through the shades in its path, but they quickly reformed themselves and joined the others to attack her. I jumped over to her and pushed the both of us out of the way, causing the ghosts to harmlessly fall into the floor as they phased through it and returned back to the room without issue. Zea picked herself up and grunted as I charged up my next attack. But we were interrupted when more ghostly hands appeared from beneath our feet in yet another attempt to drag us down. We stepped backward, avoiding another spectral sneak attack as we continued running away from them in the direction where we'd entered the prison block. We almost managed to get out, but more shades appeared directly in front the entrance, forcing us to retreat.

"I don't suppose you know how to fly, do you?" I asked.

"Don't be ridiculous," Zea said. "Even with wind invocations I don't have the control to cause the both of us to levitate."

"It was just a thought, sweetheart. Nothing to get upset over. *Fiat lux*!"

I aimed a singular bolt of light at the nearest shade, hitting it directly in what had once been its chest. The specter cried out in anguish and dissipated from sight, not able to keep itself intact from the power of my invocation.

I pumped my fist in victory, but knew it was hollow. How much power had I expended on my trip to Alcatraz? I'd forced myself to move faster and harder without much sleep or rest for weeks. Even with my immense reserves of energy I didn't have an unlimited supply of it and Zea had been forced to sleep through most of her trip, which meant she didn't have as much strength in her strikes, especially since she'd been forced to keep using her invocations since waking up. We needed to be smart about this, otherwise we'd tire ourselves out and still have two more Morior Invictus members to deal with, assuming we managed to deal with En-dor first.

Zea had been following a similar line of thought and was working just as fast as I was to work out a solution. Our link allowed us to think faster with two minds than on our own, but it wasn't perfect. However, it did provide enough of a service to each other that when one person connected an idea, the other could finish the thought process almost instantaneously.

We both knew we weren't going to win this fight if we kept running away and hitting what ghosts we could see. Eventually they would trap one or both of us and do whatever it was they'd been commanded to do to cause us to serve En-dor, which caused Zea to think up an idea I hadn't considered yet, only for me to follow suit with one of my own to complete hers. The shades weren't the real threat here and we'd wasted too much time and energy assuming they were, especially since it seemed like they were unwilling partners in this fight. Without looking at one another, Zea and I exchanged the same plan and moved to enact it swiftly.

Pretending to feint to the left, we then jumped in unison to the right, avoiding yet another set of outstretched hands as Zea sheathed her spatha and grabbed my left hand with her right hand. In midair, we pointed our held hands towards the necromancer, each adding energy to a combined strike we'd made up on the fly.

"Excelsior—" Zea started.

"—*Spiritus*!" I finished.

Having gathered our mutual power together to form in our hands, Zea and I poured the unseen energy outwards to impact our foe. The joint blast hit En-dor directly in her chest, sending her flying backwards and into an open cell. She spasmed for a moment and tried to stand, but we'd successfully knocked the wind out of her.

Sensing movement to my right, I then charged up a light invocation, but noticed to my surprise that our former assailants were ignoring Zea and I and were now hovering over to the fallen En-dor. The ghostly entourage stood silently, having ceased their wailing to instead craft an intense mutual glare that they directed at the wounded necromancer.

En-dor coughed twice and tried to pick herself up off the ground, but the combination of her erratic usage of her own evocations over the years and the impact of our attack had broken off her concentration. It was only when she tried to look at us that she noticed the predicament she was in. Had she not faltered there, perhaps she might've been able to force her will over her specters, but her fear betrayed her when the ghosts fell down upon her.

"No!" En-dor yelled. "What are you doing? I command you! Kill them! Leave me al—"

The shades descended on their former master with vitriol, causing her to shout out in despair as whatever youth she retained was slowly drained by her ex-thralls. Zea and I winced as we watched her body convulse in pain until there was no more movement from her or the shades.

We continued staring at the scene, wondering if we were next, but the ghosts turned around as one and stared at us without malice; rather, we both felt an unspoken kinship with them. However, before we could speak with them, we witnessed the shades disappear, leaving the husk of En-dor behind them.

I let out a sigh of relief and Zea soon joined me. We looked at one another and allowed ourselves a shared, brief smile before we wordlessly continued ahead, hoping that we'd find a way out of this mess as soon as possible.

CHAPTER 23

"Where are we now?" Zea asked, as we surveyed our surroundings.

"Looks like we're leading out towards an exit," I said. "The salty air's a little stronger in this direction."

"I think—"

Zea stopped, sensing something I didn't feel besides what I could detect from our link. She looked around, but couldn't find what she was looking for.

"There are more than the undead here," she said. "Christeners. Like us, but...wrong."

"What do you mean 'wrong'?" I asked.

"I don't know. I've never felt it before. No, that's wrong. It's similar to Zoë, but that's the wrong way to put it."

Confused, I expanded my awareness of our surroundings, only to be suddenly hit by an intense volley of emotion that made my mind tremble. I held my right hand over my temples and groaned, not understanding what I'd just experienced.

"Pain," Zea answered for me. "It's their pain."

"Whose?" I asked, shaking my head to clear my thoughts.

"I don't know, but they hurt and the hurt does not stop. They have felt us and are coming our way. It would be wise to hide."

"Then let's get out of here, Zee."

We did our best to suppress our power signatures and went forward, following the path we felt would lead us out of the building. However, moments later, we discovered that there was a gaping hole in what would have once led into the recreation yard. Inside this hole was another horde of zombies accompanied by one of the hulking monstrosities I'd seen patrolling the edges of the

179

island, which stood at about sixteen feet tall.

"Zea—!" I started to shout.

"—Understood!" Zea shouted back, sensing my thoughts before I could speak, as she pointed at the zombies ahead of us. "Burning Cataclysm!"

Fire rushed forward from her fingertips, incinerating the entire horde in one strike. The bigger undead was helpless next to the might of her flames and crumpled into ash with the rest of them right in front of us as it feebly attempted to swat at her, failing to get even close to Zea.

"Nicely done, Zee!" I yelled. "I was so worried by those things when I first saw them, but you made an ashtray out of it!"

Zea smiled. "It was nothing," she said, simply.

I stared at the ashes. "But this wasn't what we felt, was it?"

"No, I feel as if we should—"

Zea was cut short by an unnatural set of moans different from moaning of the ghosts. We turned to locate the source of the noise, which had started outside in the recreation yard, only to be greeted by a group of almost human-looking undead. They were all clothed in rags and their hair had grown long and disheveled, but we could both sense that they were no longer alive, except for the brief stirrings of something akin to life that they all held.

The connection I'd accidentally created with them earlier returned and those same, rough feelings from before reentered my mind. I tried to tell Zea to fight with me, but we were both stopped by the creatures when they simultaneously held out their right hands and muttered a set of incomprehensible words, causing unseen strands of energy to pelt our bodies. Zea and I cringed from the attack as we felt the attack continue and more small, invisible force bullets to hit us again and again. I'd felt a similar sensation before when training as a child to maintain concentration on my invocations. The senior teachers would shoot small bursts of energy at their trainees, causing us to continually get blasted over and over again until we could find a way to maintain a focus on whatever invocations we were being taught at the time, but this was different than that. More feral and untrained.

Using what little remained of our conscious minds, Zea and I jumped to opposing sides of the hole in the wall and leaned up against the rubble. We used the short reprieve to try and figure out what had just happened.

"What are those things?" Zea asked.

"They must be the Christeners that Morior Invictus brought here to the island to study!" I offered. "Abraxas must've used his evocations to make them mindless thralls, capable of only dishing out damage as a unit! At least that's my best guess, because their evocations aren't focused at all!"

"An unfocused evocation can be just as deadly as a focused one. We need to avoid anything they throw at us."

The Christened zombies slowly shambled to reach us, mindlessly pursuing the task of attacking the intruders. A part of me wanted to find some way to bring them back to their senses, but I knew this was only hopeful optimism trying to blind me from reality. Most of them had been dead for years and there was no invocation I knew of that could both restore a body to life and return their soul as well. We had no choice but to kill these unfortunate monstrosities.

"Any ideas?" I asked.

"They're still zombies, right?" Zea asked. "Fire should do it, but we need to be quick or we'll just get hit with that force barrage again!"

"Understood!"

Acting in unison, Zea and I rushed out from our hiding places and both crafted separate fire invocations. I focused mine on the center of the Christened zombies, in order to cause the flames to spread out to the others, while Zea had made hers appear from above them, so that it would impact all of them from a different angle. However, the flames we crafted impacted on an unseen barrier that they had conjured without our knowledge and dissipated quickly. Zea and I weren't quick enough to regroup, too slack jawed at the sudden failure of our attacks, and were hit once more with the bolts of energy that they evoked into existence to neverendingly pelt the two of us.

The mindless thralls summoned further evocations, continually hitting the both of us with unseen bolts of force. Zea and I tried to dodge them, but the recurrent barrage stopped either of us from focusing on defense or escape. The bolts weren't deadly by themselves, but the body was only supposed to take so much physical trauma before it gave out and every force bolt that impacted on us caused our nerves to go into overdrive. If we weren't careful, we could enter cardiac arrest or suffer an immense seizure within moments.

Zea steeled her mind faster than I could and placed her hands on the ground, shouting out, "Earth Barrier!"

Dirt, mud, and concrete acted as one, melding together to form a dome that covered the both of us from harm. The Christened zombies didn't let up their attack, which was now whittling away at our temporary fortress.

Zea and I caught our breath, knowing that we didn't have much time to plan our next move. Neither of us spoke at first, too tired to think either, as we tried to gather our energy to prepare something to fight back. My skin was welting up from the continued blasts, feeling as if someone had fired hundreds of pellets from a BB gun at me from every direction and Zea didn't look much better. It would've been one thing if we could've taken these zombies on individually, but their concentrated tactics would wear out the both of us even if we were at full strength. We had no way to fight back and maintain concentration at the same time. Our only chance would be to run and regroup, if providence was kind enough to let us get away from them.

The earthen dome shook violently as more of it gave way to their repeated, mindless blasts. We looked at each other and sighed as more of our protection crumbled so that we could see our foes once more, although we were low enough then to avoid their attacks.

"Guess we're outta options, Zee," I said. "We might not make it out of this one."

"I suppose so," Zea said. "Then let's fight as one."

I nodded, knowing she wouldn't see it, but that she would feel it regardless. I felt Zea raise her hands and felt a rushing surge of heat emanating from her palms as she prepared a large fire invocation to match mine.

We both knew that if we didn't take a significant amount of them out from both sides than we were both goners, but neither of us had seen our deaths yet. It was a small gift, as we knew this meant that we wouldn't have to use our final releases for now. But before we could dwell on that more two voices invoked their way into the fray, one an older woman's who said nothing except to yell, and a younger woman's, who invoked, "Fire Surge!"

A twin flow of invisible force rushed in front of me and blasted the Christened zombies into oblivion from the sheer force of the attack, destroying four, but leaving four more behind. However, before these could reach me, an overwhelming whirlpool of flame rushed ahead and incinerated the undead horde before they could strike back. The Christened zombies flailed about feebly, unable to strike against something that they hadn't seen, thus not having enough time to prepare a barrier to protect themselves. I coughed out dirt that had fallen into my mouth from the destruction of the dome and looked with Zea to see Mara and Cinderella running towards us.

Mara rushed past me and fell down to her knees, clutching Zea tightly, as Mara found herself unable to stop sobbing, as Zea soon followed suit. Zea's hands trembled as she felt a sense of relief return to her mind.

Cinderella hurried to me and bent down, grabbing me around the waist for a hug as well. I hugged her back and smiled. Moments later, she let me go once she confirmed I wasn't hurt and smiled with me.

"Ugh, that was the single worst paintball game I've ever played," I said, still feeling the stinging bullets all over my skin, even though nothing was crafting them anymore.

"Let me help you with that," Cinderella said, placing her hands onto my face. "Balm of Gilead."

A sudden rushing of rejuvenation poured through my nerves, repairing the damage my body had taken from the repeated blows in a matter of seconds. I wasn't fully healed, but I also wasn't feeling the impact of numerous mosquitoes simultaneously attacking me at once.

"Good job, kiddo," I said. "Extend the favor to Zea."

"Okay," Cinderella said, standing up, only to stop in place.

I turned to see what had stopped her and found Mara speaking softly to Zea, saying, "My dearest, I am so sorry that I could not arrive sooner. Please forgive my weakness."

Zea offered a weak smile. "Don't be upset, Mara," she said. "You saved us. You actually invoked today. I thought you weren't able to anymore."

"I would not dare attempt that attack again, dearest, but when I saw your plight, I ignored the pain that prevents my invocations from working properly and poured all that I had in your defense."

"Thank you, Mara."

The two bent their heads so that they mutually nuzzled the other's forehead. Cinderella, not wanting to break up the moment, but also knowing Zea was hurting, bent down and crafted a healing invocation to help Zea's recovery.

Zea, feeling this, removed her embrace from Mara and held a hand to Cinderella's cheek, saying, "You didn't listen to Blake when he said not to come. Thank you for thinking clearly for all of our sakes."

"No!" Cinderella protested. "I just did what I thought was right! I didn't plan anything or really know what I was doing!"

"Just like your teacher always does."

"Hey!" I shouted back, making the three of them laugh.

I fumed silently as they continued to laugh. Finally, Cinderella finished her invocation and helped Mara lift Zea up to stand and then they did the same for me. I brushed myself off and thanked them for their help.

"Well, I'm so glad everyone's sense of humor is still intact when it comes to me," I said, "but how did you two get here?"

"I did as you instructed," Mara said. "However, when I did not feel the presence of a circle on Alcatraz, I tasked Cinderella with finding a paddleboat of our own to utilize in order to reach the island. I am sorry that we were not fit enough to arrive here sooner. We were delayed by the presence of an undead shark, which Initiate Young dispatched of with well-developed skill."

"That so?" I asked, patting Cinderella on the head. "Well done, Red."

Cinderella blushed. "It was nothing," she said.

"What do we do now?" Zea asked.

"It would be wise to leave in our current state," Mara said.

"Okay, I can't believe I'm saying this," I said, "but I agree with Mara. To an extent, at least. I wanted to end things here tonight, but if this keeps up, we'll just drain ourselves. At least if we keep doing what we've been doing. No more rushing in foolishly. Even right now Zea and I are stronger than the two of you, but that won't mean much if we keep invoking attack after attack. We need to find Abraxas and assassinate him before he can make more zombies or mess with any of you. He's already raised Exosso from the dead, so it'd be best if we stop him from doing the same to Endor. We double-back, incinerate her corpse like we should've if we hadn't been in such a rush, and then stalk him until we have the advantage. Any issues with that?"

Cinderella shook her head, while Mara and Zea considered the ideas further until they eventually did the same.

"Then let's finish this," I said.

CHAPTER 24

We trekked back the way Zea and I had come from, eventually ending up past what remained of the dracolich's remains. Zea had regaled the others of our battle with the undead beast and Valefar.

"An impressive feat," Mara said, nodding as she kept up pace with the rest of us. "But it disturbs me as to what a fiend like Valefar would do with the Thyrsus."

"I agree," I said, "but there's little we can do about that now. Add it to the list of next to impossible things we're supposed to solve in the future."

"A list that grows immensely the more you blunder through life." Her tone was dry, but I'd been around her long enough to know she was secretly smiling under her scowl. "However, I am far more concerned of this 'resolve' you mentioned Valefar possessing."

"Do the Archives record anything on them?" Zea asked. "I couldn't even see it and Blake had to cheat to even know they existed."

"I didn't cheat!" I protested. "It was forcibly divulged to me in a very unsettling affair!"

Mara ignored my attention-seeking cries to say, "The term is used several times in the Archives. There are rumors that one of the founders of the Forum possessed such a resolve, but these are unproven. The medieval Moorish king Mambrino was said to possess a helmet that caused him to become invulnerable. If the reports are to be believed he had no such thing, as the helmet was misdirection for his resolve, which allowed him to manipulate events around a certain radius so that objects meant to attack him would miss. His death came about as a result of High Court member Renaud, who slew him by using poisonous gas to fill his lungs, which his resolve was unable to completely remove from the cave that they fought in. There are more that are mentioned in—"

An overwhelming presence forced us all to remain in place. My body shuddered and seemed to want to move in every direction at once. I felt as if my bones were about to shuffle to opposing locations in my body, but when I centered my mind I found that this was merely an illusionary suggestion and that the real threat was the decaying presence that was trying to kill as many of my cells as possible at once.

Icy tendrils of decayed life energy fought against our biology, forcing all of us to focus all of our power on overwhelming it before it seeped further into our very being. I didn't pretend to understand what any of that meant, but I knew that at that moment in time, we'd all had the urge to fight back, as if it was some instinctive awareness gifted by our Christening. I was glad that it had happened, because what little energy I'd allowed to enter me had almost overwhelmed me and forced me to the ground in agony. Looking around, I found my compatriots likewise in this odd turmoil, with Mara down on one knee, her head looking down at the floor. Zea had defied her self-preservation to place a hand on the back of Mara's head to offer her some of her own energy to help fight it off. As a result, the right side of her body was noticeably paler than the rest, unable to protect herself and Mara as well at once. Cinderella, meanwhile, had closed her eyes and planted her feet firmly on the stone floor, using training techniques I'd taught her to ground herself.

"Even now you resist my grand designs," Abraxas' voice said from ahead of us.

We looked over to see him walking into the room, having placed his mask back to cover his face. He glared at the others for a moment before he settled on leering at me with a gaze I could only describe as voyeuristic. Had I not then been fighting to keep myself alive from whatever evocation he'd made to hurt us I'd have been sickened, but I didn't have time for that luxury then.

"I was wondering when you were going to get brave enough to come back for seconds, Spencer," I said as snidely as possible.

I forced myself to call him Spencer in both my words and thoughts. Abraxas was a horror to deal with. The name Abraxas didn't mean anything special that I knew, but in my studies of heresies in the early church, I knew that it had been used by Gnostics for various means from as high a concept as the possible name of God or to simply be used as a charm against evil. Either way, Spencer had wanted to evoke an air of mystery and mysticism beside his renaming of himself and words had power, so if you could destroy that power you could gain power over the name you were fighting against.

I already felt the evocation attacking my body start to splinter and fade when he recoiled at my words, but he steeled himself and a renewed assault oppressed me more than the others, which was a different win, as it meant his power was focusing more on a single target. If enough time passed, the others could break out of the attack and fight while he was worried about what I would do.

But this wouldn't be enough. I also had to think of him as Abraxas too, because if I was too focused on a name he didn't wish to be associated with then my cheap shots would be weaker over time. I had to keep bringing up the old name verbally and mentally, while also fighting those thoughts with the new name he'd chosen for himself. It was ancient power, but very effective if you knew what you were doing and after all my time suffering through my training with the Fae, I was more than prepared for this match.

"It has been some time since lesser men have dared mock me," Abraxas said. "With my immense power, I was able to force them all to become my thralls. I am stronger than they ever were. I fear them no more. Nor do I fear your words."

"That so, Abraxas?" I asked. "Then why do you still keep conjuring the time you got thrown into the dumpster by Chad Erickson after he caught you talking smack about him? Sounds to me like old wounds run deeper than you want to admit, Spencer, and trust me, after what I saw that's not the only thing I could bring up right now to make you remember again."

Abraxas involuntarily stepped back once, but quickly recovered and pointed a finger at me, further increasing his evocation to focus more on me.

"You think that you understand me after witnessing my memories without permission?" Abraxas asked. "You know nothing—to have been gifted so much power only to do what? Save the lives of those far beneath you? What a tremendous waste of ability and talent! With that raw strength you could have

188

conquered the world!"

"And then what?" I asked. "You think this is some kind of game, kid? Do you know how much work that would take? I barely have enough time to enjoy what little entertainment I can find from the past because I keep having to read over paperwork that is so immensely boring, I barely even remember what I'm agreeing to half the time! But I do it anyway, because I know that the people under my care need to be given protection and to find a hope in a world that's given them none! And this is only one city! Could you imagine filing tax returns when you rule the entire world? Yeah, you don't see Doctor Doom or Lex Luthor doing that all the time, do you? Because it's boring! You can't expect to take over the world and there not be consequences for it, Abraxas, so I think I'll just stick to doing what I do so that someone else doesn't have suffer through it!"

I held out an accusatory hand at him, struggling to lift it up despite the immense pressure his spell was making me experience. He glared at me and crossed his hands regally.

"You seek to erode my will," Abraxas said. "This will not happen. I know my true worth in this broken world. I will make my own destiny and I know what I have to do to get what I want." He pointed back at me. "I desire your body."

"Why can't you people learn how to word these concepts differently?" I asked. "It's not that hard!"

"But it's the truth. I require a body as strong as your own for my machinations. Once I discover how to truly transfer consciousnesses, I can overrule your mind and use your body as well as my own as if they were one."

"Wait, if you wanted to take over my body, then why didn't you do it earlier, Spencer?"

Abraxas flinched.

"I mean, it would've been easier, right?" I continued. "I wasn't really awake to resist. Kind of a big oversight on your part, buddy."

"I—I wanted to make sure Endor and Exosso were dead, so that they didn't interfere with me!" Abraxas blurted out, as I could positively feel his pimply face growing redder.

I chuckled, enjoying his failed attempt to save face.

"Now!" I shouted out.

While he'd been focused on me, Abraxas had forgotten all about my three companions, who had broken out of his weakened evocation and were now heading straight to him. Zea was the swiftest and was about to go for Abraxas' head when a femur appeared from nowhere and smacked into her spatha, forcing her to go on the defensive. Mara's shots were intercepted by two spectral figures that rose from the ground and took the blows. Cinderella's fire invocation was likewise interrupted by more shades, who sacrificed themselves to save their master.

Abraxas grinned when he saw our confusion and smugly waved his hands as if directing someone. At that moment, we were greeted by two shambling corpses, but each of them had more vigor than their counterparts and were mumbling evocations as they approached us. Fear encroached on my heart when I recognized both of them, wishing more than ever that I'd gotten to destroy their corpses earlier.

In unison, the zombies of Exosso and En-dor strode into the room, casting maddening evocations that brought skeletal warriors and menacing wraiths into the room with us.

CHAPTER 25

We went on the defensive immediately, as Zea sent out an icy barrier in front of us to aid in our escape. I wished more than ever that Clooney was with us, as his wind invocations would be able to both hide our escape and create mini-maelstroms powerful enough to hinder anyone foolish enough to follow us.

But we didn't live in that world. We lived in the one where ghosts simply passed through the ice wall as their skeletal compatriots pummeled it into oblivion with their enhanced weapons.

I stepped forward to send a ball of light into the closest shades, hitting them before they could reach Mara, who used the brief respite to get into a better position to line up several shots from her rifle that ripped through the few skeletons that Cinderella and Zea had missed with their attacks. We had an advantage in speed and strength, but Abraxas' forces had reserves upon reserves to call upon to fight us. Eventually we would be overwhelmed, which was precisely why I'd wanted to take them out one-by-one, not that old plans mattered anymore.

The thralled Exosso and En-dor summoned even more foes to approach us, their soulless eyes showing no emotion. I bit my lip and did my best to ignore the uncanny feeling I felt when I saw them move. While the undead I'd been dealing with for the past few weeks were already unsettling, it was even worse to see someone I knew fighting, even if they were foes. Abraxas had chosen to watch this unfold, sure that we would be taken down swiftly by their numbers.

But what disturbed me more was their complete control over their thralls despite their own deaths. Christeners could be brought to life in the form of undeath and forced to use the skills that had come naturally to them when they were alive to fight, but not to this extent. It was always feral and based more on sheer power than control. It was the difference between being in a warm room versus the sheer heat of the sun's might at noon. A room's temperature could be controlled by a thermostat, but the sun couldn't be ruled over by the whims of humans. Both could be devastating under the right circumstances, but all one had to do to escape the sun would be to enter a colder environment. A person without the control of a thermostat would always be at the whim of the owner, who could choose to use more pressure as they willed it.

Yet they were both controlling their respective undead forces easily, even with the insane ramblings they made with their mouths. It wasn't possible for this to be done, even under the direction of Abraxas unless—

"—No way!" I shouted. "They've been horcruxing themselves!"

"They've been what?" Zea asked, sending forth a bevy of flames to consume a skeletal archer.

"They've split their souls and used that to put more power into their evocations! That's why some of their spells still work even after they originally died and why En-dor can still control the shades that weren't around earlier! What a stupid, reckless thing to do! No wonder they're so mindless right now!"

"How terrible!" Cinderella declared.

"Who have you been making deals with, Abraxas?" I demanded. "Who taught you to do this twisted sorcery?"

Abraxas laughed, holding out his hands to further the effect like a former Shakespearian actor way past his prime. "He has many names!" he declared. "But he came to us with the name of Death! His mastery of entropic evocation gave us the inspiration to follow his example! Now you will all meet him soon enough!"

I paused. I had never heard of anyone calling themselves Death before, not even the try-hard necromancers of my day. The concept of a Grim Reaper-esque being could be tracked to many folklores, but to our knowledge there was no such thing as a creature known as Death. But I knew from Abraxas' firm recollection of the being that this was no ordinary evoker, especially if he was naturally skilled with entropic evocations. Whoever this was would be an immense threat, but I couldn't worry about that then. Just another pin to add to the conspiracy board if we made it out of there alive.

But we couldn't do that if we died here. We needed to use a big move if we wanted to gain an advantage here.

"Zea and Cinderella, back up and prepare to strike!" I ordered, jumping backward with them.

I shared an idea with Zea, who mentally nodded. I held out my hand to her and she took it. We focused on each other's thoughts, while Cinderella moved to cover Mara. Through our link, we assessed the other's potential and current strength, using what we already knew of each other to formulate what we would need to do next. Zea knew that I unconsciously poured too much energy into my invocations, while she was collected enough to resist this unnecessary use of force to let out exactly as much as she needed. We both had to balance out the outpouring of energy I'd proposed to her if we wanted to do the next step right, but we each had face in the other's control to get the job done.

"Twin Flame—" Zea started.

"—Overwhelming Conflagration!" I finished.

Simultaneously, we sent energy into our connected hands, controlling massive bursts of flame as they appeared in front of us as two balls of orange fire. The inferno surged forward, incinerating the skeletons trying to pass over their fallen brethren to reach us and disrupting the shades' ability to remain corporeal. Exosso and En-dor both fell, but weren't completely consumed by the attack, but their lack of resistance forced Abraxas to hold out his hand and erect a shield to stop the fire from taking him too. However, he'd fallen into a blunder most fools never thought of when dealing with shielding yourself from the flames—you also had to stop the heat from getting past the shield too. Abraxas cried out in pain as his right hand that he'd been using to concentrate on his shield started to grow black from the heat sent his way. But still he soldiered on, pouring more energy into the shield with his other hand, only to see it burn in the same manner.

Zea and I held each other up, knowing we had to regather our strength after a blast that big, even with all the precautions we'd taken. Cinderella maintained her protection of Mara, who, sensing opportunity, fired of bullets at Abraxas. The gunfire was repelled by the caster's shield, but the further stress of the attack caused the necromancer to fall back.

Exosso and En-dor stirred, with their mangled and burnt corpses standing back up to renew their attacks. However, before they could do anything, Cinderella acted first.

"Final Bonfire!" Cinderella cried out, summoning flames from beneath the two undead necromancers.

The two flailed helplessly as their skin turned to cinders and their mindless gibbering was useless without the ability of their master to focus their knowledge into an attack. They fell back to the ground, now completely unusable as weapons to Abraxas, who was slowly forcing himself to retreat to the entrance of the hallway.

We heard moaning come from behind Abraxas, letting us know that he was about to be reinforced if we weren't quick enough.

"It's over, Abraxas," I said, stepping forward. "Surrender and tell us everything you found out during these hundred years if you know what's good for you."

"Never!" Abraxas yelled defiantly. "I still have something for the likes of you!"

Holding out his burnt right hand, I saw the still immaculate form of the Bone Ring. He managed to feebly form a fist that allowed him to point it at me.

"Your body is mine, boy!" Abraxas commanded.

A swirl of purple, red, and black necromantic energy surrounded the Bone Ring and I felt its enmity towards me that was separate from its current master's ambitions. I steeled myself for whatever came next, only to be let down when the energy dissipated from the ring and left it behind. That was new. Why wouldn't the ring listen to him? If anything, it made sense for it to work more for a necromancer than myself, yet Abraxas had failed.

Abraxas stared down at the Bone Ring on his finger and wrenched it off, looking at it as he placed it in his left hand's palm as if he was about to scold a child.

"The ring's useless to you!" I declared. "It only recognizes me as its master!"

I had no clue if I was anywhere close to the truth, but it sounded cool, at least, and had distracted Abraxas enough to loosen his grip on the Bone Ring. Before he could react, Zea raced forward, slicing off Abraxas' left hand with her spatha, as she caught the falling ring with her free hand and ran away from the necromancer, who yelled out in anguish at the loss of his limb. I wondered why Zea hadn't gone for a second strike to finish him, but I witnessed a horde of Abraxas' zombies entering the room to surround their master, who would have attacked her had she stayed there.

"Catch!" Zea exclaimed, throwing the ring at me.

Having already sensed where it would end up thanks to our mental link, I moved to the left and snatched it out of the air, placing it back on my left ring finger. I felt a pulsation of dark power reverberating from my body, but other than that the Bone Ring made no attempts to assert its power.

"Well," I said, grumbling, "better on me than him."

Zea appeared beside me, weapon at the ready for what was next. Cinderella and Mara were awaiting my orders, not sure what to do about the zombie horde surrounding their master, and were for some strange reason not attacking us. We'd all expended too much energy through the many fights we'd been forced into in such little time. If we weren't careful, we'd end up all looking as bad as Abraxas, so we patiently waited to gather more energy for what was to come.

A singular zombie shambled to its master and kneeled beside him in an odd form of what appeared to be supplication. Abraxas held his burnt hands over the zombie, and we watched as what was left of the zombie's life force entered its master's body, barely restoring any of his wounds as the zombie crumbled to dust.

"It's not enough, Spencer!" I called out. "You're outnumbered here, so just give up!"

"Death!" Abraxas roared. "Hear my cry and heed my words! I relinquish my soul to you! Just give me the power I need to kill my enemies!"

We watched in horror as a deathly chill surrounded us from every direction with a force much stronger than Abraxas' initial attack. I didn't know why, but I felt a resonance in this power that felt familiar, with paradoxical affection and hatred mixed into it.

To our surprise, a spectral figure surrounded by a deathly void of arcane energies came from nowhere and stood beside the wounded Abraxas. Despite the feelings I'd sensed from it, the being completely ignored us and instead gazed down at Abraxas.

The figure didn't seem to have a body, even though there was something humanoid about it simply from its general shape, but I felt as if this figure was merely an avatar of some sort.

"Pitiful, Abraxas," it said, almost like a scolding father, but with a deathly pulse of mental reverberation to match the cold air it crafted. "All those years of training and this is how you end up? All that wasted, lost time." It paused. "You wish to gift me your soul? I accept. All souls belong to Death, no matter what form I take. Here, a gift for a gift."

The figure naming itself Death bent down and held out its right hand to Abraxas, who grasped it quickly as his body spasmed uncontrollably. Death let out something resembling a cackle as eldritch energy forced itself into Abraxas' body. Then, the ritual complete, Death took one look at me and, even without a visible face, I felt it smile at me, as it left us behind, getting rid of the deathly presence we'd felt ever since it had arrived there.

But before we could make sense of anything, Abraxas' body spasmed even more as sparks of black energy surrounded his body, causing the necromancer to rise into the air, his body slowly healing itself back to where it had been before our attack. Abraxas' body swelled, his extremities staring to grow in size, as the rest of him followed suit, grabbing the dwindling life force of his zombie horde to gift him with further size and strength until he stood at a little over thirteen feet tall.

Barely appearing human anymore, Abraxas now resembled a twisted and bent man who seemed to have been kneaded like dough to form a hulking monstrosity. He lumbered forward with one overgrown hand slumping on the ground.

"I will master the Bone Ring," he said, his voice echoing with more baritone than in his previous form. "And I will have your soul to exchange for mine, Blake. I am Abraxas Reborn!"

He opened his mouth and a spiral of dark energy swirled to form a beam of power headed straight for Mara. I lunged forward to take the blast for Mara, only realizing that something else was willing to protect me from myself when a purple-black flash emanated from the Bone Ring and swallowed the evocation whole. I landed on the ground hard, but pushed myself back up swiftly, staring with the others as I felt the power surging through me and the ring. Grinning, I realized exactly what I had to do now to stop them all.

"You wanted this ring so bad?" I asked, holding it outward for them to see. "Well, you're about to get very intimate with it."

CHAPTER 26

You ever say something cool and then immediately regret it because you had no idea how to actually do the cool thing you said you'd do?

Asking for a friend.

In unrelated news, once again I'd opened my dumb mouth before I could think of the consequences and was hit by another blast of cold energy that sent me flying into the wall. I fell, the impact knocking the wind out of me, which was quickly restored when Zea rushed to my side to perform a swift healing invocation to keep me alive.

"What is going on?" Zea asked, trying to focus on her invocation and ignore the growing fear we both felt rising within our thoughts.

"This is new to me!" I declared, watching as Abraxas Reborn's body was about to move ahead to strike us. "But if I had to guess we're not doing so hot!"

"I am aware of that! What do we do about it?"

"Scatter and try to find a weakness! We're not getting out of this without putting him down for good!"

Zea nodded and dashed to my left, as Cinderella went in the opposite direction, muttering an invocation under her breath that crafted a fire veil around herself. Mara, meanwhile, had shot at the abomination several more times with her rifle, but to no avail.

"Fools!" Abraxas Reborn shouted out, chuckling madly. "I cannot be harmed by such trifles! I am infinite!"

He rushed ahead, his lumbering limbs trying to take me out like a rabid linebacker, but I was barely able to dodge under the blow and roll back to my feet to avoid him.

I grunted and tried to focus on a strategy as Abraxas Reborn recovered from his initial strike. My plan to mess with his control over his evocations was kaput now that he'd received this powerup. He'd even renamed himself, which would've been more difficult to deal with now that I had three names to worry about, so I needed a new plan.

But what the hell had just happened here? I had seen the brief glimpse of the being that Abraxas had called Death when I'd initially gazed into the eyes of every member of Morior Invictus, but our finite exchange hadn't given me more than that image, so I had no context for what he was supposed to be. Yet I had to deal with what little I knew about this person if I wanted to win this fight.

Whoever it was had to be extremely powerful to show up when summoned only by name and yet still hold power over the summoner. That could mean a myriad of things: Fae, demon, stronger evoker; the list went on and on. I had no chance on narrowing that list down, so there had to be something else I could focus on, but my mind kept drawing blanks.

"*Fiat lux!*" I cried, sending a barrage of light straight into Abraxas Reborn's corrupted face.

The behemoth staggered for a moment, but dark energy poured over the area I'd damaged and instantly repaired it.

I grunted and watched as Zea and Cinderella strike at once with a lightning and fire invocation, respectively. The lightning crackled through Abraxas Reborn, making the hulking monstrosity cry out in pain as the fire cascaded all over his body, burning him harshly. But the exact same response came as it had for my light invocation, essentially retconning their actions.

Few people could heal themselves well with evocation, especially when hit with such ferocity as Abraxas Reborn had, but it had still happened. But there was a limit to what even the most trained Christener could do. We had to overwhelm the beast without being overwhelmed ourselves. But how? What were we missing? How were we supposed to deal with a power created by an outside context problem like Death?

Wait a moment, I thought. *I have an outside context solution working for me! Nathan-Prime, I need your help!*

Silence greeted my mind.

You're worthless! I protested. *If I get my hands on you, I'll wring the life out of you!*

199

Further silence continued in my mind.

No, I said, scolding myself. *He's done enough. If he chooses to do more that means he has to. He's not saying anything right now, because I have a solution to this problem. I just need to figure it out.*

But what? Knowing I had an answer didn't automatically give me one.

I felt a pulsation ripple from my left ring finger and looked down to see the Bone Ring glowing. Was it really that simple? True, I'd swallowed the blast that had almost taken down Mara earlier, but I'd also been hit by one not too long after it.

How had I done it? Was it the ring's doing or mine? I had to find a way to permanently use its power at will, rather than on a recharge if I wanted to survive this fight. But what was the trigger?

I had a guess, but no proof, but when had that ever stopped me?

"Come on, ya necromantic weaboo!" I taunted, focusing Abraxas Reborn's attention to me. "Hit me with your best shot!"

I waved him on condescendingly and he took the bait immediately, uttering out an insane evocation that crafted another orb of arcane necromantic evocation at me. Praying that I wasn't as dumb as I knew I was, I held out my left hand and imagined it protecting me like it had when I'd jumped in front of Mara. True to form, the eyes on the dragon grew red and as soon as the orb made contact with the Ring, the evocation was swallowed whole by the ring.

I glanced down at the ring and pumped my right fist. I'd been right. Intent was the trigger for it to work. I'd been thinking about protecting Mara, so that had made the ring swallow the initial blast.

But what if that wasn't all it could do? I recalled the many times I'd been forced to use the ring to save my skin. Where did it get its power from? I hadn't empowered it with any necromantic energy, yet that was precisely the evocation source I'd felt whenever I'd used it in the past.

An idea occurred to me and I grinned. What if the ring was built to trap that very same energy so it could empower itself? It was perfect for a necromancer to use. They could store the Christening within themselves into the ring over time without truly

200

losing anything themselves. Any energy they lost would be restored within hours if they were healthy, so what was the harm in supplying the ring with occasional bits of their own power if it meant they could store it for later use?

Which meant that the energy the Bone Ring had swallowed throughout the fight was also available to return to sender.

"All right, Bone Ring, do your thing!" I called out, pointing the ring at Abraxas Reborn, who'd been distracted by a barrage of gunfire from Mara and Zea's attempt to attack him with her spatha.

Mystical death swirled around the Bone Ring, causing the very same attack that Abraxas Reborn had just sent to me to repel itself back to its originator. Before he could react, the very confused necromancer was blasted back by his own power, forcing him to the ground.

"Yes!" I cried out in victory. "I am a genius!"

Zea took advantage of the brief respite and attacked Abraxas Reborn while he was down, impaling her blade into the beast's abdomen, while Cinderella pumped a volley of fire over his legs, hoping to fully incinerate them while he was indisposed. The behemoth roared in anguish and Zea was forced back by the force of his voice, making her temporarily retreat.

"It's still not enough!" Abraxas Reborn protested, pushing himself up despite the pain. "But I know what to do to empower myself further! You two will finally be useful to me!"

Abraxas Reborn pointed to the husks of his former comrades and sent a purple-black beam out to the both of them that surrounded the corpses and forced them into the air. The corpses rushed towards him and were forcibly merged with their new master, who grew further in size from the eldritch necromantic ritual. Their faces merged with Abraxas, making a trio of mouths each fighting for control of the body.

"Oh, come on," I said, almost in a whisper.

Turning to face me, the restored Abraxas Reborn laughed with reckless abandon and held out his hands, summoning shades from nowhere that were complemented by a newly-raised horde of skeletons and zombies.

"We are here as one!" Abraxas Reborn cried out with his own voice combined with En-dor and Exosso's as well. "We are Morior Invictus united! We will rule over the world with the dead as our only companions!"

"Their souls are still around here?" I asked, cringing in further disbelief. "Just how many times did you idiots split them?"

This was no time to complain, which meant that it was the perfect time to complain, not that it would help any of us. I had to think even faster. We couldn't keep this up. I was feeling drained the more I stayed in this fight. Mara was panting, barely concentrating as she placed another magazine in her rifle, which seemed to be her last. Cinderella was almost totally worn out, hanging on merely out of obligation to the rest of us. Zea would last a little longer, but if we went down, she would be overwhelmed soon too.

But what could I do? I couldn't make a teleportation circle in time to get us all out of here in time now that we were scattered. The only thing that had been useful in this fight was the Bone Ring and I was still figuring it out as I went along.

Which was when a dastardly scheme entered my mind.

"I have a plan: the Bone Ring is empowered by drawing in necromantic energy," I said, grinning. "Now what else here possesses that type of energy?" I snapped my fingers. "Oh, right— all of you."

Abraxas Reborn's jaw fell agape as what was left of En-dor and Exosso's minds allowed them to field the same reaction.

"You wouldn't dare," Abraxas Reborn said.

"It's just crazy enough to work," I said, holding out my left hand in a balled fist with the ring pointed directly at them. "And I'm just stupid enough to test that hypothesis."

Holding out the Bone Ring again, I imagined a swirling vortex that would draw them in within the ring. I had no idea if this was going to work, but improvising and making it look like I knew what I was doing was exactly why I was still alive. To my immense glee, I watched as a tiny black hole of pulsating black and red energy appeared in front of the Bone Ring.

"You can't possibly be so foolish!" Abraxas Reborn protested. "Don't you know how the Bone Ring works?"

"Nope, but there's no time like the present to find out!" I said, attempting to sound more confident than I was.

The vortex in front of the ring grew larger with every passing second. Abraxas Reborn contemplated firing more necromantic energy to distract me, but knew this was a bad idea, so they did the smart thing and started running away.

But their momentary hesitation had made all the difference when it came to the growing power of the Bone Ring, which made the vortex swell in size to be taller than me. Rushing winds sucked in everything around the ring and I struggled to stand up straight. Zea and Cinderella had each had the clarity of mind to get out of the way as soon as their maniac of a leader had made a black hole, so I didn't have to worry about their welfare.

Abraxas Reborn attempted to grab onto a nearby pillar, but their legs were already in the air, ready to be sucked in by the Bone Ring the moment they couldn't attach to anything. My head spun as I tried resisting the ring's influence further, but I maintained my control over the hurricane as best I could, knowing it was still our best option in this fight. Or at least I was until one of the seals on my body pulsated with a strong purple coloration even being visible from underneath my clothes.

Then two things happened at once. The first was that Abraxas Reborn was forced to let go of their pillar and were sucked into the Bone Ring. The second was that my fight against the ring came to an end, but in a different way, as I felt my body remain in place, while my mind was pulled into the world held within the Bone Ring, leaving reality behind to a world filled with darkness and uncertainty.

CHAPTER 27

A mental interpretation of my own brain greeted my eyes. I was in a dark place, with the only light the placed provided being centered around the brain. I muttered an invocation and an orb of light situated itself above my head.

I looked out to see various nerve-like things filled with energy all connecting with the brain in the distance. They flashed with red and blue lights whenever I saw what I assumed to be mental impulses or thoughts moving through them. At least I think that's what it was. Truth is I had no idea what I was seeing.

"This is like some crazy mind dimension," I said. "Is this actually my brain or some kind of mental construct to ease myself into seeing it? Am I really inside my own mind right now?"

"Indeed, you are, Blake Azarel," Abraxas said, appearing beside me.

I wheeled around and charged up an attack, but he moved away from me with intense speed. To my left I barely registered Exosso in time to swerve out of the way of his attack. I heard En-dor cry out some evocation and spun away to avoid it, barely missing out on being a flame broiled chicken. Somehow when they had entered the Bone Ring the three of them had been stripped of their final form and were now back in their original bodies or spirits for that matter, as I had no idea what the four of us actually were at the time.

"Fools!" Abraxas yelled. "Don't kill him yet! If you kill him before I assimilate into his mind, then he dies, and we die with him! We must make his body and soul think that we are him first!"

"I would never share his power with you!" En-dor cried out. "Can you not sense his potential? Right now his body is fighting his fellows! The rage! The sheer might! It's just so intoxicating to the mind!"

"Yes, I can!" Exosso exclaimed. "And that is why I will claim it before any of you!"

I paused. I hadn't stopped to think about that before. If I was here in my head, then who was controlling my body? If no one was controlling it, but I was still alive did that mean it was some kind of semi-soulless shell? They claimed that it was fighting my friends right now.

Blake...Stop fighting us...I love you...Please come back to me...

That was Zea's voice. She was mentally calling to me from outside of my body. That meant they had to be fighting me right now. That wasn't good. They'd already fought enough, but to fight me while my body didn't act like I would? It wouldn't hold back the enormous reserves of power that I stored over time and nor would it be discriminatory about the range or intensity of any evocations it performed. If I didn't regain control quickly, I could wake up to find them all dead.

No. This was my mind. I was in control. To hell with these necromancers. I wanted to live.

"No more," I said, waving my hands in front of myself. "*Fiat lux!*"

Light erupted throughout the mind dimension, completely eradicating the darkness. The light swarmed around the three necromancers and forced them onto the ground I constructed from the light. It penetrated them harshly, making them all cry out in terror as I ripped through their bodies with the light.

But then I realized my mistake when the bodies disappeared from sight.

"An illusion!" I cried out, turning around to find them behind me.

Exosso clubbed me in the head with a femur construct, while En-dor kicked me in the shins. While I fell Abraxas surrounded me with a conjured straitjacket and when I hit the ground of the mind dimension I realized I couldn't get out. I knew all I had to do was wish it away, but my head was throbbing in pain. I was amazed I was still conscious.

"There will be no more light here, boy," Abraxas said. "Your body is ours."

"Yeah, I'm pretty sure that puts you on some kind of list,"

Nathan-Prime's voice echoed throughout the mind dimension.

I looked around, trying to find the source as the momentary distraction allowed me to break out of the straitjacket. The three necromancers entered defensive positions and eyed me closely, but kept on the lookout for the source of the voice.

"I'm over here, children," Nathan-Prime's voice said, allowing us to finally see him.

Nathan-Prime sat right in front of the visual representation of my brain in a rocking chair next to a warm fireplace. There was a camera crew to his right that were filming everything, and I started to have the oddest PBS flashbacks. In his left hand was a pipe that didn't have anything inside of it and yet smoke rings seemed to form every time he puffed into it. In his right hand was a children's picture book entitled *Protective Seals for Dummies*.

Beside him was the blonde-haired woman from my earlier visions, but most of her facial features were obscured by some kind of fog. She smiled warmly at me with her hands behind her back, but said nothing out loud. She shined brilliantly, with the light seemingly generated from her clothes.

"Well, hello, children, and welcome back to *Story Time With Nathan-Prime*, starring yours truly as himself!" Nathan-Prime announced warmly, while rocking back in the chair and fake smoking with the pipe.

The four of us stared at him with confused expressions on our faces. I knew that Nathan-Prime was the one responsible for the seals on my body, but he still hadn't told me what they were for. Instead he'd been needlessly cryptic and condescending, which made me realize that I was in an abusive relationship.

"Who are you?" Abraxas demanded as he called forth a wave of water to try and smother Nathan-Prime.

However, the water disappeared the moment it would have hit the "recording studio" Nathan-Prime was using. Instead, it reappeared behind us and got everyone but me soaked. The blonde-haired woman covered her mouth to laugh and gently nudged Nathan-Prime like a sibling might when their older brother made a dumb joke.

"Why I do believe that it's time for an exposition dump, wouldn't you say so, children?" Nathan-Prime asked with one of the smuggest grins I'd ever seen. "Now please, won't you take a seat, neighbor?"

A powerful force erupted behind me and picked me up before I could react. I watched as the same thing happened to the others and we found ourselves seated in chairs that appeared from nothingness. The necromancers yelled out their displeasure and Nathan-Prime motioned with his right hand, using his middle finger, index finger, and thumb to pantomime someone shutting up, causing their mouths to seal.

"Isn't it better when we all just wait our turn to speak and listen to our elders, children?" Nathan-Prime asked, sitting back in his chair. "Yes, all of you. Just because you've been alive for over a hundred years doesn't mean you hold a candle to me. I believe the word 'trillions' has been thrown around to describe my relativistic experience and that's extremely lowballing it."

Nathan-Prime rocked back and forth in the chair, obviously enjoying himself. I waited for him to speak. Clearly, he had something big in mind for us, although with every passing moment my body would be able to hurt my friends. Didn't he know that? I needed to take control now before anyone else could. Now was my chance. Why wasn't he letting me go?

"Oh, ye Blake of little faith," Nathan said, smirking. "I'm just wasting time while I repay the debt I owe you for what you did for me in Israel."

"Israel?" I repeated. "I've never been to Israel."

"Not yet at least. Well actually you have, but not in a state that would be younger than you are now. Isn't time travel just a real pain?"

The blonde-haired woman waved her hand in a continuous motion in front of Nathan-Prime's face with an annoyed expression on her face. He winked at her and chuckled. She rolled her eyes and covered another laugh.

"Fine, fine, you always know what's best, don't you, ya imaginary twerp," Nathan-Prime said with mock condescension. "Well if you'll turn to the next page of the books in front of you, we can all be on the same track, children."

Four copies of *Protective Seals for Dummies* appeared in front of the four of us and flipped over to the page Nathan-Prime had indicated. There was a very crude (surely intentional) drawing of myself there wherein I was wearing a shirt that said "I'm With

Stupid" that had an arrow pointing up to my face. I had no time to protest as Nathan-Prime continued with his newest lesson.

"Now, children, what you see before you is a dumb shmuck in his native habitat," Nathan-Prime said. "We'll call him Blake. He's a funny guy, isn't he? Thinking that he's smart and understands the world around him, but oh no, what's that in the next page?"

The page flipped again, showing the crude me now surrounding in the dark by a bunch of creatures with menacing red eyes.

"Looks like Blake bit off a little more than he could chew, didn't he?" Nathan-Prime asked. "But don't worry, children, he's fine. Because his friends are there to back him up."

The page flipped once more, revealing the presence of the Dream Team, who attacked the dark creatures and wiped them out with my help. The page after that showed us all hugging and congratulating each other on a job well done.

"Now what you see before you, children," Nathan-Prime continued, "is how things were supposed to go when people were doing their jobs correctly. Christeners looking out not for their own self-interests, but for the world's best interests. What does this have to do with the seals? Well, just be patient, children, because the story's not over yet."

The book moved forward and I was now alone, wearing the black uniform I'd seen upon meeting Tamayo. I was hiding in the shadows, avoiding the notice of what seemed to be a group of Sanguine Collective searching parties as I held onto scraps of paper from some old tome that hadn't seen the light of day for hundreds of years.

"But not all things stay gold, children," Nathan-Prime said. "Sometimes, because other people aren't doing the job they're supposed to, good people have to act outside the law in order to save others, even if it means they can't talk to their friends about it or be acknowledged for the good works they're doing. Such is the case here, where our pal Blake is doing his best to stop the bad guys from hurting the world more than they already have. But what's with those papers, you ask? Well, there's a reason nothing's written down here, because only one other person knows what happens there and he doesn't remember, although this time, he chose not to remember, outside of the amnesia he's used to now.

208

"Why, you ask? Because sometimes, children, there are dark and terrible things out there that must never be exposed to others. Evil forces that wish nothing but death and destruction upon all who would seek them out and use their eldritch knowledge. Forces that despite humans for being the favored creations of the Almighty while they were formed from chaotic energies crafted by the Fall."

The page flipped to a new two-page spread, showing me engaged with a being I couldn't properly see with my mind. I recognized myself using light and darkness invocations to combat it, but when my eyes tried to focus on the creature, I saw nothing but hazy mist.

"And because they hate humans, children," Nathan-Prime said, "these Abominations and Interlopers will do whatever they can to destroy humanity, which is why good people like our pal Blake here took it upon themselves to fight back, despite knowing the consequences for such knowledge. But that fight takes a toll not only on the body, but the mind and soul, causing our pal Blake to get hurt in ways that no human should ever suffer, for the true price would be their sanity."

The pages flipped for the final time, showing me kneeling down before two women, one with red hair and her back to the page and the blond-haired woman standing beside Nathan-Prime. The two women were holding their hands over me and seemed to be absorbing something from me, while also crafting the seals on my body. A fourth figure shorter than the others was there as well, but shrouded in darkness, although I sensed no ill intent from their image.

"And now we come to a close, children," Nathan-Prime said, smiling. "What we see here are three very brave people, who know the risks and choose to fight anyways, because they know the importance of risking everything for the good of others. They agree to take on each other's burdens, no matter the cost, which creates the initial seals placed on our pal Blake. These are made to keep his knowledge and corruption within himself, thus preventing it from spreading to others and protecting them from the eldritch untruths he understands better than anyone else on his world. But that's not all they do.

"You see, children, the seals you saw on your favorite

possession actually work twofold. They actively keep people out of his body if he hasn't given his consent for them to enter and it prevents you from jumping out of here without his say so. The reason you were able to get in here in the first place was both because he wanted to trap you here and because I was able to remotely deactivate the part of the seal that would make Blake's plan untenable. Now, if I were you, I'd start sucking up to him if you wanted to make it out of here, but we all know that won't happen, now, isn't that right, children?"

We were released from our chairs and I stared ahead at the book, wishing I could know more than was being presented to me, but my thoughts were interrupted by Morior Invictus, who clearly still didn't understand the danger they were in. The trio set aside their grievances and held the other's hands, summoning a powerful blast of entropic evocation that barreled into Nathan-Prime and the blonde-haired girl. But when it impacted them, it merely made a *tink!* noise and was deflected away from them.

Nathan-Prime looked to his companion and rolled his eyes. She waved her hand at him to get it over with and he stood up, transforming back into his normal appearance, although this time he was holding a silver sword in his right hand and a huge red, black, and silver scythe in his left. In a flurry of light and rose petals, Nathan-Prime disappeared from sight and reappeared behind Exosso, who was decapitated by the scythe at the same time that En-dor was bisected by the shining sword. Abraxas had started to run away, but Nathan-Prime appeared in front of him, blocking his escape as he sheathed his weapons and held out his hands to his right side, crafting a swirling volley of green energy in his palms.

"Star Blazer!" he cried out, sending out this green energy outwards instantly.

The sudden attack increased in size to fourteen feet in height and twenty-four feet in width, consuming everything in its path. Abraxas barely had time to scream before he was exterminated by the blast. Then, almost bored, Nathan-Prime shook his head and went back to his seat.

As he did, the world around my mind changed, this time crafting more light that allowed me to see in every direction with perfect vision. I sighed, glad that, for now, the nightmare was over and I sat back in my own chair, my fatigue catching up with me.

I became aware of a presence near me and opened my eyes, finding the blonde girl hovering over me, offering some of her energy to me. She smiled sweetly at me and returned to stand beside Nathan-Prime, as memories started flashing in my mind.

I had seen this girl somewhere before. I knew it without any doubt. But from where?

A vague memory played in my mind from the previous year, where I had seen a vision of a girl with long, blonde hair. It was only now that I had realized that I had only viewed this girl from the side, and therefore hadn't noticed that blonde wasn't the only color of her hair at the time.

On the left side of her head, she was covered with shoulder-length blonde hair. In the middle of her head, her hair was mostly black with occasional streaks of white. Finally, on her head's right side, the hair was instead a dark red, one that almost looked black in the right light. She smiled warmly at me, as if greeting an old friend she hadn't seen in a long time, but she made no effort to speak.

It was that moment that I realized that using the term "girl" was a misnomer. She didn't look it, but I had a sudden urging to realize that she was older—way older than anyone there, save Nathan-Prime. She felt and looked harmless enough with a first glance, but the more that I stared at her, the more I realized just how well-crafted this façade was. She radiated pure power, similar to Nathan-Prime's, and was clearly above my weight class.

She smiled again, somehow realizing the depths of my thoughts, and then bowed lowly to me. "My name is Naminé Créatrice Parker," she said. "I am the one who stole your memories from you."

I looked at her and then to Nathan-Prime. "Please don't tell me there's someone running out there calling themselves Xeblak or Blaxek right now," I said.

Nathan-Prime snorted. "Wrong series," he said.

"Although that is where I get my first name," Naminé said. "It's a little complicated, but it's the name Nathan gave me after he rescued me from the sorcerer who made me."

"Made you?" I asked, scanning her features further. "What are you some kind of robot? Clone?" I paused. "Tulpa?"

Naminé grinned and nodded. "I'll explain later, when we meet again for real. But for now, we need you to understand how you were able to do what you did here."

"Reckless as always, Blake," Nathan-Prime noted, "but I do love indulging optimists, so I must say it was fun to watch you make it all up on the fly. Had you not done as you did, we would not be talking now, as I am forbidden from physically appearing in your world, as you know. But I'm sure you have questions and we can answer some of them. Let's start with the Bone Ring. Earlier you asked me about the ring and its properties, and I was somewhat vague about it. For the most I will continue this course of action, save to say that only someone trained in resisting it will be able to control it well without depending on its power like its master did when he created it. Guard it with your very life, Blake. No one must gain access to its power, for its true worth is beyond what you have seen so far."

I nodded. At least it was somewhat of an answer to a question.

"Are they gone?" I asked. "Morior Invictus?"

"Had I not intervened here," Nathan-Prime said, "they would have remained as shades until eventually their consciousnesses had merged with the ring's power, causing them to lose control over themselves and perish for good. But yes, they are gone for good. Even had I not intervened you would have vanquished them, but not without cost that you were better off not paying. Their power has been added to the ring's wealth for future use should you need it."

"What's going to happen to the undead hordes across the Dead Lands? They split their souls, so they should still have power even after death."

"Normally, yes," Naminé said, "but because they died as they did that power has instead been added to the Bone Ring. Any undead constructs they formed are in the process of true decay and will plague the world no more."

"Good. If there are any survivors left, we'll send word to them to get to Corpus Christi as best we can." I paused. "Earlier Exosso attempted to mess with my bones. How did I resist his attacks? He should've been able to snap a bone or ligament to render me powerless to fight back, but he couldn't. I wasn't doing anything to actively stop this, so how was I able to no sell it?"

Nathan-Prime frowned for a moment, but swiftly replaced it

with a smile. "Because your wife taught you how," he said, simply.

"She did? What's her name? Who was she? How did she know how to do this?"

"Questions for later. I promise you the wait will be worth it."

"Don't mind him," Naminé interjected. "He's just mad I was right about who'd be the one to save this world."

Nathan-Prime grimaced at her and Naminé laughed heartily, this time not bothering to cover her face. I smiled, despite not understanding what was going on, until a sudden question popped into my mind.

"Wait—are you my wife?" I asked.

Naminé laughed even harder. "You're not my type, Blake," she said. "Sorry, but I've got another man to deal with later—also before—and trust me, he's trouble enough without bringing you into the picture."

"Fair enough. You can do better for yourself." I laughed at my own joke, but recalled the sudden appearance of Death and shuddered. "That...thing that empowered Abraxas. What was it?"

"Your true foe, who arrived earlier than should have occurred," Nathan-Prime said. "He has many names, with Death being one of them. No, he is no Grim Reaper or Shinigami. His kind has been associated with Death for some time, but he leeches off of those who have been forced to succumb to his power, transferring his soul from one unwilling victim to the next, so that he could gather power over the ages with means any reasonable person would find utterly reprehensible. But he will not attack you directly. He is afraid of a prophecy, one leaked to him by its prophet, who spoke in a manner that has caused the few who know of its existence to not know the full truth of the matter. To answer any further questions, no, you will not have to fight him for some time, but you are in this fight in order to prepare for that final bout. Perhaps it is better for you to have seen him before you were meant to, perhaps not. Either way, Blake, know that you must prepare for his true coming, no matter the cost."

I nodded. "Given that you've stopped talking," I said, "I'm gonna take that as a hint that I can't know more than what you've said."

Nathan-Prime nodded.

"Then I think I have one final round of questions," I said. "Is there a reason you chose to show yourself to me, Naminé?"

"Because we need you to save me," Naminé said.

"Save you? Aren't you here now?"

"Yes, because you saved me in my past—your future. It hasn't happened yet, but it will. Other than what you already did to help me the first time."

"Gorram time travel," I muttered under my breath.

"I understand your frustration. It was no fun being sealed away on your world, but trust me: it will all make sense one day. I did what I did to ensure the safety of your future. I'm going to help restore your memories, Blake. I promise this."

I looked her in the eyes, but nothing happened. Either I was unable to see the truth in her eyes or it was impossible to attempt it with her in the first place, but I saw the look on her face. She was sincere.

"Where are you?" I asked. "How can I free you from whatever seal's been placed on you?"

"You won't know until you find it," Nathan-Prime interjected. "Trust in your heart. The breadcrumbs will come soon, but you need to follow them. It won't be today, and it won't be tomorrow, but you will do what I cannot for my sister. It is your place to do so, Blake. Just be prepared for the consequences."

I nodded. "I don't pretend to understand, but I'll be on the lookout for them. This I swear. I give you my Word, Naminé."

Naminé smiled sweetly. "Then I know it will be done," she said.

"And with that, our business is concluded," Nathan-Prime said. "Until next we meet, Blake. Well done and may the Almighty be with you in accordance to His will."

Snapping his fingers, I watched as Nathan-Prime and Naminé disappeared as my mind was forced back to reality.

CHAPTER 28

I woke up, seeing Zea hovering over my body, which had fallen on the floor sometime in-between the last moment I'd been sucked inside the Bone Ring and now. My shirt and trench coat had been taken off and laid neatly beside my body and I felt a coolness in the air. A flash of relief filled Zea's face when she noticed my recovery and she swiftly wrapped her arms around me and hugged me. I groaned in pain, feeling muscles spasm and bones creak from wounds I hadn't been aware of until now. Zea quickly let go of me and a panicked expression overtook her former relief.

"Blake, I'm so sorry!" Zea said, placing a hand on my exposed chest, crafting a healing invocation to repair what she'd previously been unaware of before my pained cries. "I didn't know how bad the damage was and then you woke up and I was just so happy to see you were okay and—"

I held up a hand and smiled. "I know very well how you like to do your medical exams," I said, trying to smile, but stopping when it hurt to move those particular muscles. "Now please just don't make it hurt any worse."

"Understood. I'll do just that!"

Zea eyed my body, pouring more healing invocations throughout it, which were slowly repairing the damage I'd taken ever since getting slugged in the back of the head upon arriving on Alcatraz.

I nodded and looked over to see Cinderella barely restraining herself from trying to hug me too upon my recovery and a stoically calm Mara gazing at me.

"Now that you are beginning to be well, Guardian Azarel," Mara said, "would you kindly explain just what occurred so that we may understand what we just witnessed?"

"Sure," I said, feeling my jaw start to lose any strain it had suffered earlier thanks to Zea's intervention. "But first, is everyone else okay?"

"We are well. Zea and Cinderella were most capable while you were indisposed and were able to heal most of the damage that we suffered. Now please explain the events that occurred while your mind was elsewhere."

"Well that's good to hear. So what happened while I was out? Well I sucked all of Morior Invictus into my mind, fought them there, got lectured again by Nathan-Prime, watched all the necromancers get ganked, got lectured again by a triple-colored-haired girl, and then came back here."

Mara, Zea, and Cinderella exchanged mutual confused looks to each other.

"I suppose that doesn't really explain anything, does it?" I asked. "So what had happened was that the Bone Ring here is attracted to necromantic and entropic energy. I, figuring this out in the heat of battle, decided to use it to suck them into it, but got caught myself, because I'm not strong enough yet to fully control it. So when I got in there with them I had to fight their, well, mental...imprints of themselves? I think. But before I could do anything to them, Nathan-Prime and a friend talked to us, explaining that together they had both made the seals placed on my body to protect me from some nasty things from before the whole trip-to-the-future thing. They took care of the necromancers and told me that while they couldn't intervene physically, my mind or the world within the Bone Ring was fair game. Cheating, as per usual. Then they told me that I need to figure out how to regain my memories and sent me back here, while warning us about that Death guy who showed up. Does any of that make sense?"

"As much as anything does in our line of work," Mara noted. "Especially when the issues revolve around you."

"Thanks for the glowing support. Now what happened here while I was out? I could hear Zea's voice in my head, but I think those were more thoughts than spoken word, unless I'm entirely off base."

"They were," Zea confirmed. "But as to what happened, you suddenly started running around and casting evocations wildly,

216

barely using anything we recognized as a language. You hit each of us with different blasts, but we managed to recover and try to restrain you."

I paused. That was horrifying. An unhinged Christener could do a lot of irreparable damage if taken off the leash of sanity. The fact that they were all alive was a testament to their skill and quick thinking.

"I'm so sorry," I said, frowning. "But how were you able to stop me?"

Zea blushed. "Well...do you remember last year when you told me that you gave me your consent for me to control your body so I could help heal you?" she asked.

"Yes..."

"Well...you never really rescinded that privilege." She then awkwardly tapped her index fingers together. "So I might have forced you to stop moving using the same method, technically without your permission, but...with your permission, I think."

I blinked twice. "Huh. That was rather brilliant. It's a good thing I trust you, Zee."

"So...you're not mad?"

"Mad? Why would I be mad? I know how much damage I can throw out when I'm in a healthy mental state. I'd hate to be the guy who had to fight me when I wasn't trying to limit myself. If anything, I'm impressed with your rules lawyering."

Zea smiled and absentmindedly played with her hair.

"I will, however, rescind the earlier contract we made," I said. "I don't intend to let this happen a third time."

"Oh," she said. "I understand. Good plan."

"But what happened here to stop me?" I asked.

"Well, it was the strangest thing," Zea said, almost as if she didn't believe it herself. "When I took control of you, you suddenly stopped moving, like I told you to, but then you started moving again. I tried to stop you, but you told me not to worry about it. Only, it wasn't you. It wasn't even your voice. He said he was Nathan-Prime and that he was returning the favor of you using his body in Israel by him using yours now to kill Abraxas and the others."

"What? This all sounds highly inappropriate. Did he really word it like that? Of course he did, the pervert. I've never been

217

inside him." I paused. "That I recall." I paused again and then shivered. "Oh, that sounds so dirty."

"Well, anyways, he using your body simply pointed at what was left of Abraxas' body and said, 'Breath of Life: Creation Severing Slice' and this sword appeared from nowhere and cut Abraxas' body into oblivion. He didn't even move—it just happened. At least it didn't look like he moved."

I nodded. That certainly sounded like Nathan-Prime. Who else had the gall to possess a body and use techniques that the original owner of the body couldn't perform? But what was this about Israel? Like I'd said before, I'd never been to the Holy Land and if Nathan-Prime's words could be trusted, I hadn't gone there even during my missing memories, but would go there in the future, judging by his carefully chosen words.

I shrugged and cracked my neck, most of the pain removed by Zea's stellar healing words. I stood up and Zea helped me steady myself and I nodded at her in thanks.

"Okay, well, it seems, at the very least, that we aren't going to get any answers now," I said. "Guess that means we just need to be patient and grateful that we managed to make it out of this situation intact."

"Well stated," Mara said, simply. "The fact that all four of us managed to survive this rash insanity is without a doubt the gift of the Father's love for helping fools and imbeciles."

I laughed, feeling slightly better. I started stepping forward, but fell flat on my face on the concrete floor, my knees refusing to submit to my desire to move.

"Don't rush yourself, Blake!" Zea ordered, kneeling down beside me to heal me once more. "You're not ready to run around like you normally would! Not after what you've gone through tonight!"

I groaned, but before I could speak, I heard a rustling ahead of us, looking through the exposed wall to see a revolting monstrosity heading towards us. It was one of the giant zombies that had been tasked with patrolling the jail's borders, doubtless there to kill us for infringing on its masters' territory, even though they were truly dead.

Without thinking, I forced myself out of Zea's grasp and stood up, ignoring my body's feeble attempts to stop me. I briefly heard

218

Cinderella say my name, but I ran past her, intending to stop this threat before it could reach my friends.

"Those skeleton and zombie giants are still active!" I yelled, rushing forward. "We've got to destroy them and stop—" but I stopped, my vision growing cross-eyed as I then fell onto the ground and passed out, having opened up my old wounds in the process.

CHAPTER 29

I woke up once more to see Zea hovering over my body, muttering countless healing invocations designed to keep me alive, only this time she seemed madder about it. Instead of the normally, sweet sensations of repaired nerves and closed wounds, I was instead greeted by the forceful collisions of repaired skin and compulsorily manufactured red blood cells attempting to replace the blood I'd lost earlier.

Zea had noticed that her patient was awake and aware again, but was now deliberately choosing silence both physically and mentally as some form of punishment for the dimwit's actions.

I gazed over at where the zombie giant had been moments before, only to discover that its last movements towards us had been the zombie equivalent of rigor mortis. It had spent the last moments of its undeath attempting to reach us and avenge its masters, but, like the rest of the horde, was now succumbing to its creator's demise. It was then that I realized just how stupid I'd been, as Nathan and Naminé had explained that this very thing was going to happen, so I'd just rushed after a problem that had already been solved.

Looking down at me with a scowl, Zea seemed to dare me to be the first one to speak, but with rare tact, I decided to let her get the first words in this time.

"You really are stupid, you know that?" Zea asked. "Your body wasn't close to being healed and you run off to try to start another fight. You need to lie down and rest or at least wait for one of us to pick you up."

"It's what I do," I said, shrugging, only to cough when I realized how much that hurt.

"Well it's something you need to improve on. Idiot. I was worried senseless again."

"Thanks for caring, sweetheart."

Zea shook her head and looked away from me for a moment. I looked over to see that Mara and Cinderella were nowhere to be found. I tried to get up, but ended up just coughing out blood, earning me a slap from Zea as she turned back to heal the damage.

"How many times do I have to tell you to stay down, Blake?" she asked, exasperated. "I can't keep healing you forever. Eventually, even I'll run out of energy."

"I could always spare some of mine," I said. "There's plenty to go around."

"You're impossible."

I flinched. "Zea. You used another idiom correctly."

She sighed and sat down beside me, having finished patching me up. "Yeah, I guess I did."

I laughed. It hurt to laugh, but I couldn't help myself. I soon found Zea laughing beside me, as her thoughts returned to my mind. I turned my head over to look at her and smiled. She had come a long way from when I had first met her. A swirling of energy coursing underneath my ribcage made me wince, breaking off my gaze.

"Oh, it feels like there's a chestburster inside me," I said, groaning.

"Ah, the creature from *Alien*," she said, surprising me once more.

"When have you watched that?"

"I have not. I merely read about the term in the book you provided me."

"You're good people, Zea."

"Now that one was far too obvious. It is too general as a term to be a good idiom. I prefer the term 'class act,' as it presumes I am quite skilled to be called that."

"Now you're just showing off."

"I learned it from watching you."

I laughed again and clutched my chest. "This isn't fair," I said, groaning once more. "I'm gonna have a heart attack if you keep this up."

"Unlikely," Zea said, beaming with pride. "I repaired the nerves and muscles around your heart quite well. Without the help of the patient, I might add, not that I required that either."

"Listen, sister, I do the whole egotistical act here. There ain't room in this town for the both of us."

"But we are currently in a prison."

I turned to glare at her, and she laughed at me.

"I am a terrible influence," I said, sighing. "Zea...thank you. Without you I wouldn't have made it out of here alive. You're amazing."

"Me?" she asked, standing up. "I should be the one thanking you! I wouldn't be alive if it weren't for you! You risked your life by coming here to save me! For Heaven's sake, Blake, no one who came here before you ever came out alive! But did that stop you? Of course, it didn't!"

"I couldn't leave you here not knowing what they would do to you. You're my friend, Zea. Friends do stupid things to make sure they can still have someone they can call a friend. Besides, I could never live with myself if I lost you. I've lost enough. It has to end at some point."

Zea smiled, rolled her eyes, and shook her head playfully. "Do you feel good enough to let me pick you up?"

"No, but we've got to get going either way. Just help me get dressed first."

Zea nodded and carefully placed my undershirt over my barely able to rise hands, doing so despite my feeble attempts to help her. She grabbed my trench coat and put it on me without any issues. Zea then bent down to place a hand underneath my back and with her other hand she placed it under my left shoulder. Gingerly, she picked me up as I bit down on my tongue to stop myself from crying out in pain. Eventually I got on my feet, but almost slipped. Zea caught me in time to stop me from falling and our faces ended up together. I stared into her eyes closely. Had they always been so vibrant? That feeling returned to my chest and I felt my heart pound.

"Guys, Mara says the circle is r—" Cinderella said, entering the room only to stop when she saw how close we were.

Zea and I shook our heads and turned to face her.

"Hey, kiddo," I said, offering a weak smile. "Clumsy me almost toppled right over and Wonder Woman here managed to stop me. Would you mind grabbing my other side? It'll make things a little easier."

Cinderella's face was a little red for some reason, but she quickly shook her head and went to my side to help pick me up. We walked forward slowly as they carefully worked to move me in a way that offered the smallest amount of pain.

"I always knew I'd pick up a harem one day," I said, earning me a shot to the ribs by Zea.

"I'm so sorry!" she exclaimed as I cried out in pain. "I just—it was a bad joke."

"Fair enough," I said, wheezing. "I'll shut up now."

"I'll believe it when I don't hear it," Cinderella said, as Zea and she laughed at my expense.

The two women assisted me into the next room, where Mara was carefully constructing a new teleportation circle, most likely to take us straight home. Zea and Cinderella than sat me down in the center of the circle and stood in front of me, both making sure I didn't pull any other stupid stunts.

But before we left, Mara asked them to step aside and she looked down at me with some form of concern on her face. "Does the name Naminé mean anything to you?" she asked.

I paused, recalling the dream girl's name and then nodded. "Tangentially," I said, my mind a jumbled mess.

"I see. Then I suppose you will find this interesting."

She took out a note of paper scribbled on with words that hadn't been made by any of us, at least based on what little I knew of their handwriting styles. On it was the message: "Upon the successful capture and controlling of Blake Azarel, Death has told us to then seek out the heart of Naminé, who resides in Blake's control. If those dolts are still alive then they must never know about her, for Death has offered her existence only to me so that I can control her for his sake, as he seems to think she will be an issue if not dealt with properly. I am writing this note now so that if she somehow erases my memory, I will maintain a link to this idea of trapping her, as Death has said that she holds immense power over the hearts and minds of men."

I frowned. The more I learned about Naminé, the more I saw why Nathan-Prime had given her the name. Manipulating memories was an immensely terrifying ability to have, so if Death was after her it was bad news for the rest of us. I had no clue what it meant by me being the link to her, unless it was somehow

223

hinting that Death knew that Nathan-Prime would entrust me with the task of saving Naminé.

"Where did you find this?" I asked.

"In Abraxas' cloak," Mara said. "It seemed as if he was studying this woman for some reason."

"Now how did he find out about her?"

"I know not, for I did not know of her before this moment, but I suspect you are worried for her as well. Allow me to stop you before you rush into what you do not understand once again."

I chuckled. "You can read me like a book, Mara. Thanks for the assist."

"It was my pleasure, Guardian Azarel. Now please, remain still for once and allow us to leave this wretched place."

I nodded and sat in place, an immense relief washing over my mind when I looked in Zea's direction. She had her back to me at the moment, but it was more than enough to further set me at ease. She was alive and safe. All of this had been worth it.

Sensing my thoughts, Zea turned around and held out her hand. I took it and we stared at one another, saying nothing, but sharing our feelings briefly through our link. I wasn't exactly sure what I was sending to her, but, judging by her reaction, it had removed any lingering anger from my earlier self-destructive exploits.

Then, as Mara and Cinderella pressed their hands onto the teleportation circle, we all traveled miles in an instant, returning to Corpus Christi, Texas.

CHAPTER 30

1

Afsoon was the first to greet us at the circle held within the Silver Fortress. One of many would-be slaves that I'd saved the past year from the ghoulish vampires of The Horde, she had proven to be a valuable asset, organizing the reconstruction efforts of the Fortress with very little oversight needed.

"Guardian Azarel!" she exclaimed, ushering the other workers to get out of our way. "And the others!" She took out her walkie-talkie. "Initiates Dressler and Freeman as well as Secretary Dorothy: they have returned. All four of them."

With Zea and Cinderella's assistance, I stood up and walked slowly to avoid a repeat of earlier events, as they guided me to one of the many marble benches that remained within the gardens. I was feeling better, but traveling via teleportation circle was always a strain on the mind, especially after the past few weeks I'd experienced.

Not too long after this, both Clooney and Nathan appeared and ran to us.

"Blake, you're okay!" Nathan shouted out, rushing into my chest to hug me.

I groaned in pain as his head hit my ribcage at full force and he swiftly pulled back and repeatedly apologized.

"Please don't break him again," Zea said in a tired voice. "I can only fix him so much in a day."

"And it would seem you've had to do your fair share and more," Clooney said, eyeing us without approaching. "Let me guess, I bet he ran off and did something you told him not to do?"

"I would be a fool to take such a 'chump bet,' as I believe the term goes."

Before I could offer a witty retort, Dorothy had arrived and, upon seeing me in my sorry state, stopped herself from scolding me, offering a kind smile instead. "I'm relieved to see you made it," she said. "All of you."

"Well, we looked out for each other out there," I said. "Some of us kept getting into trouble."

"If 'us' could be used as a singular pronoun than yes, you would be right," Mara said, causing the others to laugh. "But enough of this, what has occurred while we were away?"

Clooney had laughed with the rest of the other traitors and then when Mara had finished speaking, he'd reached inside his coat for something, producing a large stack of papers that he offered to me.

"And what's this?" I asked, taking them.

"Oh, just a non-aggression pact and final draft of a mutual defense treaty meant to begin successful and fruitful relations between Excelsior and the Free-Zone," Clooney said, smiling smugly.

"What? I didn't authorize that!"

"Well, your forged signature says otherwise."

I flipped through the papers relentlessly until I found the parts where my signature was there, having been replicated flawlessly innumerable times.

"But how?" I asked. "Who forged it?"

"I did," Clooney admitted. "It was rather simple. I know of many children with better handwriting, so forging yours was hardly difficult."

Incensed, I almost unwittingly created an uncontrolled fire invocation, but something within me managed to calm me down, albeit briefly.

"You let this happen?" I asked, staring at Dorothy, incredulously.

"If I may be so bold, Blake," she said with no hesitation, "we both know you would've agreed to this scheme, had you been here."

I grumbled. She was absolutely right. Again.

"Okay, fine," I said, wishing I could throw my hands in the air without crying from the pain. "What does it mean? Summarize in five sentences or less. I've had enough exposition thrown at me these past couple of hours."

"When you left, Ambassador Niseweynu wished to speak with me in private," Dorothy said, "but I asked if Clooney could be there to represent the more mystical side of things, which he agreed to do. He told us that...despite everything that had happened, he was more than sure that if he helped draft an accord between our two groups that he would be able to get the treaty passed in record time, but he needed your signature. Clooney assured us that he knew enough to get the job done and signed in your place, saying that you had asked him to do what I asked him to do while you were gone. The treaty guarantees trading relationships and a call to defend either entity when faced with supernatural or mortal threats, as well as the promise to continue more talks in the future to help elucidate exactly what those ideas pertain to, remaining vague for now in the hopes of witnessing what could be done when we combine forces."

"And with one sentence to spare," Clooney noted, laughing. "Aren't run-on sentences amazing?"

I sighed, but nodded. "Well done, you two," I said. "Used my own words against me and everything. If I ever fire either of you two, you should give Álfheim your resumes. I'll even give a recommendation."

"It was not our intent to belittle your ability to lead us," Dorothy said. "We both deemed it more important to face your future wrath than to flail about helplessly if you were unable to return alive to Corpus Christi."

I furrowed an eyebrow, looking at Clooney. "I thought you said your job wasn't looking after the future of Excelsior?"

"It wasn't, but neither was I told not to do so," Clooney said. "It was simply the smarter option with the threat of limited reprisal if all went well."

"Right, well, regardless of your reasons, you two have done us a great service, especially since we were able to wipe out Morior Invictus and their entire undead army. Now we have the Free-Zone as an ally to whom we can also relay this information, proving our further worth to them. I suppose we'll need to discuss future training missions between both parties so that we can learn how to work together better—and why are the three of you smirking at me?"

Nathan broke the silence first. "Well, Blake, we already have worked alongside the Free-Zone," he said, grinning like a roguish wolf.

I looked between the three of them and waited for someone to talk. Clooney took the bait and cleared his throat.

"Despite our best efforts to not let anyone know that you had left to return Zea," Clooney said, shrugging, "that was destroyed the moment you sent the, well, Phoenix Force here, who told anyone who would listen that you'd directed them there. Thus, your exploits were inevitably leaked to the Sanguine Collective, who prepared an attack on Corpus Christi. However, what they didn't know was that Ambassador Niseweynu was on his way back to meet us while being protected by the recently restored SEAL Team Six, who, upon seeing the Collective gathering nearby, contacted us and helped us strategize so we could prepare for their assault. Having done little recon of their own, the Collective attacked en masse, falling right for the trap we'd placed for them. Nathan had crafted an illusion of the two of us leaving town, which proved too enticing an opportunity for the vampires, but in their haste, they failed to recognize the illusions and were instead mowed down by sniper fire intensified with the silver bullets that were being used. After this initial setback, Nathan and I actually revealed ourselves, using his telekinesis and my wind invocations to further take out most of their commanding officers. But when they retreated and regrouped for another assault Phoenix Force came out of hiding as we'd instructed them and was able to stop the attack before they could get into the city or take away any captives."

"Once this was done," Dorothy said, "Ambassador Niseweynu sent word to President Boone, who hailed it the first strike in retaking America from the Collective. This has swelled national pride within the Free-Zone and given us far better standing with them than we could have ever hoped for. Officially, neither of us are at war with the Collective, but both sides are aware that fighting is inevitable. However, with this unintended alliance we have forced them to pull back for now and reassess their situation. According to the Ambassador, while the President does not welcome us with open arms, he is far more trusting than he was before this attack."

"And I didn't even have to lift a finger," I said, smirking. "This is far better than I was expecting to come back to. Well done, Dorothy, Clooney, and Nathan. You three have made this job a whole lot easier for all of us."

We sat in silence for a moment and I briefly felt reinvigorated. I turned to look over at Dorothy and gave her a look, which she immediately recognized.

"With that, I do believe it's time for us to take our leave," Dorothy said, walking away from us with Afsoon and the other workers so that we could have some privacy.

"Well, Excelsior," I said once they'd left, "we've got a lot of work ahead of us, but for now, I think it's best if we take the day off. I sent Dorothy away so that she wouldn't tell me otherwise. No paperwork for this guy today."

"Well, if all else fails, I can simply forge the documents for you," Clooney said.

"Yeah, about that—next time at least tell me before you do that. Promise me."

Clooney mocked offense at the demand, but shrugged. "For you, I promise."

"Good. Now I need to get some rest. I think all of us used so much power that we're gonna need to find a mineral bath somewhere and veg out for a week. But, being that this is us we're dealing with, the world's probably gonna end within the next four hours, so use your time wisely. Team dismissed. I'm going to bed."

"Then let me take you there," Zea said. "I've—"

"No, Clooney can take me," I said. "Our rooms aren't too far from each other, after all. You've spent too much energy for my sake, Zea. Get some much-needed rest."

Zea seemed to want to protest, but nodded and left with Mara to their respective quarters.

"Cinderella," I said, smiling when I turned to look at her, "I quite literally couldn't have done this without you. If you hadn't disobeyed me, then Mara and I would be dead, and I don't even want to think about what they'd have done to Zea if we didn't show up to Alcatraz. Thank you for knowing when to listen and when to break the rules."

Bending down, Cinderella hugged me lightly, letting out a small set of tears that she quickly stopped. I hugged her back.

"I'll always look out for you, Blake," Cinderella said, grinning. "Let's keep doing it for each other."

I nodded and she stopped hugging me, leaving for her room. There was a slight bounce to her step, far more chipper than I'd expected it to be, but I decided not to press the issue. She was happy. That was all I needed.

"Hey, Nathan," I said, bringing his attention to me. "You did amazing out there. From what Clooney says your illusion crafting is far beyond what you were capable of a year ago. Keep up the good work and you'll be able to play us all for fools."

"As if I'm not doing that already," he said, smiling mischievously.

I frowned. "But seriously don't. Use your powers for good, please."

"I promise."

"Good enough for me. Now get some rest, short stuff."

Rolling his eyes, Nathan did as instructed, leaving Clooney and I alone. We stared at one another for a moment in complete silence until he broke it.

"Shall I carry you, master?" he asked, putting on a faux British butler accent.

"Sure thing, Alfred," I said. "Master needs to spend the next week asleep."

Clooney chuckled and helped me get up. We walked towards my room, spending the time in further silence until we reached my door.

Before he could help me reach the handle, I looked over to him. "Thank you, Clooney," I said, smiling. "For all you've done."

He flinched for the briefest of moments, but it was quickly replaced with a smile. "I acted as you would in your stead," he said.

"Which I don't recall asking you to do."

"No, but it made things easier for you, which means things will be easier for me."

"Well, regardless of your reasons, you saved this city and that's exactly the kind of person I need with me if we're gonna rebuild the Fortress."

"I'll try to not make a habit out of it."

Releasing his control of my body, I straightened myself, giving the appearance of further weariness as he started to walk away. Unfortunately for him, this time I was only pretending to be weaker, having gathered enough strength since our arrival for what I was about to do next.

"Oh, Clooney, I almost forgot," I said, whirling around quickly before he could react, as I picked him up by his shirt and forced him against the wall. "We need to talk about Cinderella."

Clooney, winded from my unexpected attack took a moment before he could respond, and said, "I thought you'd be happy."

"What did you do to her? If she's under some kind of *geas*, I swear to God I will end you right here and now, eternal effect on my powers and soul be damned."

"I didn't do anything. I just...I needed to know if she believed or not."

"Why? It's important, but what did that have to do with anything?"

"Because I needed to know whether her vision of you dying would come true or not!"

I stepped backward, loosening my grip on Clooney enough for him to escape and dust himself off, but he made no attempt to run.

"I don't understand," I said, shaking my head.

Clooney's face grew grimmer. "Then I suggest you start reading your Bible more," he said, his voice now a low growl. "If she were a true prophet at the time she had seen that vision, then what she'd seen would have been unavoidable."

"Why?"

"Haven't you ever read Deuteronomy? Don't you even understand how prophecies work?"

"Yeah, I've read it, but I don't see how it's relevant."

"You don't even remember," Clooney said, scowling.

"Remember what?"

"Nothing. There are many people who can see the future, but only a select few can see it for what it really is, rather than what it can be."

"Yeah, so what? Allan Kardec was a member of the High Court and he saw visions that never came to pass all the time. My dad never put much stock in him, but then again, he didn't really like the guy in the first place. Then again, I didn't either."

"And why was that do you think? How many visions have you

had before? How many of them didn't come true?"

I paused for a moment. I'd never thought about it before. Every vision I'd ever had had all come true. Why was that? Maybe I was the exception.

"You're thinking too small," Clooney said, correctly guessing my thoughts. "The answer's bigger than that."

"Then why don't you fill me in?" I asked.

"The reason there's a difference is because God specifically states in Deuteronomy that only one of His prophets can know the full future. People who don't believe in Him can get close, but often they only get what could be, rather than what will be. People like you and me—people who believe with all our hearts in the truth will always see what will be. Or so it has been in my study of such matters."

It dawned on me. It was so brilliantly simple. How had I never thought of it before?

"If Cinderella had come to faith earlier than I was done for," I said. "You asked her that to see where she stood spiritually. You didn't force her to make any stupid decisions. She did it because she believed. You needed to know if there was a chance to save me or not."

Clooney sighed. "I never lied about that and I never will," he said. "Your safety is my top priority. It was because of what my family threatened to do to me if I told you, but it ended up being because—" he stopped as if an invisible gag were caught in his throat.

I moved forward to help him, but he held out a hand and placed his other on his neck. The mystical effect of the *geas* he was under dissipated as quickly as it had appeared. A *geas* was an odd form of ancient invocation that could be used by people who studied how to use words to the point of bending reality when certain conditions were met. Mostly known for being a Celtic thing— especially since the main sufferer of a *geas* had been Cu Chulainn himself—it was actually heavily prevalent throughout the world and could be used by anyone who took the time to understand it. I'd never dabbled in it because of the Forum's law against taking over the minds of others, which a *geas* would most certainly do. But I'd never seen one this aggressive before. It had so many conditions around it that were meant to set it off. Whoever had

232

forced this *geas* on Clooney was clearly powerful.

"These lips are sealed," Clooney said, a forlorn expression on his face.

"Then let me finish for you," I said.

"There is much danger in completing what I would have said."

"Yes, but I wanted to let you know I wanted to face it with you, because you were about to say, '—I became your friend.' Right?"

"These lips are sealed."

"I'm sorry that I hurt you earlier. I wanted to be sure you didn't do anything to Cinderella, but here I find out you're just a big softy."

"These lips are sealed."

I smiled. Nothing more needed to be said. I took my leave of Clooney, who disappeared from sight the moment my back was turned as I offered the password to my room and slept for a very long time.

2

Two days later, I emerged from my slumber to hear a knocking on my door. Grumbling, I pushed myself out of the bed and headed to it, opening the door to find Mara waiting outside.

"I have awakened you earlier than you wished to be," she said. "I apologize. I shall leave and allow you to rest."

"No, the damage is done," I said, yawning. "Get in."

I walked over to my desk and sat down in a silver-painted chair, grabbing another for her to use, which she did. Mara stared at me cautiously for a while, before deciding to talk.

"I imagine you must have further questions about my connection to the Christening," she said.

I nodded. "It was a topic I was going to bring up later," I said. "But it seems to me like you want it brought out in the light now, so share as you please."

"Thank you, Blake. I must confess that there is only one other who knows as much as you will once I explain matters. It is Zea, as you might have guessed. I...had planned on not revealing any of this, but after what you have done for her sake, it would be unbecoming of myself not to tell you what you deserve to know.

"I was born in a maddening world. People like myself were

233

sought after for our power and used greedily. I defended myself as best I could, but I was never as strong as others can be with their Christening. While others decided to fight against oppression, I sought safety and shelter, arriving here to stay away from the outside world and its problems. But even with such little power, I grew…haughty. I saw myself as higher than others, because I had done more than they had while alive, especially with the task of keeping the Archives intact once that directive was given to me following the past loss of the previous Archivist. But even with that knowledge I was still unprepared for what happened next."

She paused, obviously replaying a horrifying memory.

"I…I made a mistake when I was younger," Mara said, her voice growing weaker. "I dealt a blow to an enemy who had a curse placed on him. The curse was designed to harm anyone who attacked him, causing them to lose their strength, or, in my case, my access to the Christening. The curse has stayed by my side all of these years and it is only fairly recently that I have been able to invoke in small quantities."

"To lose access to all of this," I said, staring at my hands. "To be divorced from all of that in an instant. I can't even imagine the pain involved."

"Then learn from my mistakes. I came at this man in anger for something that was my own fault, even though he was despicable in every way. Some would have called my cause just, but I know better. I deserved what happened to me."

"Is he still alive?"

"Yes."

"Do I know him?"

"I would hope not, but…knowing you the time shall come soon. When that day comes, you must promise me something."

"Anything."

"Do not attack him. Not directly at least. You will know by his power just how wrong it would be to oppose him. Use a pawn, create a hole in the earth for him to fall in, or whatever it takes to kill him without being the one who strikes the final blow. That way only leads to pain. I will not let another suffer my fate."

"I understand."

Mara stared at me with a quiet softness. "Thank you."

She stood up and began to walk away, but stopped when she

234

heard my voice saying, "You know, Mara, I barely got any proper nouns in that discussion."

"You did not," she said, not looking at me.

"Is it because you know I'll rush after the person who did this to you and try to beat them until I can return your power to you?"

"Yes."

"Then don't tell me, even though we both know I'd do it right now if I had every bit of information that I want. However, promise me this: if the time comes when it's inevitable that this person and I fight that you'll tell me everything else you're hiding from me."

She turned to look me right in the eyes. Brief memories of both of our lives played in the other's mind.

"I give you my Word," she said, and then left my room behind.

3

The next day I woke up earlier than expected, but not because of outside interference this time. Instead, my body had caught up with the time needed to regain most of my strength and gather the Christening I needed to function. Truly, I felt even fitter than before with every sign of damage I'd taken on the way to and inside Alcatraz being nonexistent.

Knowing it'd only be a matter of time before Dorothy found out about my wellbeing, I snuck out of my room and was about to leave the Fortress undetected when I found Zea waiting for me near one of the secret exits I hadn't told anyone else about.

"Oh, right," I said, frowning. "Mental link."

Zea beamed with pride. "You do need to get better at shutting out some of your thoughts, Blake," she said. "But don't worry. I won't tell. I think we both need this time to ourselves."

I grinned. "Are you really gonna play hooky with me?"

She paused, unfamiliar with the term until she sensed my definition of the word, which made her laugh. "This once at least. There's something I want to talk to you about anyways."

"Then let's do it, sweetheart!" I said, pumping my fist and opening the hidden door that led to an abandoned house on the streets above the Fortress.

We passed through the hidden alcoves as quietly as possible, both knowing just how valuable hidden exits and entrances could be in an emergency. Zea stopped me before I left the upper exit, having sensed something ahead of us. But then she stopped and ushered me ahead. I got out of there and into the room, seeing that she'd merely sensed a small group of rats that fled at our sudden appearance. I held out a hand to her and lifted her out into the room. We expanded our awareness, sensing that no one would notice us leave the house, so we walked outside. The sun was intensely bright, but we adjusted to it quickly, letting me know for the first time that it was around noon.

"So what were you planning to do while playing hooky?" Zea asked.

I brought the right side of my trench coat around to cover my face, making that part of it appear like a pseudo-cloak. "I'm going to patrol my city," I said, deepening my voice. "My people need me. I am the one who hides in the shadows, stalking after a superstitious and cowardly lot of villains before they can see me coming."

"During the middle of the day?"

I dropped my trench coat to fall back in place and held out a hand in frustration. "Can you, just once, let me have my fun?"

Zea chuckled. "No, because it's more fun this way."

"I've created a monster." I shook my head, but laughed despite it all. "All right, can we at least parkour a bit and survey the city? Make sure no mischief is being done or villainy being planned?"

"Lead the way, Blake."

"No, while we do this, I am Blakeman. No one can know my secret identity."

Zea offered a confused look, wondering if it was worth it to humor me now but shrugged and walked after me. We reached the next house over and I found that the window was open on the first floor, so I ascended it, leaping upwards to grab onto a panel on the second story. Zea followed after me with better grace as we eventually made it to the third floor, from which we had a better view of the city.

"Gaze upon the city, Day-Walker," I said, gesticulating wildly. "It cries out for help and we'll give that help."

"Then let's do so, Blake—" she started laughing, but stopped herself "—Blakeman."

236

"That's the spirit, Day-Walker. Now let us away."

I jumped over to the next building over, as the people below us watched in awe. They had seen people parkour before, but not nearly as swiftly as we were going. In a short amount of time, Zea and I had ended up several hundred yards away without breaking a sweat. We said nothing during this time, except for the occasional mental directions or observations we made about the people around us. It didn't take long for some of the populace of Corpus Christi to let everyone around them know what we were doing, and we attracted a crowd who watched our exploits, creating a shared experience for them all.

I couldn't help but smile. I'd long wanted the people of the city to know that we were there to defend them, but since I'd left, I was sure there was some small part of them who were questioning my reliability for their sake. Providentially, Dorothy, Clooney, and Nathan had done most of the work for me by successfully repelling the Sanguine Collective, but it wasn't done yet. The people needed to see us actively working out in the open. The Gray Forum was dead because they'd hidden too well. Excelsior wouldn't make the same mistakes. Instead of skulking about in the shadows and solving the public's problems without them being aware of them or having to lift a finger in their defense, we would instead give them a symbol to look towards—one that would encourage them to follow us.

We kept this up for two hours, stopping a mugging in the process, but doing little else than being seen by those under our protection. All in all, it was rather uneventful, which suited my needs more than anything else. Eventually, Zea and I stopped near the marketplace and sat on top of the tallest building there with our legs stretched over the walls we'd just ascended to get where we were.

"Are you hungry at all?" I asked, looking down at the many food stalls below.

"After what we've done, yes I am," Zea said.

I stood up and peered down at the marketplace.

"Hey, watch this," I said, holding out my hands to hold the bow about to appear. "Ageg!"

The ethereal light bow emerged from nothingness to appear in my hands. Taking some gold coins from my pocket, I willed the gold to stick to my arrow and then shot it at the nearest food stand, where the owner was making quesadillas. The arrow latched onto the table and I willed the gold to no longer stick to the arrow, leaving enough for what I was about to take next. I sent the first arrow away, creating a second one with my mind, although this one would be tied together by a rope that led back to me. I launched the second arrow, which hit two quesadillas perfectly and recoiled back to me as I caught it midair, producing my prize to a clearly amused Zea. I handed her one of the quesadillas and took the other, as we ate together.

Every now and then someone would look at us and wave and we would return the favor, but for the most part they left us alone. Despite the heat of the day, neither of us was too hot to keep this up if we wanted to do more, but I knew I was on a time limit, as news of my sudden appearance in town would reach Dorothy's ears, which meant work for me. Not that I minded as much now, especially since I'd at least gotten to go on an adventure recently.

"I'll pay you back," Zea said, making me turn my attention to her.

"For what?" I asked.

"For saving me. For saving all of us. Before you got here I never imagined we'd be like this. We've taken down some pretty big...heavy hitters is the term, right?"

I laughed. "Absolutely, sweetheart."

She blushed. "Quit distracting me. What I have to say is important. I just...I don't know how to express it."

"I've got plenty of time."

"I want—I want to help you regain your memories. You have so much missing. What happened to your parents, your friends, and...your wife. You don't even know her name. You don't even know if it's possible for them to be alive. I just...I want you to have the closure you deserve."

"That's sweet of you, but how do you propose we do that? Nathan-Prime was kinda specific on the fact that they'd only be unlockable once the time was right."

"And what if he meant for you to proactively look for a means to regain your memory? I was researching this in the Archives before Nathan brought Sedecla here. We need to find the Fae. What's left of them anyways."

238

"Why would the Fair Folk be able to bring my memories back?"

"They wouldn't, but something they captured would."

"Explain."

"In the Archives it mentions that—right before the Fae joined the fight against the Sanguine Collective—they had launched an expedition against the Norse gods, the ones that still existed anyways. They stole something from them—something that could help restore your memory."

"So are you gonna keep being cryptic or do I need to look it up myself?"

"I was getting there," she said, shaking her head. "Well, when I say they stole something I should really say it was two things: Odin's ravens. Huginn and Muninn."

"Wait a second—don't those names mean 'thought' and 'memory', respectively? They went around the world acting as Odin's eyes and ears, gathering secrets that no one else could ever access, right? Ha-ha! Zea, you're a genius!"

Zea beamed with pride. "If we were able to get a hold of at least one of them, who knows what they could tell you about what happened to you?"

I paused, taking it all in. I could know it all. The good, the bad, and the rest. I'd know what the last thing I'd say to my parents was, what had happened to Atanasio when we had gone to that barrow, the reason for how the Collective had been able to wipe out the Gray Forum, and the identity of my mystery wife. It was all so perfect.

"The only thing is I don't know how to get to Álfheim," Zea said.

I laughed. "Then leave that to me, Zee, because you're looking at the guy who knew more paths into Álfheim than anyone else in the Gray Forum."

I smiled. Things were finally going my way.

UPCOMING BOOKS

Resurrection Life

Gideon Sato is one of twelve people summoned from across the multiverses to become heroic Paragons of the troubled world of Khayim. The world is plagued by random demonic invasions called Abyssal Incursions. Gideon is betrayed and murdered. However, thanks to the help of two allies who never gave up on him, he is brought back to life, and he is determined to use his second chance to save the world.

Coming 2022

The Unseen (Sequel to Broken Veil)

After surviving the harrowing destruction of Hammer Falls, Nathaniel Goodwin and Jessie Minett are now clued-in to the true nature of the world they live in. However, finding true supernatural threats eludes them until they are drawn back to Nathan's hometown of Richardson, Georgia, where an old friend of his has gone missing. However, home has changed immensely since the last time he was there, especially since the appearance of the Unseen: an eldritch group of creatures that can cause their victims to be forgotten completely.

Coming 2023

ABOUT THE AUTHOR

M.C. Ashley has the crazy dream of being a self-sufficient author. He obtained his Bachelor's of Fine Arts in Creative Writing degree with a Minor in English in 2013. He first started writing in high school after developing an appreciation for Stephen King's The Stand. Four of his fan-fiction works, and original works, have been featured on TV Tropes where he is credited as the user "NKSCF."

He published his first book "Lost Time" in 2018. He published his second book "Broken Veil" in 2020.

He currently lives in Denver, NC.

STARVING WRITERS GUILD

We are real writers with real experience, who really want to help. Our editing service is the best deal on the internet.
Email us at info@starvingwritersguild.com

53154156R00150